"Oh, Darian, th_____ lenging. My parents are feeling quite well and are keeping close watch over me."

He tucked a stray wisp of hair behind her ear. "So you came up with an angling ruse."

"Yes." She grimaced. "Do you know how to fish? Please do! I've forgotten everything I learned as a child."

He studied the pole. "The tackle I used was somewhat different, but this seems simple. However, we do need bait."

"My goodness, I didn't think of that!"

"We'll find insects. Come, let's cross." He mounted his horse and reached for her, lifting her up in front of him and fording the stream in their usual fashion. "Sit down and catch your breath, while I hunt. Shall I pour the sherry first?"

"I'll do it," she volunteered, relieved that he was going to assume the role of handling bugs.

Sipping her sherry and watching him explore the clearing, Venetia marveled at how happy she was. She thought back on her conversation with her mother and those warnings about Darian's *experience* and could have laughed. How wrong her parent had been! Darian was perfect. He treated her as if she were made of crystal, and other than calling her by her first name, he had certainly never attempted liberties. He was an honorable gentleman, and she . . . she loved him.

—from "The Impossible Bride" by Cathleen Clare

BOOK YOUR PLACE ON OUR WEBSITE AND MAKE THE READING CONNECTION!

We've created a customized website just for our very special readers, where you can get the inside scoop on everything that's going on with Zebra, Pinnacle and Kensington books.

When you come online, you'll have the exciting opportunity to:

- View covers of upcoming books
- Read sample chapters
- Learn about our future publishing schedule (listed by publication month *and author*)
- Find out when your favorite authors will be visiting a city near you
- Search for and order backlist books from our online catalog
- Check out author bios and background information
- Send e-mail to your favorite authors
- Meet the Kensington staff online
- Join us in weekly chats with authors, readers and other guests
- Get writing guidelines
- AND MUCH MORE!

**Visit our website at
http://www.zebrabooks.com**

HIS BRIDE TO BE

CATHERINE BLAIR
CATHLEEN CLARE
HAYLEY ANN SOLOMON

Zebra Books
Kensington Publishing Corp.
http://www.zebrabooks.com

ZEBRA BOOKS are published by

Kensington Publishing Corp.
850 Third Avenue
New York, NY 10022

First Printing: May, 2000
10 9 8 7 6 5 4 3 2 1

Printed in the United States of America

CONTENTS

THE REBELLIOUS BRIDE

by

Catherine Blair

ONE

Diana Quinlan's head snapped up in disbelief. "I cannot believe I have heard you aright." Her voice was calm, but her knuckles whitened on the handle of the teapot. She steadily poured a cup of tea and handed it across the low table to where her mother reclined on the chaise longue.

"Of course you did," Mrs. Quinlan replied. "The opportunity to better the family arose, and your father took it for you. It's what anyone would have done." She waved a languid hand. "Don't be difficult, Diana. These kinds of arrangements are made all the time."

The teapot met the silver tea tray with a clang. "Well, it won't fadge. I have an understanding with John Stiles."

Her mother shrugged indifferently. "The stocking merchant's son you met in Leeds? Hardly what you would call a brilliant match. You're much better off with Lord Trevlan. He'll inherit an earldom when his profligate father has the grace to die. They haven't a feather to fly with." She took a tiny sip of tea, watching Diana closely over the rim of the cup. "It is all quite settled, you know. You can't cry off without disgracing the entire family."

Diana would have liked to shake the woman. She had been gone for two months visiting her aunt in Leeds, only to come back to find that her mother had arranged her betrothal without a by-your-leave. "Mother, I will not be bullied into an advantageous marriage like Susan and

Eleanor were." She leaned back in her chair and crossed her arms with a mutinous expression. "Look at them now, shackled to well-born tyrants who deride their background, and to in-laws who turn up their noses at them, if not their money."

Mrs. Quinlan's carefully darkened brows drew together underneath her elaborate lace cap. "You should be thankful for what you have, miss. You're passably pretty, but if you weren't rich you'd have nothing. At least your sisters had some claim to real beauty." She gave a peevish sniff. "Furthermore, Susan and Eleanor's children will be peers." Her long white fingers affectionately smoothed the fringe of her Norwich shawl as though she were soothing it. "Their husbands may be intolerable, but my grandchildren will be something more than rich commoners."

"Not that you have ever been allowed to see your grandchildren." Diana's voice was bitter. "No, Mama, we are cits, and that is all we will ever be."

Mrs. Quinlan's fingers tangled the fringe in a restless motion. "Enough of that out of you, miss. I consider it my duty as a mother to ensure that the family line is improved with every generation." Her little mouth turned down in a frown. "My mother could not read. My father was a tenant farmer who was happy to own one mule. I jumped at the chance to marry your father, even though he only owned the one cotton mill at the time."

"Yes, yes," Diana interrupted impatiently. "And the most miserable day of your life was the day you were wed. A more ill-suited pair I never saw. Your point is lost on me, I'm afraid. Our family is plagued with miserable marriages, and I am not going to marry Lord Trevlan for his ridiculous title. I've never even met the man! It matters little to me whether the entire thing is arranged or not. I had nothing to do with it, so any shame at crying off must fall on your head."

Her mother looked petulantly up as Diana rose to her feet. "He'll be here any moment."

"What?"

Mrs. Quinlan raised her shoulders in a smug sort of shrug. "Well, if you hadn't been in such a ridiculously sour mood last night, I would have told you then. I have invited the man here to take part in the house party."

Diana's eyes narrowed in suspicion. "What house party?"

Her mother waved her away. "A small thing, really. Your cousins Hypatia and Leticia, Barbara Hennings's daughter Sally, Mr. Almsworth, that dreadfully freckled Jenkins boy, Mr. Gaffield, Lord Trevlan, and yourself, of course. Consider it a chance to get to know your betrothed."

Her mother considered her daughter outmaneuvered— as though slyly making it impossible to avoid meeting Lord Trevlan would push through the whole wedding plan.

"I shall write to invite John," Diana said with a defiant smile. "And when Lord Trevlan arrives, I will inform him that our putative betrothal is off."

Her mother struggled to a sitting position in a tangle of shawls. "Diana!" she gasped. "You would never be so ramshackled as to cry off when a man considers himself engaged to you! The announcements have been sent to the papers!"

Diana turned at the doorway and coolly raised her brows. "It may shame you, and him, and even me, but I will not marry him."

Viscount Gabriel Trevlan shifted uncomfortably on the seat of the coach the Quinlans had sent for him and wished again that he were somewhere else. The piece of pasteboard covering the hole in the sole of his shoe was becoming uncomfortable. When he reached down to readjust it, his glance fell on the knees of his trousers. He scowled.

His sister Lydia had darned them quite well, but they still looked vaguely shabby. He gave them an offhanded brush and resolutely ignored them.

A pig being brought home from market: That was exactly what he was. A pig that had been bought and paid for. The well-sprung equipage turned down an elm-lined drive, and he drew a deep breath. In another moment, they would arrive at the outrageously sumptuous home James Quinlan had built from the spoils of his many successful textile mills. The home of his new owners.

It was foolish to have contracted to marry Miss Quinlan sight unseen. Would she prove a wilting, hypochondriacal, social climber like her mother? Or a bluff, uneducated, mannerless creature like her father? The idea of both their traits combined did not bear contemplation.

Well, it didn't matter what he thought of her. He would marry her anyway. Her dowry would remove the threat of debtors' prison for his father. On the other hand, at least debtors' prison would have kept the man away from the faro table. Trevlan smiled faintly. The Earl of Rochdale would find a way to lose vast sums of money even if he were locked away. His father would bet everything he had that the sun wouldn't rise tomorrow.

Trevlan absently pulled several loose threads off the cuff of his new coat. Lydia had had to sacrifice her best riding habit for the making of it. Well, he would buy her a dozen once he was buckled to Miss Quinlan.

He had hoped to be married by now. But at least the announcements had been sent to the papers, and when the Midsummer quarter day rolled around on June 24, the debt collectors would at least have the promise of Miss Quinlan's vast fortune to stay them. Perhaps Miss Quinlan could be convinced to begin the posting of the banns this Sunday.

At least the earl would have his freedom, Trevlan reflected bitterly. He himself would be imprisoned forever in an affectionless title-for-money exchange with the Quinlan family.

Two servants in blue livery appeared on the steps of the great house to greet the coach as it bowled down the drive. Trevlan had the impression they had been lurking in the hedges, waiting for him to arrive. The drive was over far too quickly. It wasn't surprising, considering that the Quinlans' house was a mere six miles away from his own. Neighbors, really. Not that his family ever would have considered them such. His father had pointedly refused to meet them even after the marriage negotiations had begun.

Trevlan removed one glove and crumpled it in his hand to disguise the fact that the fingers were irreparably split down the seams. Miss Quinlan was likely to take one look at his shabby getup and decide that no title in the world was worth it. He half hoped she would.

The house appeared to be positively swarming with servants. They scurried about like beetles in their rich blue coats as they opened the coach door, let down the steps, and ushered him up the stairs. An impressively dour butler opened the imposing front door and waved the beetles away.

"Lord Trevlan," he said without emphasis, "I will show you to the green drawing room. Someone will take care of your baggage."

Trevlan thought of his battered trunks with their crushed corners and dirty linings. Well, it couldn't be helped now. He followed the man into the dazzling salon. Gilded crocodiles and sphinxes glared out at him from every table and chair leg. An Egyptian lotus motif danced down the wall hangings, and green marble shone from every surface. He felt as though he were on the set of a play at the theater.

The butler bowed himself out, leaving Trevlan to examine the absolutely ghastly couch which sported what

looked to be gilded adders twined across its back. He sat
down gingerly and hoped the dust from traveling didn't
ruin the green silk upholstery. These voluptuous surroundings only made him appear more shabby.

An ormolu clock on the marble mantelpiece was made
in the shape of an obelisk, with a gilded crocodile grinning
out from either side. The silences between each ponderous
tick seemed to grow longer and longer. Had it only been
three minutes since he arrived? It felt more like twenty.
He got up and went to the clock to make sure that it was
indeed working.

"Hideous, isn't it?"

He whirled around. "I beg your pardon." The girl in
the doorway had a smile that was impossible not to mirror.
"Well, it is interesting," he conceded.

She laughed. "You are very tactful. I always thought it
was a bit too tempting to put one's finger into the crocodile's mouth to see if the teeth were as sharp as they
looked."

Since this was exactly what he had been doing when
she arrived, he repressed a feeling of sheepishness. The
girl could only be Miss Quinlan. He felt an unexpected
wash of pleasure. She was pretty and petite, with bright
blue eyes and a mass of dark hair dressed fashionably at
the back of her head. Perhaps his future was not quite so
dismal after all.

"I am Diana Quinlan." She affirmed his hopes. Her
even white teeth showed when she smiled, and again he
found that he could not help but smile back. "It is a pleasure to make your acquaintance, Lord Trevlan. I hope that
you enjoy your stay here at Quinlan Park. I assure you,
we have not let my mother's rage for all things fashionably
Egyptian run rampant in any other room but this. You
must think we are quite the presumptuous little mush-
rooms." There was a defiant gleam in her eyes.

"Not in the least," he protested, carefully shaking her

slender hand. "I am very happy to have been invited. I have been here several times to meet with your family." He wished he had not said that. Of course he had been there to discuss the marriage settlement, but there was no need for him to make it sound like the horse auction that it was. "I hear that you have been in Leeds. How did you find it?" His words tumbled over each other in his haste to change the subject.

Her wryly raised brows assured him that she was well aware of his blunder. She gestured that he should sit and then gracefully followed suit in a green upholstered chair as far away from him as would still allow comfortable conversation. "It was a pleasant trip."

He noticed that her blue eyes radiated silver streaks from their centers. Her expression seemed to go misty at the mention of Leeds.

"In fact," she continued, "there is something I feel I must discuss with you in private." At that moment the tea tray arrived, so she was forestalled while the butler unloaded what seemed like a hundred pieces of the silver tea service.

While he waited for the man to arrange the array of silver spoons, knives, and sugar tongs, he tried to catch Miss Quinlan's glance to get a hint of what she was going to announce. Her eyes were veiled with thick black lashes.

When the door closed, she set down her teacup with an impatient rattle. "My mother will be down in a moment, but I must say something." Her voice was suddenly urgent. "In Leeds I met someone—a man I have fallen deeply in love with." She looked perplexed for a moment. "A man with whom I have fallen deeply in love. I believe the second is more grammatically correct." The corners of her mouth trembled.

Trevlan's tea went down the wrong way and threatened to drown him. He managed to stifle a painful cough.

"Then you must marry him, of course," he heard his own voice say calmly.

"I intend to." Her entire face lit up in a way that made him uncomfortable. He pulled at his cravat.

"You must understand that my family entered into marriage negotiations with your family without my knowledge," she continued. "While I am certain that you are"—she searched for the words—"quite a nice man, I must ask that you release me from any explicit or implicit marriage arrangements." What could only be a blush was creeping over her cheeks.

He dropped his eyes to the lotus-riddled carpet. "Of course." He wasn't sure if he should feel relieved or insulted.

In an impetuous motion, she took his hands. His gloves dropped to the floor with their seams gaping open. He planted his foot on them and swept them under his chair. Her touch was light, but he could feel the strength of those smooth, white fingers. "I realize that my family and myself have caused you great inconvenience," she said, her dazzling gaze locked with his. "But once you have fallen in love, as I have, you will understand that I feel compelled to be honest with you, Lord Trevlan. Marriage negotiations should never have begun between you and my father. If I had known what was transpiring here while I was gone, I never would have allowed it."

He wanted to remove his hands from hers. He wanted to escape this horribly overdecorated room, fling himself into the Quinlans' expensive coach, and race hell-for-leather homeward. Instead he smiled. "We must all hope that we may one day experience love as you have found."

Her expression went soft again. "I wish that for you too, Lord Trevlan. Everyone should be as happy as I am. You will meet him, my John. He is coming to the house party. You will meet many other people of my acquaintance. In fact"—all the mistiness left her face, and her eyes narrowed in a speculative expression—"perhaps you will meet someone here who will suit you better than me."

"I really don't think—"

"I will ensure that you do." She dropped his hands and clasped her own together in a gesture of resolution.

"On the contrary, Miss Quinlan, while I am happy to be a guest at your house party, I have no need for you to find a wife for me."

"Well, you need the money, don't you?" she demanded bluntly.

He resisted the urge to cringe. She might be pretty, but she was as crass as any other hard-nosed daughter of a mill owner.

She interrupted his stammering reply. "If you didn't desperately need to get married, you would not have offered for me sight unseen."

"But I did see you," he countered, feeling slightly defensive. "I met you in London two years ago. We danced at some ball or other." Not a very romantic endorsement, he had to admit.

"Fiddle," she exclaimed. "If you try to tell me that you've been desperately in love with me since we danced at some ball or other, I will snap my fingers in your face. You're marrying me for my money, and I am marrying you for your title." She flung her hands in the air in an exasperated gesture. "Only, of course, I am not going to marry you at all. However," she cocked a brow, "I am generously offering to find you a substitute bride. You were going to have a bride in trade anyway; why should you not trade brides?" She looked absolutely delighted with herself.

He could not help but laugh. Miss Quinlan certainly had a ready, if quirky, sense of humor. "Very witty," he conceded. "However, I've already told you that I'm quite happy going home a bachelor." Quite happy.

"Well, I can't very well cry off without doing anything

for you," she protested innocently. "I will help you find someone else. There will be three other girls here besides myself, each one with nearly as big a portion as my own. You may have your pick."

"You are offering to sell me one of your friends?" He was incredulous.

"Nothing of the sort. They are all hanging out for titled husbands. You're frightfully handsome, if you don't mind me saying so, and therefore I can't see how any of them would have the least objection if you were to offer for them."

The creature clung to an idea like a bulldog. "Miss Quinlan, I must insist—"

She dragged him out of his chair and herded him out of the room. "Yes, yes. But now you must come and meet my mother. Do pretend she is an invalid, if you please. As to leaving here with a rich wife, you simply leave everything to me."

Trevlan allowed her to lead him upstairs feeling vaguely as though he had just relinquished the last vestige of control over his own life.

TWO

"John!" Diana looked up in delight when the butler announced his name. "Thank goodness you have arrived! It was very good of you to come on such short notice. I knew nothing of this house party until I came home."

John Stiles pressed a kiss onto the back of her hand, waited until the butler had closed the door, and then kissed her on the cheek. "Of course I came as soon as I got your message. Am I the last to arrive?"

"Yes, and Mama is furious that I invited you at all. Everyone else is walking in the gardens." She pulled back the lace curtain over the French doors and gestured at the couples walking aimlessly in the hedges. "But you have missed nothing important." She considered telling him about her encounter with Lord Trevlan yesterday, but decided it would only worry him. After all, Trevlan had taken her rejection with very good grace. The poor man, he must think them all hopelessly déclassé.

John had helped himself to a tumbler of brandy and now flung himself into a chair. "Listen, Di, I don't really want to spend my week walking about in the shrubbery. I came up here because I thought it would further our match. Have you told your parents?"

"Well, yes. Mama recalled you from the assemblies in Leeds. I'm afraid she doesn't quite approve yet." Diana bit her lip and turned to look out the window again. Lord

Trevlan was solicitously wrapping another shawl around
her mother's shoulders. The dog! Leave him alone for one
minute, and he was doing the pretty to her mother and
making it a thousand times more likely that the woman
would kick up dust that she would not have him as a son-
in-law.

"Here, John." She interrupted her beloved's monologue
regarding the things he would like to do this week rather
than squire around a collection of squealy chits. "We must
go into the garden, and you must be charming to my
mama. It is very important to me that you make her like
you."

She opened the French doors and dragged him across
the lawn. "Mama, Lord Trevlan, here is Mr. Stiles. We
are very fortunate that he was able to join us here at Quinlan Park, are we not?" She beamed up at John. He was
the most handsome man she had ever seen. No one could
possibly find fault with him.

"How lovely to meet you, Mr. Stiles," her mother said
with a languorous sigh. "Forgive me for not rising. I am
not at all well. Lord Trevlan was just telling me how his
aunt, who suffers from a malady similar to mine, was very
much helped at Harrogate. I'd as lief not go to such an
unfashionable place as that, mind you, and I can't see why
Brighton wouldn't do me better, seeing as it is very much
more a place to be seen, but Lord Trevlan insists that it
must be Harrogate."

Diana's eyes flew to Trevlan's in surprise. Was it her
imagination, or did she see a gleam of amusement in his
hazel eyes? She swallowed an appreciative laugh. It would
be most amusing to see her mother, dressed in the latest
kick of fashion, toddling about Harrogate with all of the
octogenarians in their powdered wigs.

"Would you like to take a turn in the gardens, madam?"
John asked her mother punctiliously.

The woman's drawn-on brows snapped together. "If I

can't rise to greet you, how the devil do you think I am going to take a turn in the garden, sirrah?" She unfurled her fan with a slap and plied it so vigorously that her lace cap fluttered wildly.

"Madam, I fear this is my fault," Trevlan protested in a mild voice. "I should not have insisted on the shawl. You are overheated in this warm weather."

Mrs. Quinlan seemed to recollect herself. "Perhaps I could do with a glass of cooling lemonade," she managed weakly.

"John will get it for you, Mama. I will take a turn with Lord Trevlan, if he will be so kind."

Her mother nodded benevolently. Obviously she still had her heart set on Trevlan's title. Well, first to deal with Trevlan himself.

"Just what did you think you were doing?" she demanded once they were out of earshot amongst the roses.

He gave her a bewildered look.

"Tipping the butter boat over my mama!" she snapped. "She'll be eating out of your hand in another moment."

Trevlan pointedly drew her arm within his own, and she slowed her stalking to a more sedate pace. "Am I to understand that you do not wish me to be polite to your mother?" he asked quietly.

There was something in his soft, cultivated tone that made her want to slap him. How could she help it if her own accent was broad and uncouthly stamped of industrial Lancashire? His voice would always remind her of the impassable class difference between them. She exhaled an impatient sigh. "You are not going to marry me, remember?"

"I do recall that." There was an edge to that civilized voice that made her look up at him, but his expression was impassive as he examined a bee that hovered over a bush heavy with June roses.

She scooped a fallen flower off the ground and savagely

plucked off its wilting petals. "Well, I will not have you making John look like a fool with your gallantry to her. It is important that he make a good impression on her, not you."

"I shall endeavor to stay out of the way," he replied.

She scowled and cast away the flower. "Now I've gone and said something rude." She stopped walking and looked up at him with a tentative smile. "I meant what I said yesterday afternoon. I will find you a bride. But you must also remember that I am going to be doing everything in my power to get Mama to approve my engagement to John."

Lord Trevlan's eyes crinkled up in a grin. "Has anyone ever told you that you are a most managing female?"

She could not help laughing. "Indeed I am. It comes of having very little breeding, I suppose. But, really, Lord Trevlan, I am not one of your mealy-mouthed London misses who can't say boo to a goose and fall into hysterics when their papa arranges their marriage to some ogre. Not that I consider you an ogre," she belatedly amended. Then her chin jerked in the air in a defiant gesture. "Nonetheless, I will take charge of my life."

"And everyone else's too, I fear," he murmured. "While I applaud your spirit, Miss Quinlan, I must remind you that I too am capable of taking charge of my life. I do not need you playing matchmaker."

"Fustian," she said stoutly. "You can't possibly have a clue as to who would make you a good wife. And you needn't try to fob me off with any nonsense about not needing one. You must need one desperately to offer for a cit like me."

"Please do not say that."

She could not help but feel a tendril of warmth curl through her at his gentle protest. She would always be bourgeois, but it was kind of him to overlook their differences. Honestly, though, what she needed was a man like

John Stiles. A man of her own class who wasn't after her for her money. "Well, anyway," she said awkwardly, "I see my cousin Hypatia Lane sitting by herself. You must go over and engage her in conversation. She is a very well-read creature, quite blue really, but I am certain that she is just the type of woman for someone like you."

Diana dragged him over and made the necessary introductions. She herself found Hypatia excruciatingly dull, but she was much more the type of lady a well-educated lord would approve of as a wife.

When she returned to her mother, she found her sitting alone, placidly sipping lemonade.

"Where is Mr. Stiles?" she asked.

"Gone off to inspect the stables. I never met a more insolent puppy. Your father will never approve of the match. You had better send the rapscallion packing before he gets home from Manchester." Mrs. Quinlan shook her head, desolated. "Really, Diana, I thought you had more delicacy than to develop a tendre for a shallow coxcomb who hasn't a genteel bone in his body." She took a sip from her glass and continued to wave her fan. "Especially when you have Lord Trevlan to compare him to."

"Enough of Lord Trevlan. Paragon or not, I am not going to marry him!" How infuriating of John not to at least try to do the pretty. But perhaps Lord Trevlan was right. Perhaps she *was* being too managing. There was no point in getting in a tizzy. She would not have fallen in love with John if he were not charming. By the end of the week John would have her mother around his little finger.

With an annoyed shake of her head, Diana went in to make sure the luncheon arrangements were going as planned and that the stables could properly mount all their guests for the outing she had planned for the afternoon.

* * *

Trevlan sat down at the writing desk in the sumptuously appointed guest room. His trunks in the corner looked ludicrously out of place with the maroon Axminster carpet and gold and maroon striped wall hangings. The place must have been redecorated only months before. His father could have appraised the cost of the furnishings at a glance. Trevlan wondered how much of Miss Quinlan's dowry the man would have gambled away before he heard that the betrothal was off.

Well, it was better that he should know sooner than later. Trevlan pulled a sheet of hot-pressed paper out of the desk and cut a quill. He'd best write to Lydia; who could know when his father would get around to opening his mail?

> *My dear sister,*
> *I hope this letter finds you well. I have arrived at Quinlan Park, but I must admit it is not to my liking. The place is more lavish than the Pavilion at Brighton and, if possible, in worse taste. Miss Quinlan took one look at me and decided that we will not suit, so you had best inform Father as quickly as you can. Do not mourn the loss of Miss Quinlan as your sister-in-law. The chit is irredeemably vulgar and bullying. While I would never have said before that the Trevlans have pride, I realize now that a marriage with that ungenteel creature—*

His pen stilled. He was being unfair. Miss Quinlan's character was not as black as he had painted it. True, she was managing, but she seemed to have good intentions. The girl was honestly ashamed at having called off the betrothal, and he could hardly fault her for wanting to marry a man she loved. The rich could afford that luxury. Well, in any case, Miss Quinlan was no mushroom sycophant, even if her family did wish her to marry into a title.

Was it possible that she had hurt his feelings? He smiled and laid down his pen. It was only his wounded pride that made him write such vicious comments. He had thought that rich, vulgar Miss Quinlan would fall all over herself to get herself wed to him. Well, the little blue-eyed chit had no need of him at all. He shoved the letter to the back of the desk and pulled out a fresh sheet.

His second attempt was brief, and though it let his sister know in no uncertain terms that the betrothal between himself and Miss Quinlan was dissolved, he refrained from explaining why. Of course, she would have the story out of him when he came home empty-handed, but there was time enough until then. Now at least he would enjoy the fine food, excellent wine, and amusing, if not interesting, company. He sanded and sealed the letter and then handed it to a footman to deliver as he went down to luncheon.

"Ah, you have arrived, Lord Trevlan," Mr. Stiles exclaimed as he joined the party in the dining room. "I was hoping that you could give me some advice on a hunter I am about to buy." He offered Miss Hypatia Lane a chair at his right hand, but continued to talk over his shoulder to Trevlan. "Now, I know a bit about flesh and bone, but this goer comes at a high price."

"I am sorry to say that I am not considered an expert in hunting horses." Trevlan did not wish to admit that he had never been able to afford to hunt.

Stiles dropped into his chair and continued to speak through Miss Quinlan, who was seated between them, as though she were not there. "Well, I particularly want this one because he matches my other one. In fact, all my stable matches. Every one a blood bay. Pretty dashing, you might say. Of course they cost a pretty penny, but what is that, eh? We must have our standards, wouldn't you say, Trev?"

"I was thinking that we might ride out to the abbey this afternoon," Miss Quinlan announced loudly. "The weather is fine, but it might not hold out to the end of the week. I should hate for us to miss seeing it if we were to delay."

The diminutive, blond Miss Hennings giggled. "A real abbey? Is it haunted with the ghosts of monks? I should dearly love it to be!"

Trevlan saw a wry expression cross Miss Quinlan's face. "I'm certain I don't know," she said. "We bought it from the estate next door. Papa felt that every park should have a ruined abbey." There was that half-defiant, half-deprecatory gleam in those silver-blue eyes. "We are lucky that we found a real one available. Otherwise he should have had to commission one built. And newly built ruins are somewhat unlikely to be haunted."

Miss Hennings giggled again. Trevlan prayed that Miss Quinlan would not designate her as his intended. At least Miss Quinlan had a quick understanding and a ready sense of humor. Miss Hennings seemed to possess neither. Both she and the very young Miss Leticia Lane were clamoring to know more about ghosts.

"I hope you do know the history of the place," Miss Hypatia Lane said coolly. "I would not wish to walk about in a historical place without a knowledge of its past."

"Surely you've got the odd ghost of a murdered monk or a lovesick nun," Mr. Almsworth said cheerfully.

"And I should hope it has a dungeon," Mr. Gaffield added.

The two men were as alike as peas in a pod. Both were obviously sporting men, with some rudimentary education. They were lacking Town polish, but seemed pleasant enough men. They seemed interested in little more than hunting and shooting, so Trevlan couldn't imagine why they had been invited to a party that was obviously contrived to let himself and Miss Quinlan pair off.

Miss Quinlan laughed. "You are a difficult bunch to please! If we haven't any dungeons or, heaven forbid, any phantom monks, I will make certain that Papa buys some directly. After all"—she shot a devilish look at Trevlan—"what is the point of being rich as Croesus if one can't procure those things necessary for genteel living?"

Trevlan bowed slightly in his chair. "One would not wish to be thought passé."

Her face lit up when she laughed, and he found himself wishing for a moment that he had had the chance to get to know her a little better before they'd been thrust into this bumble broth.

"Well, I will do my best to find out about it before we go," she said. "In fact, I will ask Hartfield to accompany us. He is a groom who was raised hereabouts. He will know all of the interesting stories about the countryside."

She smiled at Trevlan and then turned to Stiles. He had seen the glances she had exchanged with her beau during luncheon. The vivacity of her expression softened into something quite remarkable. She wasn't a bad chit after all. She deserved someone who could make her happy, and from those sugary looks she was giving Stiles, it seemed that she had found him.

Trevlan sighed and turned with a despondent kind of resolution to Miss Hypatia Lane.

THREE

"Lord Trevlan." Diana urged her sorrel mare forward to catch up to him. "I do not mean to cause you alarm, but you have less than one week to win Miss Lane." Despite his success with her mother, the poor man obviously had no notion of how to get on with ladies. If he would only apply himself, he could charm her cousin in minutes. Diana examined him appreciatively. With clothes a bit nicer, he would be unbearably dashing. Quite as good-looking as John, though in a different way. Truly, a titled, handsome man like Lord Trevlan would have to do very little to catch a female's attention.

He turned to her and shook his head as though he had been daydreaming. "I am not at all certain that Miss Lane and I will suit."

"Nonsense. She will make you a perfect wife. I saw that you were talking with her earlier. Why did you let her get away?"

"We were discussing the merits of Pope versus Shelley." He glanced across the field to where Miss Lane sat very upright on her mount.

Diana took a deep, satisfied breath. "Ah, very good. That is romantic. I knew you would need someone romantic."

"Why is that?" His head jerked around in surprise.

She frankly perused his even features and the dark,

more important than big houses or fine horses or fashionable clothes."

His mouth pulled to one side in a curious kind of smile. He looked almost as though he were perplexed. "You are not at all what I thought you would be like, Miss Quinlan."

A peculiar understanding seemed to have sprung suddenly up between them, and she was not sure if she welcomed it. "I am every bit what you thought of me. A rich cit whose papa can buy her anything that takes her fancy." She had meant to sound teasing, but the words came out bitter. "Well," she continued quickly, "we are not here to talk of history or of me. We must mend your manners so that you are able to win Miss Lane."

His fingers dropped reluctantly from the column, and he continued walking with her. "I admit that I am not the most polished man," he said. "I was raised in the country and have little turn for flattery. I do not trade in Spanish coin, and I have no desire to act like some dashed court card in order to impress a lady."

"There! Did you see that?" she interrupted triumphantly.

"What?"

"My cousin just looked this way with the most dour expression! She already regards you as her own." She darted another look at Hypatia, who was now walking toward them with her sister and Miss Hennings. "Now, quickly go and speak with her and watch what she does. If she opens her fan and exclaims how hot it is, that is a very good sign. If she pretends to stumble and leans upon your arm, that is an even better sign. Pay attention to how she touches her face and hair. Now go!" she hissed.

Trevlan gave her a mocking salute and went to join the ladies.

John ambled over to Diana, shielding his eyes from the afternoon glare. "I say, Di, it's a dashed hot day to be dragging us all out into the wilderness to see some old bricks."

"But don't you see, it's the fact that they are old that makes all the difference," she replied. She ran her hand up the worn stone of a column as Trevlan had done. It was cool in spite of the warmth of the day. Her fingers found a crack grown over with moss, and she gingerly caressed it. It was like touching a little bit of living velvet. "These were here hundreds of years before the Reformation. Who knows what sights they have seen?"

"You're sounding like my sister," he said derisively. "In love with all things old. I suppose that is why you like hoity-toity Lord Trevlan with his so very ancient title. I suppose that dates to before the Reformation too."

"Nonsense." She gave a disdainful shrug. "I know Lord Trevlan from my season in London." That was stretching the truth a little, but she did vaguely recall dancing with him. How strange that his unusual hazel eyes and chestnut curls had not made much of an impression on her then.

John followed her obediently into one of the small roofless rooms of the abbey. "Not much really to see, is there?" He scuffed his boot on the worn flagged floor. "Your London season, eh? Now, there was a waste of the ready if I ever saw one. What were your parents thinking when they tried to fire you off like that? Your pa's in trade and there are no two ways about it. There is no sense in cozying up to the high flyers when you'll never be one of them. You're like me, Di, a cit through and through."

He leaned carelessly against the wall and crossed his arms. "That's why we are such a good match. None of the silly if-you-please, by-your-leave manners, and none of that toad-eating that goes on in town. Once we're married we'll have the good life: lots of hunting, lots of money, and company that cares about more important things than who your grandpa was and how old his title was."

Diana looked up at him gratefully. He was right. How silly of her to have been feeling unsatisfied. This was why she loved John. She reached out to take his hand, but he had moved to the doorway.

"There's Lord Proper squiring your cousin around like a lapdog. A fortune hunter if I ever saw one, despite all his airs. Told me he didn't know about horses. I'd say that's because he hasn't had the blunt to buy one these ten years. His coat is well enough, but those breeches have seen better days. And I saw when he sat down that his shoe was mended with pasteboard. A fortune-hunting dog, I say."

Diana sighed and pulled him out to join the others. "I am well aware of Lord Trevlan's financial position," she said in a low voice. "We must do everything in our power to facilitate the match between him and cousin Hypatia."

"Who cares who he marries? What is it to you?" John demanded.

Diana ignored his comment when she realized she didn't have an answer.

"Diana!" Miss Hennings squealed. "This is so terribly Gothic! I declare I have chills in the month of June! I wish it were a little more cloudy, for then I swear I could just see a monk walking the cloister with his chains clanking."

"Why would a monk be wearing chains?" Hypatia demanded scornfully. "In my recollection, monks were not chained up. Not even in Henry VIII's time. It was mainly their fortunes he was after. In fact, the sociopolitical atmosphere was such that religious—"

"A tower!" Miss Hennings exclaimed in delight. "Oh, Mr. Almsworth, do take me up in the tower! Let us all go!"

Diana caught Lord Trevlan's eye as he dutifully offered his arm to Hypatia. His expression may have been slightly miserable, but it was hard to tell. Her cousin was launching into another detailed explanation of historical occurrences that may have influenced the turning of the popular tide against papist institutions. Perhaps Miss Hennings would have been a better choice for him after all.

"It's too hot to go up in some demmed tower," John protested. "I'd much rather be riding than traipsing around this old rock pile. This is prime hunting land." He pulled her over to look down upon the countryside spread out before them from the hilltop. "How much of this is yours?"

"I don't know. Why does it matter?" She wondered what the tower was like on the inside. Was it dark? Would Hypatia cling to Lord Trevlan in fear?

John grinned. "Well, as it will be mine some day, once we are wed, I would like to know about it." He squeezed her affectionately around her waist. "Your ma, she'll be a bit difficult, but once we've brought her around, your pa won't kick up any dust. I was thinking we should push for the wedding to take place soon. No need for the banns and all that nonsense. I'll get us a license from the bishop. In fact, I was thinking of riding over to Manchester to get it. Could you lend me the blunt? I've got it all right, just not with me. You understand." He pinched her cheek. "You'll be a June bride yet, Di."

"What?" She looked up from a daydream. "But, John, we are not even officially engaged yet. My parents have not given their consent." In fact, the world still considered her engaged to Lord Trevlan. She must see to it that the announcements in the newspapers were recanted.

"But they will," John countered firmly. "And when they do, we want to be married right away." He nuzzled into her hair.

"Oh. Yes. Of course. They've been up in the tower a long time. Should we go and see what has become of them?" She wiggled out of his grasp.

"Diana!" Leticia Lane came running across the over-grown courtyard. "Hypatia has fallen and twisted her ankle! You must help us!"

Diana took the girl's arm and ran to the tower. Lord Trevlan emerged from the doorway with Hypatia in his arms. Neither of them looked very happy.

"Miss Lane had a fall."

"It was folly to go up in the tower without proper lighting." Hypatia's mouth turned down in pain and irritation. "The stairs are simply crumbling away. Really, Diana, I can't see why you would take guests here when it is unsafe. I could have broken my neck!"

"However, you are quite safe now," Lord Trevlan reminded her. He turned to Diana. "I'm afraid that her ankle is swollen already. If she can ride, I will accompany her back to the house. If not, I will ride back and bring back a carriage."

He had assessed whether her ankle was swollen? She wondered how far up her cousin's leg he had allowed his hands to wander. She shook her head. That was unfair. Lord Trevlan was an honorable man. "You'll never be able to get a carriage up here," she said. "The lane is nearly a half mile away, and it is terribly overgrown."

"Will you please stop talking about me as though I were not here!" Hypatia struggled in Trevlan's arms, and he set her down. "I am quite well enough to ride." With one foot in the air, she listed slightly, but seemed well able to stand with Trevlan's help.

"I will ride back with you," Diana said quickly.

John caught her arm. "No, Di, you have an obligation to amuse your other guests. Lord Trevlan and the groom will accompany Miss Lane back to the house."

"Thank you," Hypatia nodded to John. Her narrow face was growing slightly more drawn with pain. "We have one man of good sense among us." She saw Hartfield approaching with her mount. "Here, man, come help me."

Trevlan bowed over Diana's hand. "Please do not let this accident make you feel that you must come home early. I, and I am certain Miss Lane, would feel terrible if this slight misfortune were to intrude on your pleasurable outing." There was a glint of amusement in his eyes.

Diana opened her mouth to give him some useful advice about how to make the best use of his time alone with Hypatia, but she stopped herself. She smiled, murmured something noncommittal, and then turned back to her other guests who were emerging from the tower. Lord Trevlan didn't need any help if Hypatia was going to throw herself at him. Accidental twisted ankle indeed!

Trevlan smiled and tried valiantly to look fascinated as Miss Hypatia Lane lectured him on the proper ways to reduce swelling in a wrenched joint. Apparently the young lady was blessed with a wealth of information on every topic and considered it her duty to disseminate this knowledge.

"Are you feeling any better?" he asked, wishing it were not quite such a long ride to the house.

"No. And I imagine that I won't for at least another forty-eight hours. Now, if only I can manage to get my aunt's servants to listen to me when I tell them how to make up this poultice . . ."

He wondered what Miss Quinlan was doing. She must think him quite poor-spirited if she thought he would meekly allow himself to be fobbed off on one of her relations. She was a termagant all right. Too good by half for the swaggering popinjay she was looking to marry.

"Why, Lord Trevlan, you look quite the thundercloud!" Miss Lane's voice dragged him out of his reverie. "I know how you feel. As a peer, you must find it even more provoking to be unable to find good help. My mother maintains that one should never employ servants that are related to each other. It keeps them from fraternizing and badgering one constantly to find positions for their dozens of brothers and sisters. What does your mother do?"

"My mother passed away some years ago. My sister runs the household now. We are fortunate that our help has been with us for a long time." There was no need to tell her that the help at Newland Lodge consisted of Betty, the maid of all work, and that he had acted as his own valet, groom, and coachman for years.

Would they never arrive at the house? He cleared his throat. "The weather certainly is fine for this time of year."

"Indeed it is fine. But I don't quite know what you mean by 'for this time of year.' June is the only time of year where we can possibly count on good weather. May is always cold and July unbearably dusty. I can't even begin to think about August. Happily we always spend August in our house in Edinburgh, but really, even there it gets dusty. And what's worse is the state of the roads there!"

Trevlan nodded in cheerful agreement. Surely a discussion covering the state of Scottish roads would last until they got to the house. Then he could turn Miss Lane over to her abigail and think over what was to be done. There was no point in staying at Quinlan Park if Miss Quinlan was not to be had. It was better to escape now and not have to hand over the vails that the servants would expect for a week's stay.

Yes, he would be gone in the morning. It was still early June. There was always the chance that he might find another wealthy bride before the end of the quarter. Or perhaps his father would have had a run of luck at the tables and could be convinced to part with some of it to stave off at least a few duns. If Diana Quinlan wished to buckle herself to a boor like John Stiles, it was no business of his, but he certainly was not obliged to sit around and watch his erstwhile intended give her pretty smiles to another man.

FOUR

"Lord Trevlan." Miss Quinlan came striding down the hall just as he closed the door to his room. "I have been to see Hypatia, and she seems to be doing quite well. You were wonderfully brave, you know."

"No," he replied with a smile, "I wasn't. Perhaps Miss Lane misinformed you. There were no highwaymen, fires, floods, or other difficulties that might have necessitated courage encountered on the way home."

She rolled her eyes. "You are a very difficult man. Here, walk with me on the lawn for a bit." She pulled him toward the stairs. "I was trying to praise you, and you insist on being irritatingly modest." Once outside, she drew a deep breath and lowered her voice. "So, how did you fair?"

"I am certain I don't know what you mean." He knew exactly what she was after, the little minx, but it was so much more fun to infuriate her.

She jabbed him in the arm, her mouth pinched in mock annoyance. "Did you progress in your wooing of Hypatia? She was very pale when I saw her. Perhaps you frightened her with your passion." She arched a brow at him meaningfully.

"That was probably it."

"Well, what did you say?" she prodded.

"I believe the conversation began with poultices and ended in Edinburgh," he replied mildly.

She shot him a look of disgust and swept up a battledore that lay on the lawn near the battledore-and-shuttlecock net. "Well, if you are going to be disagreeable, Lord Trevlan, I will not help you. You can go home as much a bachelor as when you came." She picked up a shuttlecock and bounced it on the racket with an expression of utmost unconcern.

She really was a piece of work. "Please, Miss Quinlan," he said contritely. "Don't abandon me entirely. You know I am a man of unpolished manners. I know nothing of seducing young ladies."

"I said nothing of seducing," she snapped. She repressed a smile and hit the shuttlecock over the net. "You only need to be charming, and no woman could help falling in love with you."

He picked up the second racket and ducked under the net. "You mean in love with my title." He gave a dismissive shrug. "I daresay I needn't even be charming." He tipped the shuttlecock back to her side.

"Impossible man!" she laughed, running for it but missing. "There is no point in pretending that it is not an advantage. Just like there is no point in pretending that you were not going to marry me for my money." She stopped his protest with a warning gesture. "No more of that. You must tell me about Hypatia. Did she cry?"

He looked at her in surprise. "No."

"Oh." She hit the shuttlecock back to him. "Did she look up at you from under the brim of her bonnet?"

"No."

"Hold on to you long after you had set her down off her horse?"

"I believe Hartfield helped her dismount. You will have to ask him."

"Thank you profusely in a breathy voice?"

"Well, she did thank me, but I can't recall anything special about her voice." He swung and missed. "There," he said triumphantly as he leaned over and picked up the shuttlecock; "we managed to keep it up fully six returns and nearly as many questions."

"If you were as good at witty repartee as you are at battledore and shuttlecock, you would have been married long ago," she replied dryly. "So, she thanked you. I suppose we must be content with that. What are your plans for this evening?"

"I hoped for another fine meal, a sample of your father's cellars, and a little entertainment after dinner."

She set her hands on her hips in an attitude of impatience. His serve landed the shuttlecock at her feet, but she ignored it. "Hypatia plays the pianoforte well. I will ask her to play, and you will turn the pages for her. Be sure that you lean closer to her than you have to."

"Poor Hypatia, to be so conspired against!"

She ignored him and picked up the shuttlecock. "And fix her with one of those looks you have."

"Which look do you mean? The one that says I am desperately in need of a rich wife?"

She hit the feathered missile so hard that it went several yards out of bounds on his side. "The one where you allow your lids to sink down ever so slightly, while still looking very, very intent."

He looked over his shoulder when he leaned down to retrieve the shuttlecock. She was blushing slightly.

"When did you see me make a ridiculous expression like that?" He walked up to the net.

"Well," she faltered, "I believe it was at luncheon. I can't quite remember what we were talking about." It was the first time he had seen her disconcerted.

"Ah, then it must have been made in appreciation of the very fine beef tongue that was served."

She pretended to threaten him with the racket. "I believe we were talking about—oh dear, you just did it."

"What?" he replied, knowing very well what she was talking about.

He could see that her cheeks were very pink as she dove after the shuttlecock he had dropped. When she stood up, they were face to face, with only the battledore net separating them.

"Yes, well"—she cleared her throat—"you know the look I mean, then. I think that it would do very well if you were to turn it upon my cousin." She seemed absorbed in watching her racket as she twirled it between her fingers. "She may seem like a bluestocking, but I happen to know that she is very much addicted to romantic stories of chivalry. With an expression like that and a few sweet words, she will be yours by the time the tea tray comes in!" Her laugh sounded a little artificial.

"But I'm afraid the look must be properly inspired," he said softly.

"Oh!" She looked up at him in alarm, her blue eyes very bright. "Well! Oh, look, here comes John!" She turned quickly and hailed the man as he came across the lawn.

"Ay up, Di," Stiles nodded an offhand greeting to the two of them. "Your mama says you must come in and change for dinner. I said I'd come after you, since I wanted to ask Trevlan here a thing about hunting lodges. Have you got one in Scotland? I've heard it said that all the blue-bloods do. I want to get one for myself. Always fancied my own grouse moor."

Trevlan clamped down his irritation. Perhaps it was for the best that they were interrupted. Beginning a flirtation with Miss Quinlan was at least futile, and at most, extremely unwise.

* * *

Diana stabbed at the piece of needlework she held and jerked the stitch tight. Would the men never finish their port? What could they possibly find interesting to talk about for so long? Probably John was telling one of his off-color jokes. She cringed. Lord Trevlan must think him a complete buffoon. He must think her even more of an idiot to have chosen John over him.

But John was right; she and he were cut from the same cloth. She would never have fit into Trevlan's world anyway. They would have had a miserable existence, lavishly financed by her family's money in a society that would never accept her. She had never forgotten the snubbing she had received during her one London season. While her money had ensured entrance into some of the ton's parties, the best of doors had remained closed to her.

"Diana, do refrain from tapping your foot like that. It is driving me to distraction," her mother remonstrated. Diana flung down her needlework and went to open the window. She straightened a painting on the wall, relit a candle near the window that the evening breeze had blown out, and then looked around for something else to do. Her mother scowled at her as she began to restlessly prowl the room.

"Would you like to play whist?" Miss Letitia Lane looked up and asked. "With Miss Hennings and Hypatia, we could begin a rubber before the men join us."

"I do not wish to play," her sister announced pettishly. "I should not have come down to dinner at all, but to keep you from coddling me. I knew if I stayed in my room, you would keep running upstairs all evening to make sure I was not lonely. I cannot bear coddling." She adjusted her bandaged ankle on the footstool set in front of her and winced. "I feel certain that if your cook had prepared the poultice recipe I gave her in the manner which I specifically outlined, I should be very much better this moment."

Letty shrugged. "Well, perhaps *you* wish to play, ma'am." She turned eagerly to Mrs. Quinlan.

Diana's mother agreed to make up a fourth, and they sat down to play. For a time the silence was broken only by the snap of the cards on the green baize table. "There, another trick for you and me, Miss Letitia. Diana's not playing well tonight." Mrs. Quinlan smiled in some satisfaction as she tallied their score.

"Sorry." Diana glanced contritely at her partner, Miss Hennings. The door to the drawing room banged open, and they all jumped in surprise.

"Ladies, ladies, what's this?" John bellowed as he sauntered over to the table. "At cards already? Penny for a point, I'll wager. Dull business indeed." He grinned at Diana, and his hand slid intimately around the nape of her neck. She saw her mother's eyes widen in disapproval.

"Now! Who's for a real game of cards? Trevlan? Almsworth?"

The smell of port on him make Diana wrinkle her nose.

Lord Trevlan bowed slightly to the party of ladies. "Perhaps later."

"Indeed, we are finished, gentlemen. I am afraid Miss Hennings and I have been utterly routed." Diana stood up and shrugged off John's hand. "Perhaps we can convince Hypatia to play at the pianoforte."

Trevlan turned to her cousin. "If you are feeling up to it, Miss Lane, we have heard that you are very skilled." He took a chair beside her and clasped his hands between his knees. "If it pains you to walk, I could carry you to the instrument." Diana thought she saw him flick a mischievous glance in her direction.

"I think not. I am not feeling at all the thing, and I do not wish to play," Hypatia replied with a frown. She gestured to her sister. "Letty, bring the lamp closer so that I can see my whitework."

John dragged a chair over to the whist table and sat

down. "There. She does not wish to play. Now there's no reason we can't play cards."

"Why don't *you* play, Diana?" Hypatia leaned her head against the sofa back and closed her eyes wearily.

"Oh, I don't think—"

"Yes, do. Letty will fetch me another pillow, and we will all be comfortable. I know for a fact that Miss Hennings can't play, so you needn't ask her."

"Not a note," Miss Hennings tittered. "My papa couldn't bear the noise, so I never had lessons."

"Smart man, your papa," John nodded. "No sense kitting a girl out and giving her graces like a duchess, when she is nothing but a mercer's daughter." He laughed at Miss Hennings's affronted gasp. "I meant that as a compliment, m'dear."

Diana sent him a meaningful glare and stalked over to the pianoforte. She sat down with very little grace and began a sweetly romantic ballad that bore very little resemblance to her present mood.

"I'm afraid we lingered a bit too long over the port," Lord Trevlan murmured regretfully at her elbow.

She missed a note. "What are you doing here? Go back and talk to Hypatia." She kept her eyes on the music, but could sense that he was smiling.

"I'm afraid that I cannot obey you, Miss Quinlan. Your mother ordered me over to turn your pages."

"Drat that interfering woman," she muttered. "Very well, turn now, if you please."

When he leaned over to do so, she caught the scent of his soap. How strange that she had never noticed before how nice a man could smell. John smelled only of port and smoke. She felt a sudden wave of annoyance with Trevlan. He was so irritatingly perfect all the time.

"You play quite well." His voice was low and soothing.

She turned to look at him, but his face was so close to hers that she fumbled at the keys again. "Obviously I do not." She focused resolutely on the music in front of her. "Did you get John drunk on purpose? To make a fool out of him?"

"No," he said gravely; "that honor goes to Mr. Stiles himself."

"But you are glad of it," she hissed. "You are happy to look so noble and gentlemanly compared to John. You think that when I compare you to him, I will regret my choice. But you are wrong. John understands me. Neither of us belongs in your world."

He breathed a laugh that had no humor in it. "I have no world. With no fortune, I am excluded from my world and from yours."

She looked at him, but he was staring sightlessly into the flames of the candles that lit her music.

He recovered himself and smiled at her. "You mistake my intentions, Miss Quinlan. I have no desire to cast your intended in an unfavorable light."

John was laughing uproariously at something Mr. Jenkins had said. Diana sat up straighter on the pianoforte seat. "I will be betrothed to him as soon as my parents allow it, and nothing will set me off it. Not you, not my mother, and not John himself."

Trevlan leaned over to turn another page. "I wish for you to be happy, Miss Quinlan. From the moment you told me that you were in love with someone else, I released you from any obligation to me."

His low voice so close to her ear made the hair on her arms raise. Hypatia should be the one playing the piano-forte; *she* should be the one longing to slam down the lid and throw herself into Lord Trevlan's arms.

Diana felt an unaccountable heat rise in her cheeks. "My mother still labors under the delusion that you and I will wed."

"Would it be easier if I were to tell her directly that we

have decided we do not suit?" he asked. "That will leave the way entirely clear for yourself and Mr. Stiles."

Her fingers stilled. "No," she whispered. "I . . . I don't think that is necessary . . . just yet." She tried unsuccessfully to swallow the lump that had formed in her throat.

"Diana! What is the matter with you tonight?" Her mother cried out with an arch expression. "You have been in a dream all evening. As you seem entirely unable to keep your mind on your playing, we must entreat Lord Trevlan to promenade the room with you until you compose yourself." She smiled coyly and waved a white hand at her daughter in a dismissive gesture. "I suppose we shall have to do without music after all. And I had dearly hoped to have the young people roll up the rugs and set to dancing."

"I suppose we shall have to play at cards after all, eh, Mrs. Q.?" John grinned and expertly shuffled the cards.

Lord Trevlan offered his arm to Diana with a neutral expression, but she did not take it. A headache was forming behind her eyes, but she couldn't, as hostess, excuse herself. "I don't wish to walk about," she said. "I'll play whist with you, Mr. Stiles, if anyone else cares to join us." She forced a smile and went over to join John. Mr. Almsworth and Mr. Jenkins agreed to play and sat down with the two of them. She felt her mother's scowl burning between her shoulder blades.

"Perhaps you could read aloud to us, Lord Trevlan," Mrs. Quinlan said sweetly. "I think that poetry would be nice. It is always enjoyable to have someone read something romantic after dinner. What would you like him to read, Diana?"

She shot her mother a look of faint exasperation. How humiliating to have Trevlan thrown at her head. "Read Pope to us, Lord Trevlan," she said coolly.

"Oh, dear, not him," her mother protested. "Pick someone contemporary; Pope is too satirical. You would rather hear something romantic, wouldn't you, Diana? Ladies?"

Diana lifted her shoulders and let them drop. The cards let out a little purr as John shuffled them. She turned her attention to the whist table, but was vaguely aware that Lord Trevlan had gone to fetch a book from the library.

She lost three tricks in a row.

"Come on, Di. You're not paying attention." John frowned and dealt another hand.

" 'Epistle II. To a Lady,' " Lord Trevlan began.

Diana forced her lips not to smile. It was a particularly witty poem, though scathingly critical of women. As he began to read, she wondered why he had picked that one.

> *"Papilla, wedded to her amorous spark,*
> *Sighs for the shades— 'How charming is a park!'*
> *A park is purchased, but the fair he sees*
> *All bathed in tears— 'Oh, odious, odious trees!' "*

Trevlan's eyes flicked to hers. He grinned and continued on.

She smothered her laugh and listened with pleasure to the way his cultured, steady voice rolled over the words.

John slapped his cards impatiently on the table. "Now, Di, I won't be your partner if you are not going to play right," he chided, not bothering to lower his voice.

She gave him a curt nod and took the cards Mr. Jenkins dealt her.

"Demmed silly poem if you ask me," John grumbled when Trevlan was finished.

"You don't think it is witty?"

He shrugged. "A poem about how women are always impossibly featherwitted? I call that truth, not wit!" He laughed loudly at his own joke.

"I certainly hope you are not such a misogynist as Pope, Lord Trevlan." She shot him a wry glance.

"Not in the least. Shall I now read 'Epistle I'? I believe it discusses the merits of men." He looked mischievous.

"Very nice, Lord Trevlan." Mrs. Quinlan covered her yawn with a limp, beringed hand.

"Couldn't you read us some Byron instead?" Letty begged him.

"But do so quietly," John growled. "Some of us are trying to play cards."

Diana clenched her jaw and resigned herself to a long evening of misery.

FIVE

"Letty, if you would just hold the parasol so that it covers the both of us, I could complete this sketch without entirely ruining my complexion." Hypatia twitched the edge of the lace umbrella so that its shadow fell across her face and then continued drawing the copse of willows on the far bank of the pond. "I do wish you could keep the boat from bobbing."

"You said you wished to get closer," Diana protested. She pulled once more on the oars and then allowed the small rowboat to glide across the surface on its own momentum. Across the pond, the two other boats were racing each other. She could hear Miss Hennings's shrill squealing as her boat, manned by Mr. Gaffield and Mr. Almsworth, broadsided the other one containing John, Mr. Jenkins, and Lord Trevlan. She sighed.

"That's quite close enough, Diana. I just wanted to get a view of the house beyond the trees." Hypatia squinted critically at the scene. "If I draw it as though the house were turned this direction, add more flowers, and leave out the mill on the hillside in the background, it will be sufficiently picturesque."

Miss Hennings was now attempting to change places with Mr. Jenkins. The boats were rocking dangerously, and Trevlan stood up and put his hands around the girl's waist as she laughingly pretended she was about to lose her balance.

"Lord Trevlan is quite the gentleman," Diana said with studied carelessness.

"Yes, he is very kind," Hypatia agreed without looking up.

Diana watched her cousin closely. Perhaps she was blushing underneath her straw Gypsy bonnet. "He knows just how to make one feel comfortable." She thought of their conversation at the battledore net. She had not felt precisely comfortable then. "Well, in any case, he is not in the least bit toplofty."

"Not at all," both of the Lane sisters agreed.

"And so very handsome," she reminded them.

"Well, certainly not unhandsome." Hypatia continued to sketch the willow grove, but the sunshine on the water made her blue eyes sparkle brightly.

Diana cleared her throat and tried not to watch Miss Hennings make a spectacle of herself on the other side of the lake. But then again, perhaps Miss Hennings would make a better match for Trevlan than Hypatia. Perhaps he would prefer someone more vivacious. But what if Hypatia had already fallen in love with him?

Letty looked at her sister and then at Diana. "It sounds like someone is head over heels in love," she said archly.

Diana bit her lip. It was too late; Hypatia was besotted. She could kill Sally Hennings for being such a cruel flirt. How was she going to convince Trevlan that he must remain constant to Hypatia? She squinted across the water and tried to think of a way to remove him from Miss Hennings's rapacious claws.

When the sun was at its hottest and the boaters had sufficiently tired themselves out, she directed the party to a shady glade where they could lay out the luncheon they had brought.

"I cannot get out of the boat!" Miss Hennings squealed. "It is too muddy on the bank and I shall ruin my shoes."

"Then I suppose you shall have to take your luncheon where you are," Diana said tartly as she guided her rowboat to the shore. "I shall bring you out some cold chicken once I have settled everyone." She was surprised to hear an irritated edge to her playful words.

"Nonsense! You would never be so cruel!" Almsworth protested. "Miss Hennings, if you will allow me, I will carry you to shore."

This set Miss Hennings to giggling, and Diana could barely keep from rolling her eyes. If Trevlan really did prefer the silly creature, she would have to seriously question his good sense. Trevlan waded into the water and caught the bow of her own boat. He pulled it aground. "With all the tomfoolery, I suppose we should all be glad that our luncheon is not at the bottom of the pond."

She smiled reluctantly over her shoulder. "Oh, do refrain from calling it a pond. My father would have a fit. It is a lake, if you please."

"Of course." Trevlan grinned. "My apologies. It is actually more like a sea than a lake."

Miss Hennings began shrieking in terror as Almsworth carried her over three feet of slightly muddy ground. "Mr. Almsworth has put us all to shame with his chivalry," Trevlan continued. "May I offer you the same service?" He held his hand out to her.

"Not at all," she said with forced cheerfulness. She handed him a basket of luncheon things and prepared to get out of the boat without his help. "Pull over that piece of planking and we shall walk across on that."

"Come on, Di." John picked his way across the mud. "Give me your hand." He picked her up as though she were a child and bore her off to where the rest of the party was setting up luncheon.

"There is no need to manhandle me, John. I am not a

bag of grain." She tried to keep the sharpness out of her voice. Perhaps it was only the heat of the day that was making her cross. She twisted around in his arms. "You will help Hypatia, won't you, Lord Trevlan?"

"Of course," he replied amiably as he bowed to Miss Lane.

She looked to see if Miss Hennings noticed as Trevlan carried Hypatia and then Letty from the rowboat. She seemed to be much more interested in flirting with the other men on the shore. Diana turned her attention to the luncheon with a lighter heart.

"What can I do to help you?" Lord Trevlan asked, flinging himself onto the grass beside where the lunch was laid out on a linen cloth.

"Well, if you had not taken your time carting young ladies about, you might have helped me," she teased. "As it is, there is nothing left to do but carve." She handed him a knife. "We sailors must eat after our sojourn across the Mediterranean."

Luncheon passed pleasantly enough, with John amusing everyone by pretending to eat chicken bones and making rude noises with the jellies. Diana laughed, but she could feel herself blushing. If only he would be a little less crass. However, she had more to worry about than John. If Hypatia loved Trevlan, but Trevlan admired Miss Hennings, and Miss Hennings was merely toying with his affection . . . well, it could be quite the bumble broth.

The meal was long over before Diana had a chance to corner Trevlan. "I was thinking you might walk with me to gather some of the lilies that grow by the temple," she said urgently as the others were formulating a plan to search for early strawberries.

"Certainly." His brows drew together in an expression of mild curiosity, but he did not question her further. He helped her to her feet, and they walked in silence toward the mock-Grecian temple that stood at the edge of a man-made cove of the lake.

"Is something the matter?" he asked at last.

"No," she dragged the word out reluctantly. Now that she had him to herself, her worries seemed silly. "I'm anxious about Hypatia." She tapped her fan across her palm.

"Why? Her ankle is much better, surely."

She squinted out across the lake. Its sparkling surface was blindingly bright. "No, it is not that. I'm worried that she might not suit you after all." She opened the fan and then shut it with a snap. "Do you think you would prefer Miss Hennings? She is a very lovely girl, you know. And so very vivacious . . ." She opened and closed the fan again. "I should have known that you would prefer someone with some spirit. I should have thought of her in the beginning, since she is so very—"

"Miss Quinlan!" He grabbed the fan by its sticks to still her. "Enough! I do not prefer Miss Hennings."

"You don't?" The air rushed out of her lungs.

"I don't. In fact, I believe she has conceived a bit of a tendre for Mr. Almsworth."

"Has she?" She looked up in amazement. His hazel eyes were laughing down at her. "How could I not have noticed?"

"Perhaps you yourself have been too in love to have noticed anyone else in the same state."

Her gaze dropped to the fan they both still held. "Yes, of course," she said in a dull voice.

"Well," he continued cheerfully, relinquishing the fan, "are these the flowers you wanted?" He kicked at a clump at the base of the temple steps.

"Yes. They're pretty, aren't they? However, I must apologize for the temple. It is the most ridiculously ostentatious monstrosity ever built. I can't imagine what my father was thinking."

He walked inside and glanced around impassively. "So abbeys are allowed, but temples are not?"

She hung in the doorway. Perhaps it would not be quite right to disappear into the temple with Lord Trevlan. As its columned sides were artfully tumbled down, it was quite open nearly all the way around, but people might talk. "I dislike it because it was built only for show," she said. "A real temple might be different. Although why there would be a Greek temple in the middle of Lancashire, I couldn't begin to fathom."

Trevlan appeared to lose interest in the structure and rejoined her outside. She looked over her shoulder from where she was gathering some flowers and saw that he was watching her with a faint smile.

"What about Letty?" she asked with a frown.

"Letty?"

"Miss Leticia. You cannot tell me that you missed the look she was giving you as you carried her from the boat."

"I did not." He sat down on the steps and watched her as she continued to sporadically rip up lilies. "Miss Leticia is a child. I would be surprised if she is a day over sixteen. I have no desire to wed a mere infant."

"Oh." She straightened. "Well, I didn't suppose that you would."

"I think the gardener will be quite distraught when he sees the havoc you have wreaked on his lilies," he said mildly after a moment.

She stared in horror at the fistful of flowers. Their earth-covered roots dangled in an ugly clot from the bottom of her bouquet. "Oh, dear. I suppose I was a bit too enthusiastic. Well, Lord Trevlan, I feel much better for our little talk." For some reason, she did not feel very much better at all. "I was hoping that you would not break Hypatia's heart by falling in love with another woman."

"I think there is very little chance of that."

The stems of the flowers bent under her grip. "Good."

There seemed nothing else to say, so they began slowly walking back toward the glade. Diana walked at the edge of the path so that there was no chance of her bare arm brushing against his sleeve. Good; at least Hypatia's happiness was safe.

"Di, where have you been?" John demanded when they reached the clearing.

"I went to pick some flowers." She shoved her mangled bouquet toward him.

"Well, you should have come with the rest of us. Miss Hypatia found half a worm in the strawberry she was eating. Had to be revived from a dead faint!" He laughed loudly. "Must have swallowed the other half, and I'll be damned if she didn't turn quite as green as the worm itself."

He gestured over to where Mr. Almsworth and Mr. Jenkins were supporting a very unwell-looking Miss Lane. Trevlan went to her and began making quiet inquiries. Diana tried to work up the energy to feel satisfied, but she suddenly felt very tired.

"John, there is enough room in the other two boats for everyone. Why don't you and I row back together?"

"Suits me. I don't want to be stuck in a boat with that shrieking Hennings chit anyway."

It was hard not to feel better once they were floating on the serene surface of the lake. She leaned back and shaded her eyes with her fan. It looked like the rest of the party were getting into the boats at last.

"You're awfully quiet, Di," John grumbled. He gave another pull on the oars and then rested them on the gunwales.

She shut her fan and tapped it against his knee. "It was unkind of you to tease Hypatia; she was quite distressed."

"Aw, come off it. It was only in fun. The ape leader has no sense of humor."

"She is my cousin, and I am very fond of her," she frowned.

John shrugged and gave another pull at the oars. "I didn't say anything against her; I just said she had no sense of humor. It's a fact. Besides, Trevlan was willing enough to coddle her."

"Yes," she said faintly. Of course Trevlan was kind to Hypatia. She wondered how long it would be before he proposed.

The other two boats were rowing homeward. In the late afternoon sun the whole valley was gilded with warmth, and the rippling reflections of the boats on the water gave the whole scene a pastoral serenity. She felt jarringly out of place in it.

"Trevlan's an odd one," John continued. "Never really know what he's saying. Them blue-bloods think they're too clever by half, even when they haven't got a feather to fly with. I've a fancy your mother had an eye on him and his title for you."

She shrugged dismissively. "She will be happy enough to have my family allied with yours." Hypatia was talking animatedly while Trevlan listened. Diana saw him nod in response, obviously hanging on every word she said. She found herself ungraciously hoping the worm Hypatia had swallowed would give her indigestion.

"Right. Well, so I was thinking that we should marry right away."

Her head jerked up. "Right away?"

"Work on your parents tonight about our engagement. They'll come around. I'll ride out tomorrow for the license, and the day after that we can have the vicar marry us. What do you think about that, Di? Day after tomorrow you could be doing your wifely duty." He leered suggestively.

She pressed back the feeling of horror. No; she had promised herself to John. After all the fuss she'd made, she couldn't very well cry off. Besides, John loved her. She looked across the water to where Trevlan was handing Hypatia out of the boat. "Yes," she heard her own voice say steadily; "let us marry immediately."

SIX

Trevlan was certain that he was dying. His gaze drifted to the ceiling in the vague hope that it would cave in suddenly and put a swift end to his misery. He had never been so bored in his life.

The rest of the men sat around the dinner table as the port made its circuit. It must have been hours since the covers had been removed. He sank lower in his chair and stifled the urge to groan. Perhaps it was for the best that there was no longer any sharp cutlery left on the table.

". . . So I bet the whole lot that my bay gelding would throw his rider before Holben's gray threw his. I never laughed so hard in my life! You should have seen the man tumble when he came to the stone wall at the bottom of the hill! I won back everything I had lost." Stiles laughed uproariously and then drained his glass.

"Someone else was riding your horse?" Trevlan asked. He must have drifted into a stupor partway through the story. He had stopped drinking long before, knowing he could not keep up with Stiles. Jenkins was already face-down on the table. Trevlan envied his state of unconsciousness.

Stiles looked at him as though he were an idiot. "I bet Holben that my bay was worse-tempered than his animal, so we hired a few mill workers to see who would be thrown first."

"Ah." Trevlan smiled thinly. What did Miss Quinlan see in this man? Obviously he minded his manners more in public, but— He told the voice in his head to be quiet. The kind of man Miss Quinlan found attractive was entirely her own business.

Mr. Gaffield and Mr. Almsworth embarked on a detailed analysis of the proper technique necessary for clearing an obstacle while following the hunt on a downhill grade. Trevlan watched Stiles refill his glass.

"How did you meet Miss Quinlan?" The voice in his head blurted the question aloud before he had time to stop it.

Stiles gave him a slow, port-heavy grin. "Di? I met her in Leeds. Heard Jim Quinlan was rolling in the ready and decided the gel was just my type." His laugh was thick. "It's dear indeed to keep up my style of living, and I ain't nearly as flush as you might think."

He lowered his voice to a level that Trevlan was obliged to assume was conspiratorial. "It's hush-hush until I'm leg-shackled, but Miss Quinlan and her moneybags came like an angel from heaven in my time of direst need." He gave a sage nod and took a gulp of liquor. "I knew you'd understand which way the wind blows, eh, Trev?" He gave Trevlan a violent nudge with his elbow. "You know what it is like to need to wed a golden goose, don't you?" Stiles made a floppy gesture toward Trevlan's feet. "You with your mended shoes and your darned shirts. You know what it's like."

His blue eyes opened widely, and Trevlan had a rather ghastly view of the abused blood vessels in them. " 'Course it's a good deal more dear to keep someone like me in funds. You wouldn't catch me in a darned shirt, that's for damned certain."

Trevlan's jaw clenched. "You're marrying Miss Quinlan for her money."

Stiles slid his elbow down the table until he was practically lying down. "Now, now, don't come up all moral on me. I know very well that you had hoped to get your hooks in her yourself. But I got her first, fair and square, so there is no point in pokering up like an archbishop. Besides," he continued, mercifully oblivious to the fact that Trevlan was very near planting him a facer, "Diana loves me."

The statement burst Trevlan's rage like a bubble. She did love Stiles. He thought of her expression when she spoke of the man on the first day he met her. "But you have deceived her," he said icily, annoyed that he even cared.

Stiles shrugged. "A bit. But I understand Di. I understand what she needs and wants a damn sight better than a down-at-heel blue-blood like you."

Trevlan smiled blandly, but his mind was racing. Perhaps, if Diana knew what Stiles was really like . . . Then what? Then she would chose him instead? He could only offer her a mountain of debts and a title she obviously cared nothing for. But at least he held her in high regard. Hell, he was practically in love with the girl. The notion made him wonder if he had drunk too much port after all.

Stiles slapped his shoulder. "But no hard feelings about the chit, eh? What say we tear off for a bit of shooting in the morning? You fancy that, lads?" Stiles turned to Gaffield and Almsworth, who had moved from the fascinating subject of taking fences on a downhill grade to that of taking them uphill.

Trevlan leaned back in his chair and began mapping out his battle plan.

"Lord Trevlan, I am very disappointed in you." Miss Quinlan put her hands on her hips and regarded him with a teasingly severe expression. She looked to see if anyone was coming up the stairs and pulled him into the gallery.

"Why?" he asked innocently.

"Last night when we played crambo, you did not take the opportunity to make a sly little rhyme about Hypatia's beauty."

"Hypatia is a very difficult name to rhyme," he protested.

"And you did not contrive to be on her team in charades."

"I preferred to watch her."

"And then this morning, when she expressed disappointment that the weather was bad, you might have offered to walk with her along the gallery"—she gestured to the portraits behind her—"or asked her to sketch your portrait, or taken her to see the new kittens in the stables."

"Why would I have wanted her to draw my portrait?"

"Then you could have praised her, you dolt." She rolled her eyes. "You could have sat very close to her and talked about what a very fine artist she is."

He sighed and ran his hand through his hair in a gesture of frustration. "I just don't seem to be able to do it." He collapsed onto a bench in despair. "You must give me lessons."

"Lessons?" She looked down at him with that adorable little line forming between her brows.

"Yes." He leaned his head against the oak paneling and closed his eyes. "Lessons in flirtation."

"Ah." She thought for a moment. "Well, you certainly could use some aid. You really hardly spoke a word to her last night. And when John was teasing her so dreadfully about that worm, you might have jumped to her defense. You might have taken the opportunity to pat her hand, for example."

"You see?" He heaved a dispirited sigh. "I never would have thought of that. You must teach me what to do."

She sat down beside him on the bench and turned to him. "I think you know very well what to do. You just don't know when to do it. You cannot go plowing in and declare yourself or you will frighten her."

He had a difficult time picturing Miss Lane frightened of anything. "Very well. You play the part of Miss Lane and I will play myself." He sat with his hands on his knees and watched her expectantly.

"Well, you can't very well expect me to start the conversation. Say something innocuous." She composed herself and pretended to be extremely interested in the carpet.

He cleared his throat. "It is a very fine day."

"We're inside," she hissed.

"Can't we pretend we're outside? I plan to make my great play for her heart when we're outside."

"It's raining!"

He threw up his hands. "Fine. We're inside." He hid his smile with a ruthless swipe of his hand. "What a pity it is raining and we cannot go outside."

"Yes, I would have liked to have gone for a walk," Diana replied in a high voice that was nothing like Miss Lane's. "See, she means a walk with *you*," she explained in her own voice.

He nodded gravely. "Where would you have gone on your walk, Miss Lane?"

"I love to walk amongst the roses," she simpered.

"But you would put them to shame with your loveliness."

Diana laughed delightedly. "Ah, very good. A little heavy-handed, but we shall not deduct points since you are a novice. Now Hypatia will blush and give you a light slap on the arm with her fan, or perhaps her fingers if she is not carrying a fan."

"We must hope she is not carrying a parasol or a large stick," he said dryly.

She shot him a look of reproof and then rapped him on the sleeve. "La, sir, how you do go on."

The silver streaks in her eyes were like a starburst. He

was suddenly possessed with the vague urge to count each ray. "Now what do I do?"

"Well, you will continue to make inconsequential conversation, but you must watch her very closely. If she turns on the seat toward you, that is very good. If she touches her fan to her cheek, that is even better. Blushing is good; breathless is excellent."

"Yes?" He savagely repressed the laugh that twitched the corners of his mouth.

"Oh, yes. You must only pay attention in order to know where you stand with her. Now, at some point you should lean closer to her. Just a little, mind you. If she does not lean away, I think we can safely assume that she is very amenable to your suit."

"Very wise advice. Is this sort of thing taught in books these days? No wonder I am still a bachelor! Where were we? Ah, yes, 'La, sir, how you do go on.' " He rubbed his chin and drew a deep breath. "You think me merely flattering you, Miss Lane," he began in a low voice, "but I must assure you that I am quite sincere."

Diana had been fumbling with the handle of her fan, but she looked up, and he held her gaze.

"I know I am overstepping my bounds, and I would never do anything to distress you . . ." He leaned closer. Diana swayed slightly but did not retreat. The color was high in her cheeks. "But I can no longer suppress the feelings I have for you. Miss Lane, I lo—"

Her fingers flew to his lips. "Oh, don't say love," she said quickly. "It is too soon. You will frighten her."

"I admire you?"

Their voices had sunk to whispers. "Yes, and then she will most likely look down, very modestly. . . ." Her own brilliant blue eyes were veiled by dark lashes.

"And then I could lean even closer. . . ." The tiny dark tendrils at her hairline trembled under his breath.

"Yes. . . ." Her voice was almost inaudible.

"And I could lift up her chin. . . ." Her expression, when he turned up her face, was one of anxiety mixed with longing. He was carrying this too far. He should lean back, laugh, and begin some other conversation. But he couldn't tear his eyes away. He couldn't even blink.

"Yes?" The one word she breathed through her parted lips removed any resolution he had.

His mouth was so close to hers that just speaking would touch their lips together. "And I could kiss her."

She made a tiny noise that wasn't exactly a sigh, and closed the infinitesimal space between them.

With a strength he didn't know he had, he moved away at the last possible instant, his lips brushing her cheek. God, he longed to kiss her just once. Just to know what it was like. Just to know what he would be missing for the rest of his life. He sat back with the horrible feeling that his emotions were transparently displayed on his face.

They stared at each other for a moment in stunned silence. "Oh!" she breathed at last. "You did not kiss me after all."

"Diana—" his voice was hoarse.

She rushed on as though she had not heard him. "Well, I daresay you remembered at the last minute that it was me. Still!" She pressed her hand to her heart and laughed. "It was quite intense. You have a natural aptitude for seduction, I think. I daresay if you kissed Hypatia she would faint dead away. And then you would have to call for aid. That would ruin the moment, I can tell you."

"Diana, listen—"

"Good heavens, I'm quite flustered! How silly of me. How cross John would be if he knew I'd let you do that, even though you were only pretending. The poor man's ridden all the way to Manchester in the rain to get a license for our wedding."

"Wedding?" he repeated stupidly.

"Of course." She met his eyes innocently, but her hand

crept to her throat and she began to began to toy with her necklace. Her slim, white fingers shook slightly. "John hopes that if we have a license, we will convince my parents that we are in earnest."

"Yes. Of course." His voice sounded hollow. He rose and bowed briefly over her hand. "Forgive me, Diana." She had told him from the first time they met that she loved Stiles, and he had refused to believe it. In his arrogance, he had thought he could change her mind.

She laughed rather high in her throat. "Oh, you needn't ask my forgiveness. I quite enjoyed our playacting. Though you mustn't worry that I mistook your meaning, for I know you were thinking about Hypatia when you did it. I suppose I should say that I was thinking about John, but to be honest, I am not sure there were any thoughts going through my head at all!" She jumped to her feet and tucked her hands behind her back. "Well, I'm sure I should be glad that you stopped when you did. I should not like to think that my first kiss was from someone who was pretending I was someone else! Really, I think I must have been quite swept away in the moment, for I—"

"Diana," he cut her off. "That was very wrong of me. I took advantage of the situation in a dishonorable manner." He stood up and took her hands in his.

"Oh, don't be silly, Lord Trevlan! I don't blame you if your passion for Miss Lane overcame you. Please don't give the matter another thought. Now, while you're still feeling amorous, why don't you go and find her? I believe she and Letty are in the conservatory."

Trevlan nodded dumbly and started down the stairs. At the last moment, he looked back at her. She had sunk down onto the bench again. One white forefinger moved slowly against her lips as she stared unseeing into space.

* * *

The conservatory seemed unbearably hot after the coolness of the rest of the house. Even in June, the braziers were blazing and the water boys continued to pour cold water over the coals. Clouds of steam rose up from them to make the air chokingly thick with humidity. The room looked like what he imagined the West Indies to be like. It was dense with potted plants and trees whose flowers emitted a cloyingly sweet aroma.

He tugged at his neckcloth and found it rapidly losing its starch. Who would willingly spend their time in here? Even the walls of the room appeared to be sweating as tiny beads of steam condensed on their surface.

He had failed. He had basely tried to seduce an engaged woman and had been entirely rebuffed. Furthermore, his idiotic ruse of using Diana's cousin as his pretended interest had likely served only to convince that young lady to expect a proposal from him.

He forced his steps in the direction of the voices he heard through the veil of vapor. Miss Lane and her sister were seated in a tropical bower. Their fans stirred the tendrils of steam as they half-heartedly continued a languid quarrel.

"Lord Trevlan, how kind of you to join us!" Letty jumped to her feet. "I was just reading aloud to Hypatia from *Romance of the Forest*. This did seem like the most appropriate place to read it. Do you not agree?"

"Indeed." He forced himself to smile. More like *"Romance of the Jungle."* He half hoped he would instantaneously succumb to yellow fever.

"In fact," she continued brightly, "we would be fortunate if we could prevail upon you to read it to both of us. You have such a lovely reading voice. I enjoyed the poetry you read the other night more than any poetry I think I have ever heard before."

"Do be quiet, Letty," her sister cut her off. "You are prattling like a great fool."

Trevlan clutched his hands behind his back and forced himself to continue with what he had decided must be done. "I was hoping that you might like to walk for a few moments with me, Miss Lane."

Her brows rose. "Of course. If you wish. Though I must tell you my ankle is not quite well, so I will not be able to go very far."

He took her arm, and they walked in silence through the glistening foliage. Tendrils of exotic vines and broad flat leaves the size of platters crowded across their path. Miss Lane seemed as cool as though this were a walk through the woods in November. He himself felt as though he were drowning in the wet thickness of the air. "Miss Lane," he began awkwardly. "I am afraid that I must return home unexpectedly."

"Really? How unfortunate." She opened her fan and plied it so slowly that it barely stirred the steam around them. She stared at him when he didn't continue, evidently waiting for him to explain his comment. "Is there something you wish for me to do?" she asked at last.

"Well, I was hoping— That is—" He felt as though he were strangling in the damp heat of the room. "I was hoping that you would do me the honor . . ." His voice died in his throat. Water hit the coals in a brazier with an irritated hiss.

She stopped and looked at him in shock. "Are you proposing to me?"

"I think so," he replied miserably.

"Well, I must say, Lord Trevlan, I am very surprised." Her voice was slightly censorious. "You must have a rather high idea of yourself with that title. Though I can't say that I blame you, what with the way everyone has been toad-eating to you the past few days." She waved her fan at the cloud of steam that rose from the brazier. "In any case, I know you will appreciate my complete honesty in this matter. Everyone knows your family is quite encumbered, and, to be quite frank, I don't believe my family would be prepared to go to bail for yours, even if you are due to inherit an earldom at some vague date. A rather recent earldom, if my memory serves correctly."

"Ah." The air rushed out of his lungs.

"Letty will tell you differently, of course, because she has developed a ridiculous schoolgirl's tendre for you, but it will not do you any good to ask for her hand either, because I assure you that my father will not allow it."

He was free. If he had led Miss Lane to believe she should expect a proposal of marriage, he had fulfilled any obligation and Diana could not accuse him of having duped her cousin. Even his father could not fault him for not having attempted a second match after Miss Quinlan's rejection. He and Miss Lane must have distanced themselves from the pans of coals, for he began to feel slightly better. He bowed over her hand and smiled the first genuine smile he had managed since he had found her. "I thank you for your honesty, Miss Lane. You have saved me from a good deal of grief."

SEVEN

Diana was not sure how she had managed to make it through the day. Certainly she had laughed while Mr. Almsworth, Mr. Jenkins, and Mr. Gaffield entertained the party with their own invention of indoor cricket. She had presided over the luncheon table and told witty anecdotes about her season in London. She had even instigated a game of "Hunt the Squirrel," which had ended in the discovery of Miss Hennings and Mr. Almsworth embracing in the linen closet.

This last event had upset her more than she would like to admit. Seeing them in each other's arms had brought back the memory of the morning's debacle in a surge of shame. How could she have let Lord Trevlan very nearly kiss her? Even now she found herself wondering what would have happened if he had not stopped himself. At the same moment when John was riding through the rain to obtain a license so that they could be married, she was wishing desperately that Gabriel Trevlan wanted her as much as he wanted Hypatia Lane.

"It is a pity that Lord Trevlan did not wish to play with us." Letty sighed and flung herself onto a sofa.

Diana assumed an air of nonchalance. "Yes, I have not seen him all day."

"Didn't he tell you he was leaving?"

Her heart stopped. "Leaving?"

"Well, yes," Letty loosed another despondent sigh. "He came and told Hypatia and me good-bye when we were in the conservatory. What a shame he had obligations at home arise so suddenly."

"Has he gone already?" Diana heard the panic in her voice, and willed herself to remain calm.

"I don't know."

She barely heard her. She took the stairs two at a time and flung open the door to his room. It was tidily bare of any evidence he had ever stayed there.

The upstairs maid walked by with her arms loaded with linens. "Where is Lord Trevlan?" Diana demanded.

The woman's brows rose at the unaccustomed sharpness in her voice. "I think he's gone out to the stables, miss."

She tried to keep from running, but her legs kept breaking into an undignified trot. It didn't occur to her to send a servant to the stables or even to take an umbrella as she ran across the courtyard. The rain was coming down heavily, and she arrived in the stables panting and wet. "Is Lord Trevlan still here?" she called out into the dimness.

"He is." She saw him stand up from where he had been sitting on his trunk.

"Where are you going? How dare you go without taking leave of me?" Her relief at finding him turned to anger. She marched over to him.

"I had every intention of coming back to the house to explain myself," he replied calmly.

She saw several grooms pretending to be busy nearby and motioned them away with an irritated gesture. "Why are you leaving?"

"I'm not. Your coachman refuses to set out in such weather."

She pushed her wet hair back from her face with an impatient hand. "You know that is not what I mean."

He sighed. "I came here in order to marry you. We

have decided to call off that match, so there is no point in my staying." His shoulders lifted in a shrug.

"What of Hypatia?" she heard her voice go shrill.

He rubbed his hand across his forehead, but did not meet her eyes. "Miss Lane has also refused me."

The breath went out of her. Hypatia did not love him. "Oh, Trevlan . . ." she stammered. "I'm so sorry."

He still did not meet her gaze. "It is for the best. We did not suit. To be honest, my pursuit of her was only to please you." His laugh did not really sound like a laugh.

"What?"

"Look at you. You're quite soaked. You didn't come racing out here just to find me, did you? What a ridiculous creature you are." He threw his coat over her shoulders. "Now, since I am unable to go home until the weather improves, we shall both go back to the house."

"You never loved Hypatia?" she repeated weakly.

His hands stilled on her shoulders. "You should know better than anyone that for someone in my position, love has nothing to do with it. I am in need of a rich wife, if you recall." She could not see his face, but his voice was bitter.

She turned and looked up at him. His hazel eyes were impossible to read. "But if you are not in love with Hypatia, why—"

Trevlan was not listening to her. His attention was caught by the sound of a horse's hooves clattering across the court. Two grooms brushed by them to take the rider's steaming animal. The man flung himself off and stomped into the stables.

"Damned awful weather," he said, taking off his hat.

"John!" Diana cried out. She realized belatedly that she sounded more horrified than pleased.

"What are you two doing here?" he demanded heartily. "Waiting for my return?"

"Unfortunately, I have business at home to attend to,"

Trevlan replied. "I was hoping to leave today, but Miss Quinlan and her coachman have convinced me that the weather is far too inclement."

"Not too inclement for me," John puffed out his chest. "But I had my Diana to get back to." He wrapped an arm around her waist and gave her a proprietary kiss on the mouth.

"I'm glad you're back, John," she murmured, wishing she didn't feel so awkward.

"Well, so am I. Let's go into the house and give your parents the good news."

"Oh. I suppose you got it then," she stammered.

He patted his chest pocket proudly. "I've got it. We can be married tomorrow."

She could not stop herself from looking at Trevlan. He was absently watching the rain roar down outside the doorway. His expression was of absolute boredom. "If Mama and Papa agree, you know," she reminded John with a frown. "And I am not at all certain that they will."

" 'Course they will, Di. They won't deny their youngest daughter anything she has set her heart on." John flicked Lord Trevlan's coat off her shoulders. It landed in a heap on the mud- and straw-covered floor. She turned back for it, but John took her by the elbow, tucked her beneath the arm of his own greatcoat, and trotted her back to the house.

"Diana," James Quinlan shook his head. "Are you certain that this is what you want?"

She smoothed the skirts of the dry dress she had changed into and mutely nodded her head.

"Are you out of your mind, James?" Her mother's voice rose shrilly. "She has the chance to marry into the peerage, and you would allow her to marry the son of a stocking maker?" She leaned her head back against the settee.

"Really, Diana, I don't understand how you can spend three days in the company of both men and not be able to tell chalk from cheese."

Her father crossed his arms. "If she wishes to marry Stiles, she shall have Stiles."

"She only wishes to be perverse," her mother insisted. "Honestly, she has only known Stiles for a few weeks. We never should have let her go and visit your sister in Leeds. *She* put these ideas into Diana's head." Mrs. Quinlan pulled her shawl closer around her and sniffed indignantly. "Until then Diana had been willing to make a good match like Susan and Eleanor. Trust your sister to be filling her head with romantic nonsense just to spite us. She was always jealous that our girls married well and her own son Philip only managed to marry into shipping."

"John is a . . . is a very good man," Diana said defiantly. For some reason her eyes were beginning to sting. She blinked hard. If she burst out crying, her parents would never be convinced.

Both of them ignored her. "The Stileses are known to have plenty of the ready, even if they are a hard-gaming kind of family," her father leaned forward to say to Mrs. Quinlan. "It's a good enough match. You have two daughters buckled into jumped-up, ill-suited marriages; why do you need another?"

The lace on her mother's cap was trembling in suppressed fury. "I want Diana to better herself. If she marries Stiles, she will never be anything more than the wife of a cit."

"And that isn't good enough?" he roared. "If it was good enough for you, it is good enough for Diana!" He rose to his feet. "Diana is marrying this John Stiles tomorrow, and that is the end to it." He marched out of the room.

Diana sat silently for a long time while her mother wept.

"Tomorrow," Diana said at last in a hollow voice.

"Tomorrow," her mother repeated dourly. "And what does that man expect you to wear? We've no time to make up a proper trousseau. I had started one when we were contracting with Trevlan, but of course it isn't ready yet."

Mrs. Quinlan sat up and shook her finger at the chair James had vacated. "I suppose your father wouldn't care if you were married in a riding habit three years out of fashion, but I won't have it, I tell you! We'll have Madame Tonnard up from Manchester, and you will have a proper wedding gown if I have to help her stitch it myself. No one is going to say that a daughter of mine was not turned out in style. Stiles! Why did you have to go and pick a man like Stiles! I could understand if he were handsomer than Trevlan. All you young girls think about is looks. But Trevlan is nothing if not handsome, and you turn your nose up at him as though you were a princess. He will be an earl someday!"

After this violent and somewhat incoherent outburst, her mother collapsed back onto the settee.

"I suppose I had better go and tell everyone," Diana said in a weak voice.

"I don't know what the vicar will think of us with this havey cavey business. We'll have the whole county saying that you are with child."

"Mother!"

"Well, there is no sense in being missish about it, Diana. You know as well as I that that is what will be bandied about. And honestly, if you go and get impregnated right away so that the baby is born nine months from now, I swear I will have your hide, I really will."

"Mama! Enough! I have enough on my mind without worrying what the neighbors will think if . . . if that happens. I am going downstairs to our guests."

"Well, really, Diana," her mother continued as she left the room. "It would be most embarrassing. If you must marry a man like that—"

Diana closed the door. She leaned her head back against it and tried to collect her senses. Tomorrow. By tomorrow she would be married to John. Which was exactly what she wanted. Wasn't it?

EIGHT

It wasn't until after dinner that she got up the courage to tell anyone. Perhaps it helped that Trevlan wasn't in the room. Maybe it was only guilt that was eating away at her. After all, her willfulness in marrying John meant that he would be forced to continue in poverty until he found a rich wife. She had wasted his time.

"Are you all right, Miss Quinlan?" Miss Hennings asked in an undertone.

She started. "Yes, yes, of course. In fact, I am very happy indeed. Ladies," she raised her voice so that Hypatia and Letty could hear over their quarreling. "I have accepted an offer of marriage from Mr. Stiles. We will be married tomorrow."

"Mr. *Stiles?*" Letty echoed incredulously. "You mean Lord Trevlan."

Diana's head jerked around. "Why would I mean him?" None of her family had breathed a word of the proposed match!

"Well, you looked as though you had developed a tendre for him," Miss Hennings replied for the gaping Letty.

"We all thought so," Letty chimed in.

"How ridiculous. I hardly know the man."

"But you said when we were boating how handsome and wonderful he was." Letty's innocent eyes opened wider. "I think he is handsome and marvelous too, but of course if he had the choice between you and me, he would pick you."

"Nonsense! Besides, he told me he offered for you, Hypatia." Diana's head was beginning to ache. She walked over to the pianoforte to escape the tirade of exclamations. Now that the rain had stopped, the windows had been opened to let in the cooling breeze. She inhaled the fresh, damp air and felt slightly soothed.

"I confess, I was surprised to have received an offer from him. After all, he never showed a partiality for me in the entire time we have been here." Hypatia shrugged prosaically. "In any case, Diana says she will have Mr. Stiles. May I offer you my felicitations, Diana."

"Thank you," Diana murmured. She sat down at the instrument and began to play. She realized it was the same tune she had played the night that Trevlan had stood beside her and turned the pages of music for her. She abruptly began another piece.

"Did you say you were getting married tomorrow?" Miss Hennings cocked her head to one side and looked slightly perplexed.

"Well, we hope to. It is not quite set with the vicar yet." Despite the freshness of the air, she began to feel as though she were choking. "You will all attend?"

"How could we not attend? We are staying at your house," Hypatia said reprovingly. "It is the last day of our stay, though, so it is a fitting end. Then we may go home and you may go on your honeymoon. It is very like a theatrical comedy to end with a wedding."

Diana didn't feel as if it were a comedy. It must just be nerves. "Well, we shall start the celebrations early. Shall we dance tonight? Mama had her dinner in her room, but she promised me that she would come down afterwards. Perhaps we can prevail upon her to play the pianoforte."

"A' up, ladies," John burst into the room with his customary after-dinner exuberance. "Are you ready to drink to my health tomorrow?" He clapped Letty on the back. "In fact, we shall drink to the health of my affianced and myself tonight. Billings? Where is that butler? Billings, bring in some champagne."

Diana meant to keep her eyes on John, but they were somehow drawn to Trevlan. He was absorbed in removing a piece of lint from his sleeve.

"Miss Quinlan says that we shall have dancing," Miss Hennings announced. She took Mr. Almsworth by the hand and danced across the room.

It took only a few moments for the footman to roll up the rugs and slightly longer to convince Mrs. Quinlan to come downstairs to play the pianoforte. She insisted dolefully that she did not know any tunes suitable for dancing, but admitted under duress that she knew a few Christmas songs that might do for a country dance.

As there were an odd number of gentlemen, Mr. Gaffield and Lord Trevlan vied for the honor of sitting out, but in the end Lord Trevlan was forced to give in and take his place in the set with Letty as his partner. Diana could not help wondering if the girl was hoping to throw herself at Trevlan now that she knew him to be unattached.

Her mother began a slightly ponderous version of "The Holly and the Ivy." Sally Hennings and Letty were thrown into fits of the giggles. It was a bit odd to be dancing to Christmas songs in June. Diana suddenly felt very provincial and annoyed with herself for caring. After all, her life and her upbringing had always been good enough for her before.

"John, I was thinking," she began quietly as he stood up beside her. "Must we rush the wedding so? I mean, it is quite an inconvenience to our guests to expect them to attend a last-minute wedding on their last day here."

He looked at her in surprise. "But it's all set for tomorrow! I thought you were chafing at the bit to get the thing settled. Aw, come on now, Di. There is no use putting it off when we know it is what we want. I don't want a long engagement, and I know you don't either. Otherwise you'll just have time to get all fidgety."

Diana was feeling very fidgety now. "Perhaps just a few weeks?" she suggested weakly.

"Nonsense. Tomorrow is better. Married the 24th of June, Midsummer day. That sounds nice, now doesn't it?"

The figures of the dance separated them and she could not respond. Not that she knew what she would say anyway. The next figure dictated that she take hands with her counter partner, Lord Trevlan. She raised her eyes tentatively and found him smiling down at her.

"Congratulations, Miss Quinlan," he said softly. "I wish you every happiness." His hand was warm and reassuring, but she felt that all the former intimacy between them was gone. There was nothing between them but a neutral acquaintanceship.

How dare he be so kind, so understanding? Now it was too late. She was promised to Stiles, and any latent hope that her parents would refuse their consent had evaporated. There was no way out of it without causing an enormous, disgraceful scandal. Her heart began racing uncomfortably fast.

Tomorrow night the house party would be over, Trevlan would go home, and she would never see him again. Tomorrow night she would be irrevocably changed into Mrs. Stiles. She was breathing as fast as she could but still couldn't seem to catch her breath.

"Are you all right?" Trevlan asked sharply.

"Fine," she gasped. "I'm just feeling a little dizzy." The room was beginning to darken around the edges. "I think I need to sit down for a moment."

"What are you doing, Diana? A little too much wine at dinner, eh?" John took her about the waist and pulled her over to a chair. She looked up at Trevlan, but he had already turned back to the dancers.

* * *

"Well, I am certain that the dress will not be ready until two minutes before the ceremony, but at least no one can say that you were not properly turned out." Mrs. Quinlan sat before her dressing table and allowed her dresser to run a comb through her hair.

Diana, who sat crumpled at the end of her mother's bed, did not reply.

"I must say, I am most gratified that Barbara Hennings is coming. She shall see that your wedding is a great deal finer than her oldest daughter Mary's was." She dabbed on a bit of rouge and examined the effect critically. "We shall have real turtle soup, while she only had mock. And there are ells and ells of lace on your gown. I'm certain it cost a good deal more than anything Mary wore." She held up a necklace to her bosom, shook her head, and chose another. "Why, I think that—"

"Were you miserable on your wedding day?" Diana interrupted.

"Miserable? Of course I was miserable." Her mother's eyes darted to hers in the mirror. "But the initial pain goes away after the first time or two, and it becomes nothing more than an inconvenience."

Diana sank lower. "I didn't mean that. I meant about the idea of marrying Papa. Of being married to him forever."

"No, you're making it too poufy. Do you want me to look ridiculous?" Mrs. Quinlan scowled at her dresser and flattened the woman's handiwork with a vicious palm. She looked back at Diana. "Your papa was considered a very good match. There were twelve girls in the county who were panting to marry him. I was the prettiest." She smiled at her reflection.

"Oh."

"I do wish this wasn't such a rushed affair. I really do

think that we could have hired musicians from Manchester if we had given enough notice. After all, you will only get married once, one hopes." She batted her dresser's hands away and began inserting plumes into her hair herself. "I should like to do the affair right."

"Only once." Diana's brow furrowed. She clutched her hands around her knees and rested her chin on them.

"At least the roses were early this year. We should have quite enough. Barbara Hennings will be beside herself. Mary was foolish enough to be married in October and there was not a blossom to be had for love or money. We shall have orchids from the conservatory at every place setting. I shall put the largest one at her setting just to see the woman go green." Mrs. Quinlan turned around. Her coif was so full of plumes she looked as though an enormous pink ostrich had taken up roost on her head. "Where are you going, Diana?"

Diana turned with her hand on the doorknob. All her listlessness was gone, and there was a strange light in her eyes. "I wouldn't bother finishing, Mama," she said with an odd laugh. "I don't believe there will be a wedding today after all."

Trevlan felt like kicking himself. He should have insisted that the Quinlans' coachman drive him home yesterday. How was he going to stand in the Quinlans' parish church and watch Diana marry someone else? He drew a deep breath and finished tying his cravat. Fate had a very ill-bred sense of humor sometimes.

He went downstairs to the breakfast room, but he could hear the sound of feminine chatter through the door. Miss Lane and her sister were quarreling vociferously over what they would wear to the wedding. He decided he was not hungry.

The library was cool and dark. Through the windows

he could see the gardeners stripping the rose bushes of every available flower for the coming celebration. He flung himself into a chair. There was no escaping it.

He was not sure how long he had been sitting there, blue-deviled, when he heard voices. The angry tones penetrated the door separating the library from the adjoining study. When he caught the sound of Diana's voice, he leapt to his feet.

"Be reasonable, John! You cannot wish me to marry you when I do not love you."

"You can't cry off the day of the wedding!" Stiles's voice was rough. "You said you would marry me and you will."

Trevlan's heart stopped. He should leave. This was not a conversation he should be hearing.

Stile's voice grew more desperate. "You must marry me. I'll be in a terrible state if you don't."

"Let go of me. You're hurting my arm."

The blood was ringing in Trevlan's ears. If Diana was really in danger, he should interrupt. She sounded more angry than frightened, though. Perhaps she would resent any intrusion into their lovers' quarrel, which was probably only the result of wedding-day jitters. He hesitated, his fist clenched on the door to the study.

Stiles's voice continued in an irritated whine. "It's the 24th of June, Di. Debts come due today. If you don't marry me, I'm finished."

"What?" There was a silence. "I thought you said your family business was doing well." Another silence. "You dog! Another man who wants me only for my money!"

Trevlan's skin stung as though she had slapped him. God, she had lumped him together with Stiles. His fingers ached to throw open the door and beg for a chance to explain.

"I do love you, Di!"

"Get away!"

"You can't cry off!"

"Stop it!"

"I'll kill you if you do, Di, I swear I will. I've got to—"

They both looked up in shock when Trevlan burst in. Diana threw off Stiles's arms and stood back from him, panting. Her face was red, and her hair had come partly loose from its pins.

"What are you doing here?" Stiles roared.

Trevlan approached him with all the coiled serenity of a loaded pistol. "If you touch her, I will kill you."

Stiles's handsome face twisted derisively. "Playing the knight errant, Lord Smug? Are you hoping to win Diana's moneybags now that she has thrown me over?"

"Get out of here, both of you!"

They ignored Diana. "You told her, didn't you?" Stiles hissed. "You waited until the last minute, knowing how much I needed it, and then you told her I was marrying the golden goose."

Diana inserted herself between them. "You knew?" she turned to Trevlan. "You knew he was a fortune hunter, and you did not tell me?" Her starburst blue eyes begged him to deny it.

He glared over her head at Stiles. "I didn't tell her. I said nothing because I knew she loved you. And I foolishly credited you with the brains to love her in return."

"You knew?" Diana repeated.

"I'll sue you for breach of contract, Di. You said you would marry me. I have a marriage license with your name on it!"

She did not appear to hear Stiles. Her eyes were still fixed on Trevlan's face. He could not meet her gaze. He turned to Stiles instead. "If you bring suit, the courts will laugh at you. Miss Quinlan has every right to cry off."

Stiles started to reply, but Diana gave them each a hard elbow in the chest. "Listen to you, fighting like schoolboys over a toy. I am not an object to be squabbled over."

Her voice shook with emotion. "Neither of you gives a pin for me or my feelings! To you I am just so many pounds per annum. Fortune hunters, the both of you!"

She stomped over to the door and flung it open. "Well, I'm the one with the money, and I get to decide." Her eyes narrowed. "And if both of you are not out of this house in a quarter of an hour, I will personally see to it that every single one of your debts are collected to the full amount." Without even waiting to see the effect of her dire pronouncement, she slammed the door shut behind her.

NINE

"I told you from the start I knew what was best for you," her mother said for the tenth time.

"I know."

"You should have married Lord Trevlan while you had the chance."

"I know." She sat on the floor next to her mother's settee and leaned her head against the seat.

"Chalk to cheese, I always said. At least with Lord Trevlan you knew where he stood. It's one thing to marry for money openly, but Stiles was trying to do so on the sly, and, well, that's something I could never stand for. And not even a title to go with it!"

Diana sighed. "Well, it matters little now. At least I didn't marry him." She pressed her hands to her cheeks and tried to collect herself. "I only wish that someone wished to marry me for myself."

Her mother prodded her on the shoulder. "There you go talking nonsense again. Be happy you have a fortune behind you. It's your trump card. If you had been born with a title, it would have been nice, but having a fortune means you can buy one, so be happy your father was successful in business."

"Thank you, Mother," she said with a touch of sarcasm. "I feel ever so much better." She got to her feet and smoothed her gown. "I must be getting back to our guests. How shamble-mannered they must think us."

"Dearest, while you are downstairs, tell Cook that she needn't plan on serving the wedding breakfast. Although I suppose it is too late now. We'll likely just have to eat it anyway. Good heavens, and tell that poor seamstress that she can stop working on your dress. The creature has been up all night. She'll charge us a fortune whether we have the wedding or not." Mrs. Quinlan sank back onto the settee. "And, love, could you have Cook send up a tisane? I feel all this excitement has overset my nerves."

Diana closed the door to her mother's room, and saw Lord Trevlan coming down the hall. He looked up, his expression grimly neutral, and then continued toward the stairs between them.

"Wait!" She choked out the word just before her throat closed off.

He stopped, one foot hanging over a step, his face level with hers.

"You must think me very nearly insane." She laughed weakly. "Twice now I have come to beg you not to leave." He said nothing, so she went on. "I should not have said what I did. You are not a fortune hunter, and you never deceived me."

"I should have told you what I knew about Stiles," he said in a low voice.

"I know why you did not. It would have looked as though you were making angry accusations out of pique because I broke off the match between you and me."

He was making this harder. Why couldn't he simply laugh, shake her hand, and tell her to forget everything? Instead he stood there looking achingly sad.

"I knew you loved him," he said at last. "I thought things might work out all right in the end."

Her fingers dug into the newel post. "I didn't love him

after all. That's why I couldn't go through with it." She waited for him to react, but he said nothing.

"Well," she shrugged. "I suppose since we are both unattached, we could go through with the original plan." She tried to laugh as though this were a joke.

He looked down at his hands and rubbed his thumb along the brim of his rather battered-looking hat. "Perhaps," he said after an agonizing pause, "we could try a proper courtship."

She took a deep breath to overcome the sudden pain inside her. "Yes?"

He smiled faintly. "If you do not object, Miss Quinlan, perhaps I might visit you on occasion? I do not actually own a carriage at the moment, but if you wished to go driving on a fine day . . ." There was a faint wash of color on his cheeks that she was possessed with the sudden urge to caress.

"I would like that." She realized how much his offer meant. His father's debts must have come due today too. He was offering her time, though he himself had none to spare. It was his way of showing her that it was not about her dowry.

"I will call on you." His mouth curved up and his face lost its tenseness. "Thank you, Miss Quinlan."

She offered him her hand, and he bowed over it. The warmth of his breath on the back of her hand made her entire body feel wiltingly boneless.

He released her hand, and they stood in silence for a long moment before he at last turned and continued down the stairs.

"Trevlan!" His sister Lydia flung herself into his arms. "Where have you been?"

"At the Quinlans', you knew that." He disentangled himself from her and looked down into her anxious face.

"You wrote five days ago to say that you were coming home immediately. Did you marry her after all? Please say that you did!" She wrung her hands.

"What is happening?" He looked past her. The house was all in commotion.

"The bailiff's men have come for the furniture. Oh, Trevlan, they are taking everything! Papa has put them off for too long. And then, once it was out that you were to marry into the Quinlans' fortune, he got enough credit to lose five thousand pounds at faro."

"But I wrote you to tell him that the engagement was called off."

"It was too late. He hasn't come back from his last gambling session. And now we've been set upon by these, these . . . vultures!" She pushed aside one of the men who was struggling out with a chair. "What will we do?"

He dropped his hat onto a side table and ran his hand through his hair. As the side table had been removed to the wagon outside, his hat fell to the floor. "I don't know. It is all legally theirs."

"Not the pianoforte! Oh, Trevlan, don't let them take my pianoforte!" Lydia darted back and forth between him and the instrument as the men prepared to move it onto their wagon. "Why couldn't you have married Miss Quinlan? Was she so very terrible?"

"She was wonderful."

Lydia stopped still in her revolutions. "What?"

"And she was betrothed to someone else."

"But you had made a marriage settlement with her parents!" She set her hands on her hips and regarded him suspiciously. "What kind of double dealing is this?"

He shrugged. "It matters little now. We did not marry, and now you and I must solve our problems on our own."

Lydia's sigh deflated her. "How?"

He went to run his hands through his hair again, but

stopped himself. "You will have to go and live with Aunt Mary."

"And you?"

He shrugged. "I shall have to find some kind of employment. Who knows?"

His sister batted away the bailiff's men and collapsed on the settee they were attempting to remove. "I hate Miss Quinlan. I really do. How could she go and promise herself to someone else when everything was settled with you? She has ruined our lives, and I truly detest her for it."

Trevlan turned to the window and watched the rain begin to fall. "Well," he said grimly, "I had the misfortune to fall in love with her."

"Now, Diana, there is no point in fancying yourself going into a decline." Mrs. Quinlan pulled her shawls closer around herself and took a fortifying sip of tisane. "You have been wandering about the house like a lost soul for two days. Of course it was a bit of a disappointment about the wedding, but, really, my dear, even your father has admitted that Stiles was not in the least bit suitable."

Diana continued to stare out the window. The battledore net billowed out in the breeze like a sail. "No," she agreed vaguely.

Her mother sniffed indignantly. "No indeed. After all, *I* am the one who must suffer the unbearable sympathy of Barbara Hennings. But there is little point in refining upon it. We must begin thinking of who else might make a suitable candidate."

"What?" Diana looked up with a perplexed expression. "Oh, yes, of course." She picked up the teapot and walked out of the room. What was keeping Lord Trevlan? He had said that he would call. She heard her mother shouting after her, but continued down the hall.

It was strange that she hadn't given a second thought to John once he had left. Shouldn't she be at least a little heartbroken? As it was, she felt a vague sense of irritation and an enormous dose of relief.

It was amazingly easy to admit that she had been wrong about John, that her parents had been right, and that she had fallen in love with Gabriel Trevlan. She rubbed her fingers across her forehead. She stopped in front of a potted palm, absently watered it with the rest of the tea, left the teapot sitting in the middle of the hallway, and went into the room that Trevlan had stayed in.

She closed the door behind her and drew a deep breath. He had been gone for two days, but she could imagine the room still held the smell of him. She remembered the scent of him so well from the evening she played the piano and he had leaned close to her to tell her that she should marry John.

Perhaps she should write him to tell him that she would marry him, courtship or no courtship. He might not love her, but, as her mother always said, her money was her trump card. Trevlan still needed her money, and perhaps, once they were married, he could come to love her. She went to the desk and pulled out a piece of writing paper.

She squeezed her eyes tightly closed and tried to think of the right words. When she opened her eyes, they lit upon a piece of paper that had been written on. As she read the slanted black writing, her hand began to tremble.

"Do not mourn the loss of Miss Quinlan as your sister-in-law. The chit is irredeemably vulgar and bullying. While I would never have said before that the Trevlans have pride, I realize now that a marriage with that ungenteel creature

Trevlan's unfinished tirade of abuse hung in the air as though he had spoken the words aloud. Had he really writ-

ten that? Her mind reeled. They were all terms she had
cheerfully used to describe herself dozens of times, but
seeing them before her in his handwriting hurt her more
than she knew was possible. She had thought he didn't
care about her background. She had thought he . . . liked
her.

But, for all his kindness, for all his renewed offers, he
despised her. She thought of how he had looked intently
into her eyes and pressed her hand when he took leave of
her. Good God, his family must be in desperate straits if
he wished to marry her despite the fact that he found her
personality repulsive.

She violently ripped the paper into small pieces.
"There!" she panted. "Be glad you are rid of me!" She
stood for a moment, surrounded by bits of paper on the
floor, then dropped to her knees and ripped each bit into
even tinier scraps.

"Miss," the butler opened the door. His eyebrows rose
the merest fraction when she looked up with an expression
of rage. "There is a gentleman here to see you."

"I am not seeing anyone," she snapped.

"But it is Lord Trevlan. He said you were—"

"Him!" she cut the butler off with a hiss. "Oh, yes, I
have a thing or two to say to him."

TEN

The parlor door bounced off the wall when Diana flung it open. Trevlan turned from where he was examining the teeth of the crocodiles on the mantel clock. It was exactly the attitude in which she had found him the first time they had met. The memory made him smile. "Diana." He held out both hands to her.

She locked her fingers behind her back. "Hello, Lord Trevlan. Why are you here?"

He stared at her in confusion. Her voice had been sharp and ungracious. "I . . . I needed to talk to you."

Her face was paper white and her eyes sparkled dangerously. She allowed him to draw her to the green silk settee, but slipped her hands from his and clutched them in her lap. His hands felt empty without hers in them.

"I brought you something." He took a book from the table beside him. She did not even glance at it. He tried again. "I came to tell you good-bye."

"I believe we already took leave of each other two days ago," she replied coolly.

"Well," he gave a short laugh, "now I am off to seek my fortune. My family has run into . . . into slight troubles, so I am taking my sister to our aunt's house, and then I am going to seek a position in Town." He resisted the urge to shuffle his feet like a schoolboy. "I will be back as often as I can, and I had hoped that we might spend some time together . . ." He was beginning to become incoherent under the weight of her icy gaze. "I thought perhaps if you wished to go for a walk . . . riding. . . ." God, she was looking at him as though he had just proposed she eat a slug.

"So you've decided that even real work is preferable to a liaison with a rich bourgeois bride?"

He recoiled in horror. "Diana! What's—"

"You great snob!" She spat out the words. "You think that you are so much better than me and my family simply because of your birth."

This was not going at all as he had hoped. "What has happened to make you hate me so?"

"I found your letter." Her chin went up. "I know what you really think of me."

"The letter?" His mind was a blank.

She leapt up from the couch as though she couldn't stand to be near him any longer. "The letter you wrote to your sister saying that I was a vulgar, bullying thing and you dreaded marrying me." Her chin lifted defiantly.

He felt as though someone had hit him very hard in the stomach. She had found the letter he had written in a fit of smarting pride when she had rebuffed him. "Oh, God, Diana, I wrote that in a moment of anger. It was nothing. I was insulted that you did not want to marry me. I knew it was cruel and untrue, so I never sent it." He knew even as he spoke that she would accept no excuses.

"All I ever wanted was to be loved for who I am and not for my money." Her voice shook with fury, but her eyes were steady and hard. "Our relationship was about my dowry from the start. John pretended to love me to get at my fortune, but at least he was one of my kind. At least he didn't think he was better than me because of who I am and who my parents are." She rose to her feet and looked down at him. "Now, Lord Trevlan, I will thank you to be on your way."

He sat stunned for a moment. What was there to say? Anything he said now would ring false. She waited impatiently, her breath coming in quick, angry gasps. Her knuckles were going white as she gripped the mantelpiece to steady herself.

He was defeated. With a few strokes of the pen he had destroyed any hope he had of happiness. At least when Diana was to marry Stiles, he could pretend that he was being noble in bowing to her wishes. Now, worse than hurting himself, he had wounded her.

He walked to the fireplace and took her chin in his hand to force her to look at him. Her bright blue starburst eyes were expressionless. "Diana," he said softly, "what I did was unforgivable, so I cannot ask for forgiveness. What I ask is that you look back over the time we spent together. If you are impartial, you will realize that I never loved Hypatia. That was a charade you and I both played. I certainly never pretended you were her." He cocked an eyebrow meaningfully. Her eyes dropped to his mouth, and he saw her cheeks pinken a little.

"I knew from the moment I saw you that I loved you, and I was going to try my damnedest to win you away from Stiles," he continued. "That was probably more wicked than writing a foolish, prideful letter that was never sent. Think of everything that has passed between us and see if you can truly believe that I do not love you." He took her hands and looked intently into her eyes. "The duns have come. Everything is gone. I have no need of your fortune anymore. I don't need your dowry, your parents, your Grecian temple, your pond, your abbey—I don't need anything. All I want, all I need, is you."

There was nothing else to say. She stood and stared at him as though she had not heard a word. He bowed swiftly over her hand and left the room.

* * *

Every afternoon for four days, Diana relived the scene in the drawing room. It would be so easy to simply forgive Trevlan for his hasty words. But somehow they rang too true to be easily brushed off. Besides, though he said they were written in a moment of irritation, she only had his word for it. For all she knew, he had written the letter the afternoon after he had nearly kissed her in the gallery. The memory of that day gave her a strange, very physical pain in her chest. Why, when she had always been comfortable with herself and her trade background, did she suddenly care what Trevlan thought of her anyway?

"Diana, what are you doing sitting here all by yourself?" A voice roused her from her reverie. "Good heavens, you must have been in here for hours. No one had the least notion where you had got to."

"Hello, Hypatia. Why are you here?" Even turning her eyes to her cousin was painful.

"My mama wanted a recipe for your mama's tisane."

"Oh. Perhaps she is considering becoming an invalid as well." Diana forced herself to smile and stand up. "Shall I ring for tea?"

"Tea is not very good for the constitution, I believe," Hypatia replied, glancing down at the slim book that Diana had put down on the gilt and onyx table. "It is said that it aids in digestion, but I find that in more cases than not, it causes a disagreeable giddiness and vivacity in those who indulge too much."

"And one must repair to the necessary every ten minutes."

"Really, Diana!" Hypatia shook her head. She held up the book. "What is this?"

"A book."

"Yes, I can see that it is a book. It is a volume of poetry by Pope. How nice. Do you remember when Lord Trevlan read us some of his work? He did a very creditable job of it, really. I must say, most men do not read poetry well at all. They always seem to think they must stop at the end of every line. Of course, one might argue that all of our great poets are men, but that wouldn't necessitate their reading poetry well in any case. Writing it is likely an entirely different matter altogether."

Diana took the book from her cousin's hands. The same slanted handwriting she had seen in that horrible letter graced its flyleaf. She had memorized every word.

> Miss Quinlan,
> I will always think of you when I read the last lines of 'Epistle II:'
> "The generous god, who wit and gold refines, and ripens spirits as he ripens mines, Kept dross for duchesses, the world shall know it, To you gave sense, good humor, and a poet."
> You have always had sense and good humor, and now please accept from me a gift of the last.
>   Yours,
>   Gabriel Trevlan

"Oh, it's from Lord Trevlan, is it?" Hypatia glanced over Diana's shoulder.

"Yes." She slapped the book closed.

"How kind." Her cousin took her arm and pulled her toward the door. "Here, I'm driving myself in the gig today. You must come for a drive with me. You're looking frightfully pale, and a little air will do you more good than pints of tea.

"It is interesting that Lord Trevlan would give you a book," Hypatia returned to the subject once they were in the gig. "I have heard that he had to sell off the entire Trevlan library."

"Oh?" Diana was glad her bonnet hid her expression.

The last thing she wanted to do was discuss Trevlan with Hypatia. There wasn't a romantic bone in that woman's body.

"Indeed. And that one book might have got him a rather good price. It is a first edition."

"You certainly looked carefully," Diana frowned.

"I have a sharp eye." Hypatia turned the gig down a shady lane. "It is a pity I could not marry Trevlan to help out his family," she said after a few moments.

Diana felt a sudden cramp in her stomach. "Why didn't you?" she asked, feeling an overwhelming sense of dread.

Hypatia regarded her steadily for a moment. "Because he was in love with *you.*"

Her nerves gave a painful tingle all at once. "No, he wasn't." She kept her eyes on the road in front of them. His declaration of love meant nothing. He was only trying to weasel himself into her good graces after learning of his fatal blunder.

Hypatia shrugged. "Well, it seemed that way in any case. I feel a bit sorry for the man."

"Sorry!" Diana snapped, "He was only hanging out for a rich wife!"

Her cousin's mild blue eyes were calm. "Of course. But how perfectly dreadful to know that one has nothing to recommend oneself but a title. Auctioning oneself off to the highest bidder, really." She gave a languid flick to the reins. "It doesn't matter whether he was in love with you or not. He must marry whoever buys his title."

Diana folded her arms. "I don't suppose I thought of it that way."

"Yes. At least when you're rich, you have choices. Lord Trevlan does not."

"He is going to try to get a position in Town. Though I can't see what he would be suited for."

"Is he?" Hypatia looked mildly interested. "Well, then, I suspect he will be fine. I really did think that you would marry him. Especially once you came to your senses about John Stiles."

"Well, I'm . . . I'm not going to marry him." She heard her voice quaver.

"Very well," Hypatia sighed. "I'm not in the business of matchmaking, so I will not try to convince you."

"He thinks me bullying and vulgar and ungenteel."

Hypatia smiled. "Well, you are, my dear. Well, not vulgar, but certainly bullying. And if not ungenteel, direct to a fault. You're really quite shockingly managing. I suppose that is why we all love you." She ignored Diana's affronted gasp. "I fancy that is why Lord Trevlan loves you."

"A gentleman like Lord Trevlan could never want a wife like that," she protested. "He could have the most ladylike and well-bred wife in England."

"Well, apparently he wants a bullying, vulgar, ungenteel one," she shrugged.

"I cannot believe—"

"Hm." The horse clumped to a stop in response to Hypatia's reins. "I may be obliged to add addle-witted to the list." Her grave face split into an affectionate smile. "Don't be proud and miserable, Diana." She gestured to the house they had stopped in front of. It looked as though it used to be a small hunting lodge of some sort. But the roof was badly in need of repair and the whitewash was peeling off of the walls. A wagon stood in front of the door, and a man was loading battered trunks onto it.

"Trevlan," she breathed.

He paused to wipe his brow with his sleeve and looked up. An expression of surprise followed by misgiving crossed his face.

"Trevlan!" She leapt down from the gig and ran to him. In a moment his arms were around her and she was laughing into his shirtfront.

"What are you doing here?" he murmured into her hair.

"I am here to rescue you." She looked up at him and smiled.

He held her out at arm's length and regarded her seriously. "You don't have to be noble, Diana."

She wiggled her way back into his arms. "I'm not. I'm being very, very greedy. I love you, Gabriel Trevlan. If you don't promise to marry me in a shockingly short amount of time, I shall sue you for breach of contract."

"You know I never meant those things I wrote. Not once I got to know you."

"I know. And it doesn't matter if I *am* nothing but a managing, bourgeois cit. As long as you don't mind."

"Of course I don't mind. I would not have it any other way." He pulled her into his arms and kissed her.

"Trevlan," she whispered dreamily at last.

"Yes, my love?"

"Is your sister single?"

His eyes narrowed in suspicion. "What are you thinking, Diana?"

"Well, we can give her a marvelous season in London. I know a large number of very eligible men. And I was thinking that if Hypatia and perhaps even Letty were to come with us . . ."

"Run, Hypatia! Run while you can," Trevlan called out to her cousin, who still sat placidly in the gig.

Hypatia snapped the reins over her horse's back and turned the gig around. "London does not agree with my constitution," she replied. "I think that all the coal soot in the air cannot be good for the lungs. And with the hours they keep in Town, it is little wonder that everyone is not dead of fatigue by the end of the season. Having one's dinner so late at night cannot be healthy either . . ." her voice drifted back faintly from the lane as she drove away.

"Oh, dear." Trevlan kissed down Diana's neck behind her ear. "She's escaped." With one last kiss he reluctantly stopped and put an arm around her waist. "Let's go inside,

Miss Matchmaker. I must introduce you to Lydia, your victim."

"You know, Trevlan," Diana said, affectionately leaning her head against his shoulder, "it was always so important to me to find someone who loved me for who I am instead of for my dowry." She grinned up at him. "But now I think being betrothed to you because of my fortune was the greatest good fortune of all!"

THE IMPOSSIBLE BRIDE

by

Cathleen Clare

ONE

It had been an unseasonably hot day and a trying one for twenty-one-year-old Venetia Woodbridge, who was caught up in the unenviable task of attempting to assist in two sickrooms at the same time. In the late afternoon, both patients fell into a troubled sleep, allowing their constant attendant to step outside on the balcony for a breath of fresh, though humid, air. It was not a pleasant day to be ill, if indeed any day could be so designated, but Venetia was not overly concerned about her elderly parents. They had a touch of grippe which, in addition to their other minor infirmities, made them miserable, but they were far from mortal danger. They were just . . .

"Demanding," she whispered, exhausted.

Her parents simply refused to submit to much care by the staff. They permitted their personal servants to perform such chores as would be deemed indelicate for a young lady, but in all else they called upon Venetia. Only their daughter could bring their meal trays and help them eat, running back and forth between the chambers. Venetia alone brought them drinks of water, read to them, plumped their pillows, tucked their covers, fanned them. This was the way things were done in the Woodbridge family. She was the youngest. Her brothers and sisters were married and gone from the area. It was—and had been from time immemorial—the task of the youngest daughter to care for the parents in their old age. There would be no husband and family for Venetia. This was her lot. Daily, she resolved herself to accept it.

With a sigh, she passed a hand across her brow, wiping away beads of perspiration. She should have escaped to the banks of the nearby stream where a breeze would surely be blowing. Perhaps tomorrow . . . if a miracle caused them again to sleep at the same time.

Hoofbeats drew her attention to the front drive. Down the avenue of oaks at a rather unladylike gallop came her best friend, Sally Colfield, riding as usual in her irrepressible, carefree way. Spying Venetia as she drew to a halt, she waved her crop.

"Come down from your perch and hear all the gossip! The neighborhood is set on its ear!"

"Shh!" Venetia swiftly placed a finger over her lips, but her friend didn't see it. Sally had already hopped from her horse and darted toward the house. Venetia hurried to intercept her before she came clattering up the stairs and awakened her mother and father.

"Venetia!" Sally cried up from the hall. "He is handsome beyond belief!"

"Wait down there." She quietly descended the stairs. She was in no doubt as to whom her friend had referred. The whole county knew that the Marquess of Enville was visiting his brother, who had recently bought an estate in the district. The event had created quite a stir, especially since His Lordship was wealthy and a bachelor, a *prize catch* as the *ton* would say.

"Oh, I cannot wait to tell you!" Her friend was nearly jumping up and down in her eagerness. "He danced with me, Venetia. Really! He actually chose *me*! It wasn't a waltz, more's the pity, but I did get to touch him!"

Venetia felt a stab of jealousy, not because she thought anything would come of Sally's meeting with the marquess, but because the girl at least had the opportunity to participate in the excitement. Nothing like this had ever happened in the neighborhood. It probably never would again, unless His Lordship made a repeat visit.

She took Sally's arm and directed her to the morning room. "You must have been thrilled beyond all belief."

"I was. To say nothing of Mama! She was so-o-o proud. And Papa . . . Well, you know him! He stood there, chatting with friends and smiling benignly, but he was impressed. Oh, yes, he was!"

"So am I. And pleased as punch for your success." She ordered tea and seated her friend by the open French doors overlooking the garden for which Woodbridge Manor was famous.

Eyes sparkling, Sally leaned forward. "I will tell you how he looks. I vow I have never seen a more handsome man."

"I'm sure his being titled and very wealthy has nothing to do with that," she said wryly.

"Certainly not!" Sally feigned insult. "I would think the same if he were nothing but a common stable lad."

Venetia chuckled. "Somehow I doubt that."

"Venetia!" Her friend pursed her full, heart-shaped mouth into a pout. "If you continue making jest of me, I shan't tell you a thing."

"Very well." Her chuckle became a light laugh. "I apologize. Do tell all. I am waiting on pins and needles!"

Sally briefly eyed her suspiciously, then continued with great enthusiasm. "His hair is quite dark, almost black, with just a few gray hairs at his temples which make him look so distinguished. His nose is that straight, slim, aristocratic kind . . . do you know what I mean?"

Venetia didn't, but she nodded to spare herself a lengthy explanation.

"His mouth . . ." Sally's cheeks glowed pink, and her eyes grew dreamy. "His lips are made for kissing, Venetia."

That was too much. "For heaven's sake! How would you know that?"

"I just do," she claimed pertly. "You would too, if you saw them."

Venetia took mercy. "Well, I doubt I ever will, and I shall probably never kiss anyone, so I will take your word for it, Sally."

Her friend regarded her sadly. "My dear, you must do something about your life."

"Dear heavens, let us not initiate a discussion on that topic! Continue telling me of Lord Enville. That is far more interesting."

"He has dimples . . . no, they are really what one might call 'smile marks,' charming indentations at the corners of his mouth." She sighed. "But his eyes, Venetia . . . oh, my! They are a wondrous dark blue. *Dark*, mind you, not pale and washy. And they are framed with the longest, thickest dark lashes you've ever seen. A lady would simply do murder for eyes like that. Think of the flirtations one could commence by batting such luxuriant eyelashes. Such drama, such mystery! I always envied your nice long lashes, Venetia, but they do not hold a candle to his."

They ceased the conversation while Branson, the Woodbridge butler, brought in the tea tray. Venetia poured a cup for her friend, adding Sally's requisite sugar, then served herself. She glanced at the clock, surprised that she had been allowed such a long respite from the sickrooms. She hoped it would go on. For the first time in two days, she was beginning to feel rejuvenated. Of course, part of it was due to her friend's uplifting chatter. Thank heavens she had received some benefit from Lord Enville's visit!

Sally nibbled a macaroon but put it down, unwilling to relinquish talking for eating. "Venetia, his shoulders are nice and broad. He has no need for the tailor to pad them! His legs are those of an active gentleman. He is definitely no layabout."

Venetia laughed. "My goodness, you made a thorough study of him."

She nodded vigorously. "Oh, but that is not all. His bottom . . ."

"Sally!" she cried, flushing deeply. "Surely that is outside of enough!"

Her friend trilled. "Venetia, we have been friends forever and we can speak of anything. Do not tell me you have never looked at a gentleman's derriere!"

"Well, I will tell you that, for I have not!"

"Then you are missing one of the finer things in life."

Cheeks burning, Venetia shook her head. "I think not. My friend, I love you dearly, but do spare me a description of Lord Enville's posterior."

The young ladies looked at each other and burst into laughter.

"But it is so very shapely," Sally protested.

"Nevertheless, you have told me enough to convince me that the marquess must be the most handsome gentleman in England," she giggled.

"In the world," her friend corrected.

"In the world, then." Venetia reached out to squeeze her hand. "And I wish you all good fortune in capturing his heart."

"Oh, would it be possible!" Sally's expression assumed a far-off, pensive look. "Can you imagine what it would be like to be the Marchioness of Enville?"

"I truly cannot." Venetia thought it would be quite wonderful just to be a kind gentleman's wife, to have happy children, and to be the mistress of even a modest estate. The fabulous life of a Marchioness of Enville was beyond even her wildest dreams. But someone would have him. Such a lofty peer must do his duty to his lineage.

Sally finished her macaroon. "It does seem that one other good thing has come from this meeting. Mama has convinced Papa that I must have a Season in London. I am nineteen, you know, and there are simply no gentlemen in the area with whom I intend to make an alliance. Papa consents to afford the Little Season, so we shall be going up to town in the fall. Unless, of course, I land *this* prize catch."

Prize catch! Venetia could suddenly picture Lord Enville as a big trout, swimming about in the stream, with Sally feverishly angling from the bank. She smiled and sipped her tea.

"Do you think," her friend mused, "that I have even the remotest of chances with him?"

"He asked you to dance, so he must have thought you attractive," she said carefully.

"He danced with a number of others as well."

"Did he ask anyone twice?"

"Oh, no." She shook her head. "But in all truth, Venetia, he will probably wed a lady of very high *ton*, won't he?" Ordinary girls like us do not stand a chance, do we?"

"Probably not," she said quietly. "Such noblemen usually wed within their own ranks."

"Still . . ." Sally brightened. "I will have a Season from all of this!"

"Yes, and you will doubtlessly shine like the diamond you are!"

"You are so kind, my friend, to be enthused about me, when you—"

Venetia shifted uncomfortably.

"You cannot have accepted the idea of remaining a spinster!" Sally objected. "You cannot do it! I know you cannot want that!"

"I have no choice." She finished her tea and set it aside.

"You must appeal to your brothers and sisters."

"It would do no good. This is the way of the Woodbridge family. They are all too glad that the responsibility of caring for our parents rests on me."

Sally set her jaw. "Don't you want a husband and family?"

Venetia lowered her gaze. "Of course I do."

"Then rebel!"

"How?" she cried. "Every gentleman in the county knows of the Woodbridge custom. No one will come to court me. My goodness, even if such a miracle did occur, it would be a clandestine affair. My parents would not permit anyone to call on me. Then we would have to fly to Gretna Green. My father would never, ever give his blessing. I would be a disgrace! That is no way to begin a marriage. Let us face the facts, Sally. No gentleman has the nerve to take an interest in me."

"But you are so pretty! And you are just as beautiful inside as you are on the outside." She squared her shoulders. "We must think of something. Yes! I know just the thing!"

Venetia shuddered inwardly.

"I will go to London and snare a husband," Sally said confidently. "Then you shall come to visit me, and we shall find a gentleman for you among his friends."

Venetia smiled patiently. "How could it work? I can seldom be spared to attend local social events. I would never be permitted to go away on a visit. It is all impossible, Sally."

"But it must not be!"

"It is. Seek your own heart's desire, my dear friend. Think of me as having a true vocation. I shall be fine."

Sally bent her head and fell silent.

As if to underscore Venetia's situation, Branson scratched on the door and softly entered. "Miss Venetia, Madam is asking for you."

"Very well. Thank you." She smiled at her friend. "You know I must go immediately."

"Yes." Sally made a mouth of distaste.

"We did have a nice long talk." She glanced at the

clock. "You have cheered me immensely. I am now refreshed and up to date on everything."

"Including Lord Enville's bottom!" Sally added, her
very wickedness lifting her spirits again, too.

The stark black horse picked his way along the leaf-
mold path that led, Daniel said, to a stream which marked
the estate boundary. Except for the normal natural sounds,
the chirping of birds and the slough of a light breeze
through the trees, it was quiet in the woods. Even the soft
plock-plock of the stallion's hooves did nothing to disturb
his master's reverie, if indeed it was worth disturbing. In
truth, it was not.

Darian, Lord Enville, was telling himself how bored he
was. He had looked forward (that was a lie; he never
eagerly anticipated anything) to this visit to his younger
brother's new property. It should have been interesting to
see Daniel married and settled, given his sibling's wild
youth, but the couple were still billing and cooing like
two lovebirds, even though it had been over a year since
they'd wed. Their little kisses and touches were quite dull
and ridiculous to the onlooker. Surely it was past time
they should begin to behave like other *ton* wedded pairs
and take each other for granted. But Daniel and Fanny
did not seem to wish to cease smelling of April and May.
They pretended to be in love, whatever that meant.

The marquess deigned to arch a perfect, dark eyebrow.
Enough was enough! And this was outside of enough! He
longed to leave, to what destination he did not know, for
one place was just as dreary as the next, but he was
trapped. Little Fanny had planned too many more activities for his doubtful entertainment. She had obviously
tried so hard to provide for his enjoyment that he couldn't
disappoint her. He was fixed in this jading environment

for several more weeks, and as usual, he must watch his step.

Whenever Lord Enville entered a community, he caused a great stir. He was titled; he was wealthy; he was handsome; he was a bachelor. Those irresistible components never failed to ignite hope in the hearts of every unmarried young lady and her mama within a very large radius. Invitations were pumped out in dozens. Dressmakers worked far into the night, making so many gowns that they could probably retire from their trade and live off their profits for the rest of their lives. Elaborate snares were concocted, causing Darian to shy from all the dropped handkerchiefs, offers of strolls in dimly lit gardens, even sweet coquettish smiles. He knew he was desirable, and he wouldn't have traded it for anything, but it did become wearying very quickly. If only people would treat him like everyone else. But they would not, because he wasn't.

Casting that thought from his mind, he began to look forward to his lonely sojourn by the stream. He could smell the freshness of the water and hear it babbling over the rocks, before the trail widened and opened into a bright, grassy clearing. The spot, which Fanny claimed made her want this estate above all others, was just as pretty as she'd promised. The two lovebirds picnicked here often, either in the sun or under the shade of the spreading oaks that fringed the area. Daniel had caused the grass to be scythed as close as a lawn, but allowed the yellow daffodils and fragrant poet's narcissus to bloom undisturbed. There was white wrought-iron furniture, and even a hitching rack. Darian laughed to himself. It was rather romantical, but who would have expected anything else from Daniel and Fanny?

He dismounted, tethered his horse, and strolled to the bank of the stream. Angling might be a diverting pursuit. He hadn't fished since he was a lad. He might not even be good at it anymore. But it was an event in which he could partake without interference from anxious hostesses, scheming mamas, or chattering girls. He glanced down into the water and saw a school of minnows. Hmm, little fish indicated that big ones might be there in the deep holes, didn't they?

As he straightened, he saw her and half startled. The young woman was sitting silently on the bank across the stream, legs drawn up and arms encircling them, her head resting contemplatively on her knees. She had probably been there when he arrived, viewing his imperception with vast amusement. Flushing slightly, he doffed his hat.

"Good morning, ma'am."

She lifted her head, the breeze stirring tendrils of rich, shiny, brown hair. "Good morning, sir."

He was somewhat taken aback that she did not say more. After his acknowledgment, young ladies usually gushed forth with endless pleasantries. This one did not. Her reticence actually made him feel awkward. He tried again.

" 'Tis fine weather we're having."

She nodded. "Quite so."

Like a novice at meeting ladies, he shifted from foot to foot. "I was wondering about fishing . . . whether there was anything here to be caught."

"My brothers fished here when they were at home. They caught fish."

Two sentences! Things were looking up. Conversing with this lady had become a challenge.

"I thought I might try it. But do allow me to introduce myself." He bowed most elegantly. "I am Enville. I am visiting my brother who owns this estate."

"I know." Polite manners forced her to rise and curtsy. "I am Miss Venetia Woodbridge, my lord. My father owns the property that marches with Lord Terrell's."

So she realized who he was, but she wasn't throwing

herself at him. She must be engaged, or in love with someone else. After all, every young unmarried lady attempted to snare the Marquess of Enville. But perhaps it was a trick. Perhaps in appearing that she was not trying to trap him, she was really *trying to trap him*. She knew who he was. She may have been coming here for days, hoping he'd come along.

Darian mentally shook himself. That was ridiculous. She was obviously a lady who would have been invited to the local entertainments, but she had not attended. She was rather striking, so he would have remembered her.

Once again, he was at a standstill in communication. He gestured to the clearing. "Daniel and Fanny must spend a great deal of time here."

"Apparently." She nodded pleasantly. "They were kind enough to offer its use to me, but I seldom come here anymore. I do not wish to disturb them or their guests."

"This guest does not mind being disturbed. Won't you come across?" In retrospect, he glanced up and down the stream, but saw no bridge or safe stepping stones.

She laughed lightly, a sweet tinkling sound. "Wading would not be proper."

"I could carry you," he gallantly offered.

"That would be *more* improper." She laughed again. "No, my lord, I believe we are destined to stay on our opposite sides of the brook."

He suddenly, desperately, wanted to see her up close. "I don't think so."

As he slogged into the water, she momentarily looked as if she would flee. But she held her ground. Perhaps she was as curious about him as he was about her.

"My lord, your boots!" she cried as he gained the shore.

"My valet will doubtlessly murder me." He paused to look at her, happily finding that she was well worth ruining footwear in order to view.

Miss Venetia Woodbridge was of medium height, slender, but nicely endowed in the places a gentleman appreciated. Her long, silky hair glistened with red and gold sparkle when the sunlight glittered on it. Her oval face was classic with a slim, fine nose, delicate cheekbones, and gently defined pink lips. But her eyes . . . A man could lose his soul in those emerald orbs. For a gentleman jaded by pulchritude, Darian was impressed.

"Have you quite finished your perusal?" she asked pertly.

"My apologies, Miss Woodbridge." He bowed his head. "You must know that we of the male gender are deplorably obvious in our appreciation of feminine beauty, of which you do possess an overabundance. Do forgive me my weakness."

She seemed disconcerted, lowering her gaze.

"I truly did not wish to offend," he went on.

She licked her lower lip, unawarely exciting his further male prowess.

He moved forward.

She stepped backward, gazing at him directly with those wide-open, marvelous eyes.

"Definitely, Miss Woodbridge, I do not wish to cause you alarm."

"You must excuse me, my lord. I have much to do." Abruptly, she turned on her heel and dashed down a path into the fringe of trees.

"Dammit," said Darian under his breath. He had ruined his little tête-à-tête by being overly appreciative. Miss Venetia Woodbridge was not accustomed to a gentleman's warm regard. He did not know why. She was so pretty that she must have been outrageously admired by countless members of his sex. But she wasn't interested in the Marquess of Enville.

"Dammit!"

He retraced his steps across the brook and remounted

his horse, turning toward Highlawn Hall and Daniel and Fanny, water dripping from his soggy boots.

Changing and freshening for luncheon under the auspices of his grim, aggravated valet, he descended the stairs. He was not certain whether to ask his relatives about the elusive Miss Woodbridge. The slightest show of interest might invoke Fanny's matchmaking skills. But as they shared the delicious rib of beef, his curiosity got the better of him.

"This morning by the stream, I chanced to meet Miss Venetia Woodbridge."

Fanny dabbed at her mouth. "Now, that is a rare occurrence."

"Indeed?" He lifted an eyebrow, hoping not to appear too interested.

She nodded vigorously. "Poor Miss Woodbridge! I vow the whole county feels sorry for her."

"Why?"

"Her parents are elderly and often unwell. As the youngest, it is her duty to take care of them."

"Are they too poor to hire servants for the task?"

"Oh, no." Fanny laughed. "From my understanding, the Woodbridge family has always designated the younger daughter for such a chore."

"That's ridiculous!" he erupted.

"Indeed, but that is the way they have always done it." Fanny took up her fork to continue with her meal.

"Do you mean that's all she does?" he prodded. "She doesn't participate socially or . . . or anything?"

Fanny shook her head. "Miss Woodbridge is evidently well aware of her duty, and has accepted it."

"There's one lady that you can't charm, Darian!" Daniel chuckled. "Miss Woodbridge is as unavailable as a nun."

Darian failed to find humor, but he smiled good-naturedly. "I had the feeling I was safe from her clutches."

"We called upon the Woodbridges when we moved to

the neighborhood," his brother went on. "They weren't bedfast, but they seemed on the verge of becoming feeble."

"Were they pleasant?" he inquired.

Daniel raised a shoulder. "Actually, it was neither here nor there with them. Miss Woodbridge was, but the older people . . . I think they merely put up with us."

"I disagree," Fanny put in. "When I admired her viburnum, Mrs. Woodbridge offered me a rooting."

"Yes, love, but did she ever send it over?"

"Spring is the time for transplanting," his wife informed him. "Perhaps I should call and sow greater interest. The plants were quite beautiful."

"If you decide to do so, I would be honored to escort you," Darian tried to say casually.

His brother eyed him piercingly, but said nothing.

"Darian is interested in Venetia Woodbridge," Fanny stated as she and Daniel paused on the sofa to share a glass of wine before bed. Because of a flock of afternoon callers and the evening entertainment at Lord Burridge's residence, they had not had the opportunity to discuss the luncheon conversation.

"He is taken with her," she continued.

"Balderdash!" swore her husband. "You don't know Darian. She was but a fleeting curiosity. I could see it in his eyes."

"She is most attractive."

He laughed. "Think, my darling, of the beautiful ladies who throw themselves at my brother. Miss Woodbridge is merely a simple country maid in comparison to their stylishness."

"I know." She thoughtfully sipped her sherry. "That's why I am alerted."

"No." Daniel firmly shook his head. "I fear you are wrong in this, darling."

"He must wed sometime."

"Not necessarily." He stretched his arm across her shoulders to draw her closer. "There's a very good possibility that he will not. You, sweetheart, may be the mother of the future Marquess of Enville."

"Fustian!" she scoffed.

"It's true. Darian seems very satisfied with his long parade of mistresses."

"Really, Daniel!" She made a mouth of chastisement. "We shan't talk about such things."

His eyes danced. "You don't believe that your dear brother- in-law keeps a bit o' muslin?"

She squealed and batted her hand at him. "I don't want to think of that."

Daniel sighed. "A man needs an . . . outlet."

"I want him to fall in love," Fanny protested. "I want him to have what we have."

"That will never happen. Darian is far too cynical. He doesn't believe in love. If he weds, it will be for pure duty." He hugged her. "Now let us forget my brother and tend to our own marriage. He is perfectly capable of making his own match, and it will not be to the unattainable Miss Woodbridge."

She lifted her chin to kiss his jaw. "Nevertheless, I have decided that I shall pursue obtaining those shoots. You may accompany me to the Woodbridge estate if you please, but I am persuaded that Darian will be more than willing to escort me!"

Daniel groaned.

The morning following her meeting with Lord Enville, Venetia was still shaken. She had been quite a fool in the handsome nobleman's presence. First, she'd behaved like a tongue-tied, naive country girl; then she had actually immaturely fled from him. Even though he had regarded her in a manner too warm for comfort, a charming young lady of *ton* would have parried his enticement with wit and elegance. Not she! The encounter by the stream had been her only chance to meet the legendary peer, and she had ruined it. At best, the gentleman probably thought her shy. At worst, he'd decided that she was a brainless bumpkin. But what did it matter? She would never see him again.

Leaving her chamber, she went at once to her mother's bedroom and was delighted to find that the lady had improved. Her eyes were brighter, and her expression was not nearly so strained. She was sitting up in bed and had actually allowed her abigail to serve her tea and a muffin.

"You're looking much better, Mother," Venetia smiled.

"Only somewhat. I'm sure I'll be several more days in bed." She sighed mightily.

"You're missing your lovely spring flowers," Venetia said, hoping to tempt her. Mrs. Woodbridge's gardens had always been her pride and joy.

"Am I, dear? Well, it cannot be helped." She sighed again. "Old age and infirmity are terrible things."

Venetia patiently plumped her pillows. "You are not so old, ma'am. You have many years left to direct gardeners and plan beautiful plantings."

"Huh!" scoffed the lady. "Not the way I feel."

"Now, now. It's only the summer complaint."

Venetia realized too late that she'd made the awful mistake of downplaying her parent's illness.

"Only!" Mrs. Woodbridge returned her cup to its saucer with a sharp clink. "Young lady, you would not be so glib if you felt the way I do!"

"I am sorry, Mother. I suppose I'm engaging in wishful thinking." She bowed her head to underscore her remorse. "I do so want you to feel just like new. I remember the days when you so ably trotted around the gardens, creating beauty wherever you went."

"Those days are gone."

"I know. Do forgive me my nonsense."

"Yes. Well . . ." She flicked her hand. "Go see your father and hasten to return to me with a report on his condition."

"Yes, ma'am." She gratefully left the room before her mother could embark upon further lectures on the plight of the elderly.

She was happy to find that her father was also feeling better. He was even seated in a heavily padded chair by the window! His temper, however, had not improved.

"So, daughter! It took a long while for you to appear this morning. Overslept, hum?"

She nodded. It was easier to agree than debate.

"Slothfulness is to be deplored."

"Yes, sir." Again she found herself bowing her head. "It shall not happen again."

"But it will. Sometimes, Venetia, I seriously wonder about your sense of responsibility. Your mother and I must depend upon you for our very lives. Do you take this as earnestly as you should?"

"Oh, yes, Father, I do."

"Then you must put all else from your mind," he directed.

"I shall." She attempted a smile. "But do tell me how you are feeling today. Mother is anxious to know."

"I am a bit better, though still vastly feeble." He glanced toward the door which connected his room to his wife's. "Perhaps I shall join her for a short interval this afternoon. You can read to us."

"She would enjoy that." She fluffed the pillows at his back.

"Stop that! I was already comfortable!"

"Yes, sir." She dropped her hands to her sides.

"Go and tell her that I have improved," he ordered; "then see to my breakfast. Jenkins has served my coffee, but I want ham and boiled eggs."

"I'll see to it at once." She withdrew to the door, where her father's valet lurked. "I'm sure you heard what he said?"

"Yes, miss."

"When you fetch the tray, scratch on Mother's door. I'll come to the hall and carry it to his room."

He nodded.

Venetia returned through the adjoining passage to Mrs. Woodbridge's chamber. "Father has improved. He plans to attempt a full breakfast."

"That is good news." She motioned her daughter to remove her tray. "His health was always much better than mine. I have been delicate all through my life."

Venetia remembered when both of her parents frequently rode to the hounds. Mrs. Woodbridge hadn't been dainty then. She'd been an admirable horsewoman.

What had happened? She could not recall when the two had begun to decline. She suspected that they had entered their late middle age, started to experience the little aches and pains which apparently accompanied that period, and had not had the fortitude to resist succumbing to them. But it made no difference now. They were convinced that they were ill, pitiful, and helpless, and nothing could change that. This was the way life was going to be.

"Father believes he will be able to join you this afternoon for a reading session," she announced.

"If I am rested," the lady replied, but there was a pleasant spark in her eye. "Go and tell him that I will let him know after lunch if I may withstand the visit."

"Yes, ma'am." Venetia returned to her father's room to relay the message.

"Very well, but where is my breakfast?" he demanded.

"I shall fetch it soon."

"Soon is not good enough. I am hungry now."

"Yes, sir. I will go hurry matters along." She started toward the hall door.

"Wait!" he called. "On your way, do tell your mother that I shall hope her state of health is well enough to allow her to participate in my outing."

"Yes, sir." Venetia went to her mother's chamber, imparted the sentiments, and went out into the hall to await Jenkins.

She heard him huffing and puffing on the stairs even before she saw him.

"You know how the master hates cold food, Miss Venetia," he panted, thrusting the tray into her hands. "I hurried fast as I could."

"Yes, Jenkins." She rushed to her father's room. "Here you are, Father; just what you wanted."

"It could have been presented in serving dishes with a lighted candle."

"We . . . I . . . couldn't carry that much, but see? There is a spring posy from Mother's garden to cheer your spirits. Now, if you immediately commence to eat, I believe you will find everything most hot and tasty."

"I am not a dog to gobble my food without ceremony."

"Of course not, Father, but this is the best we can do." She spread his napkin and removed the silver domes from his plates.

He sampled the fare. "Passable. Perhaps I should have requested bacon."

Venetia gritted her teeth and thought of the many steps to the kitchens.

"A sick person's appetite should be tempted, you know," he expounded. "Food possesses strengthening powers, but when one is ill, one does not often wish to eat."

"Yes, Father."

"You needn't stand over me," he complained. "Go and see how your mother is."

Venetia strode toward the door.

"Return in half an hour. You can help me back into bed and fan me a bit. It is growing very warm."

"Yes, sir." The able-bodied servant, Jenkins, would be forced to stand aside while Venetia escorted her father to bed. The gentleman would lean on her, strain her back, and complain that her knees wobbled. The same would occur when he visited his wife's chamber that afternoon. The Woodbridges didn't need a slender daughter to care for them. They needed a strong, stalwart son for this physical labor!

Slowly shaking her head, she set aside those uncharitable thoughts. This was her lot in life, and there was no point in bemoaning it. She thought she had accepted matters, but Lord Enville's visit to the neighborhood, Sally's enthusiasm, and her own escape to the stream and subsequent meeting with the marquess had made her so very dissatisfied with things. But she must put the unattainable out of her mind. It would only serve to make her horribly unhappy.

"Is Mr. Woodbridge enjoying his meal?" her mother asked as she entered the room.

"Yes, Mother, it would seem that he is." She hoped the lady wouldn't ask her to dash back to her father's chamber with another message. She felt she'd been running for hours.

And so it continued until after luncheon, when she assisted her father into Mrs. Woodbridge's room for the reading session. She had scarcely opened the book when Mrs. Dawes, the housekeeper, quietly entered.

"Ma'am, sir, Miss Venetia." She eyed them doubtfully. "There are callers."

"Tell 'em to go away," said Mr. Woodbridge.

"Who are they?" simultaneously inquired his wife.

Mrs. Dawes glanced anxiously from one to the other. " 'Tis Lady Terrell and . . . and the Marquess of Enville."

Venetia's heart leapt to her throat. Enville? Here? Calling on them?

"We must send our regrets," Mrs. Woodbridge declared. "I expect that Lady Terrell is hoping for the viburnum start I promised her. Our gardener will deliver it right away. Venetia, will you see that it's done?"

"Indeed, Mother." Unsteadily, she rose to her feet.

"Seat yourself, dear. I only meant for you to advise the gardener. Mrs. Dawes will inform our callers and explain that, due to illness, we cannot see them."

"I am not ill," Venetia said softly.

"No, but we need you."

"Heed your mother!" commanded her father.

Venetia thought of the handsome marquess below. He had actually come to call! Her heart throbbed wildly against her ribs. What would Sally think of this? Could Lord Enville be interested in her?

She pushed away that foolish thought. He was merely escorting his sister-in-law. Her husband must be otherwise occupied, so he had volunteered to do the pretty.

Mrs. Dawes turned to the door.

"No!" Venetia burst out. "I shall go."

Her parents gaped.

"It is only proper," she swiftly explained. "I shan't cause you to wait long for the reading. I'll exchange polite pleasantries and bid them good day. But . . . but I must freshen myself first, so please tell them, Mrs. Dawes, that I shall greet them shortly."

Before they could mount a protest, she sped from the room.

Hands clasped behind his back, Darian viewed the long vista of the Woodbridge front lawn. If the owner of this estate was feeble, he must have a very good steward. All was neat, trim, and attractive. But also, perhaps, Miss

Venetia Woodbridge was an excellent overseer. Was the young lady as efficient as she was pretty?

The housekeeper entered the room and curtsied. "My lord, my lady, Miss Venetia will be along soon. I shall bring refreshments."

"Well!" said Fanny when she'd departed. "I am almost surprised. Gossip has it that the parents are very jealous of their daughter's time."

He smiled. "Then we are to be greatly honored."

"I do believe so. From what I hear, even the marvelous Lord Enville would have no effect on the Woodbridge habits."

"Maybe you listen too much to false, wagging tongues."

"That is not the case!" she defended. "My sources are unexceptionable. I assure you that all I have told you about this family is true! It is their tradition that the youngest daughter remains unmarried, at home with the parents."

"It seems outlandish," he nearly scoffed. "What sort of parents would not wish a match for their daughter?"

"The Woodbridges!" she cried. "Do not make sport of me, Darian. Ha! If you had not believed me, you would not have accompanied me. Not from the way you shy from anything remotely resembling a marriage plot."

"Perhaps I was curious."

"Never," she vowed. "If you had suspected a daughter of marriageable age in residence, you would have run the other direction."

"Would I now?" He laughed. "Fanny, my dear, I am quite adept at escaping matrimonial schemes. This should not be any different."

"Except that there are none."

Darian feigned a yawn. "Very well, the last word belongs to you."

It was true, for at that moment Miss Venetia Woodbridge glided into the room. "I am sorry to have kept you waiting. We have illness in the house, so I was not prepared for visitors. Your call is most welcome, however. It breaks up a very long day for me."

"Then we shall not regret disturbing you at an importune time." Fanny smiled. "I believe you have met my brother-in-law, Lord Enville?"

Darian bowed.

"How do you do, my lord?" Miss Woodbridge executed a graceful curtsy, inadvertently revealing the soft, rounded tops of nicely endowed bosoms.

Murmuring pleasantries, the marquess was rather entranced, but he took care not to allow his gaze to linger. He certainly did not wish Miss Woodbridge to take offense in front of his sister-in-law. If she noted the direction of his interest, however, she gave no indication.

"Do sit down, my lord," she invited, seating herself on a settee and demurely smoothing her skirts.

He was tempted to join her on the loveseat, but thought it best for the ladies' peace of mind if he did not. He chose a chair next to Fanny, where he could get a good direct view of the interesting young lady. He was rewarded with a lovely smile.

"How are your parents?" Fanny inquired. "I hope their ailments are not serious."

"A summer complaint." She dimpled. "An *early* summer complaint, I suppose. They are recovering nicely, though they still need much care. I vow I am fair run off my feet."

She did not make the last sentence a grievance, rather laughing lightly.

Darian and his sister-in-law smiled too, but he wondered if the Woodbridge family was short of servants to cause the daughter of the house to be so active in the role of nursing. One didn't receive that impression from the physical surroundings, though. The estate looked prosperous. The house was tastefully furnished. On both occa-

sions he'd seen her, Miss Woodbridge was pleasingly, if
simply, attired.

Fanny must have had similar musings. "Miss Woodbridge, please do not think I am stepping beyond my
bounds, but my old nurse is retired and living with us.
She would be overjoyed to be of use to you. She is in her
element when she is presiding over a sickroom. May I
send her over?"

A look of longing crossed Venetia's face, but she shook
her head. "I do thank you so for your offer, but I must
refuse. In their debilitory state, my parents are awfully
fussy and require that I alone perform most of their care."

Fanny did not look surprised. "Of course."

"I wish . . . I imagine your nurse is far more adept at
such a task than I," Miss Woodbridge said ruefully. "Ah,
but that is neither here nor there."

There was a brief, awkward silence, happily broken by
the arrival of the tea tray. The young lady served
flawlessly. Darian couldn't help but notice the grace of
her slender hands. They would be better employed by . . .
what? Caressing a gentleman's cheek?

"When we were informed you were present, my lady,"
Miss Woodbridge went on, "my mother remembered how
much you desired a shoot from her viburnum. Our gardener will dig one and bring it over."

"Capital!" Fanny cried. "I do so appreciate it. Please
tell Mrs. Woodbridge how delighted I am."

"She will be pleased."

Fanny turned to Darian. "Mrs. Woodbridge must have
one of the finest gardens in England."

He eyed the daughter. "I would like to see it sometime."

She was flustered. "Gentlemen are not . . . usually . . .
interested in such things."

"Perhaps you have not met many gentlemen who are
appreciative of beauty, Miss Woodbridge." He casually

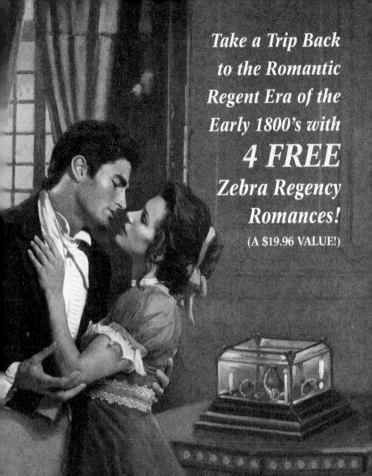

We'd Like to Invite You to Subscribe to Zebra's Regency Romance Book Club an Give You a Gift of 4 Free Books as Your Introduction!   (Worth $19.96!)

If you're a Regency lover, imagine the joy of getting **4 FREE Zebra Regency Romances** and then the chance to have th lovely stories delivered to your home each month at the lowest prices available! Well, that's our offer to you and here's how you benefit by becoming a Regency Romance subscriber:

- **4 FREE Introductory Regency Romances are delivered to your doors**

- **4 BRAND NEW Regencies are then delivered each month (usually befo they're available in bookstores)**

- **Subscribers save almost $4.00 every month**

- **Home delivery is always FREE**

- **You also receive a FREE monthly newsletter, *Zebra/Pinnacle Roman News* which features author profiles, contests, subscriber benefits, bo previews and more**

- **No risks or obligations...in other words you can cancel whenever you wish with no questions asked**

Join the thousands of readers who enjoy the savings and convenience offered to Regency Romance subscribers. After your initial introductory shipment, you receive 4 brand-new Zebra Regency Romances each month to examine for 10 days. Then, if you decide to keep the books, you'll pay the preferred subscriber's price of just $4.00 per title. That's only $16.00 for all 4 books and there's never an extra charge for shipping and handling.

It's a no-lose proposition, so return the FREE BOOK CERTIFICATE today!

lifted an eyebrow. "I assure you that I admire beauty in *all* its many forms."

Her cup suddenly chattered against its saucer. She set it aside, blushing becomingly. "I am sure you do, my lord."

Fanny eyed them speculatively. "Darian is not only a Corinthian of masculine sport, Miss Woodbridge. My brother-in-law possesses a high regard for the gentler, refined facets of life. He is not merely being polite. He *would* enjoy seeing the garden."

Miss Woodbridge seemed almost worried, actually holding her breath.

"I know you are too much occupied today with your parents' care to indulge my fancy," Darian said hastily, to put her at her ease again. "If you will allow me to come, once more, at a more suitable time?"

She exhaled. "Certainly, my lord."

He would come again. Seeing her this second time had not dispelled his curiosity. He was intrigued by her. And he still found her attractive on second sight, as was not often the case, given his jaded outlook on women. Her emerald eyes were just as clear, brilliant, and mesmerizing. Her hair still glistened with dazzling highlights, although its glory was somewhat hidden by the bit of lace on her head. She was too young to proclaim herself a spinster by wearing the little cap. What a waste!

"I am considering redesigning the gardens at Enville Hall, my country seat," he fibbed.

Fanny's mouth dropped open, but she quickly hid her gape by dabbing at her lips with her napkin.

Miss Woodbridge nodded. "My mother will be honored by your interest, my lord, and I know she'll be delighted to give you many pointers. May I ignore modesty and say that she is quite renowned in her hobby?"

He didn't want attention from her mother. He grinned

charmingly. "I'll wager you've inherited your mother's talents. Am I not correct?"

She did not have the opportunity to reply. There was a flurry in the hall. The door opened, and in popped a young lady clad in riding attire. She was vaguely familiar; Darian must have seen her at some of the recent gatherings. Rising, he tried to recall her name. He couldn't.

"Lady Terrell! Lord Enville! How marvelous to see you again! And Venetia . . ." She curtsied and extended her hand to him.

Darian politely bowed over it.

"As often as I can, I try to visit my poor friend in her distress," she bubbled, plopping down beside Miss Woodbridge. "Dear Venetia, how are your parents?"

"Much better, thank you, Sally." She smiled. "My lord, my lady, you are acquainted with—"

"Oh, yes," her friend broke in. "We have met at ever so many social events!"

A footman entered with an extra cup and saucer and a fresh pot of tea.

"Lord Enville is the finest dancer it has ever been my privilege to stand up with," she enlarged.

"You are too kind," Darian murmured, still unable to remember her name.

Fanny came to his rescue. "Do not spoil my brother-in-law, Miss Colfield. He is already far too conceited for his own good!"

She fluttered her eyelashes. "Surely not!"

Darian smiled at his brother's wife. "Fanny exaggerates."

"Fustian!" his sister-in-law fired back, then returned her attention to Miss Woodbridge. "We were discussing garden design."

"Oh, dear." Miss Colfield feigned severe distress. "I recognize a rose among other flowers, but that is about all."

"Then we should change the topic," Darian said gallantly.

"We could discuss the Bascombs' ball," the young lady suggested.

Miss Woodbridge, of course, was at sea on that subject. Darian glanced hastily at Miss Colfield's expression, but there was no malice in it. The girl caught his eye.

"Venetia does not go out in Society, but she loves to hear of our doings." She hastened to squeeze her friend's hand. "We are the best of companions and have been so forever."

"Indeed." Miss Woodbridge smiled fondly. "Tell me of the Bascomb ball."

The Bascomb ball had been provincial. The maternal marriage brokers had been present in force. Darian had been subjected to so many coy smiles, sighs, and battings of eyelashes that he would rather forget the whole affair, but he realized that it had been a very important event in this neighborhood. Gad, he was weary of being fawned over! He hadn't conceived how much, until Miss Colfield's arrival. Miss Woodbridge's calm, polite manner had been like a desert oasis.

"Dear Venetia." The young lady actually bounced on the seat. *"Everyone* was there. I have never seen such glitter, such elegance!"

"I'm sure it was quite grand."

"Oh, yes." She flushed, simpering at Darian and Fanny. "You must think me terribly naive. London parties must be so much finer. I will be going to London for the Little Season."

A fleeting glimmer of wistfulness crossed Miss Woodbridge's face.

"You will highly enjoy it, Miss Colfield," Fanny kindly predicted.

"I know I shall. Will you be there, my lady? Will you, my lord?"

Fanny nodded with kind understanding. "I hope you will attend my parties."

"I would like that above all things!" she exclaimed, searchingly glancing at Darian.

"I may still be at Enville Hall, redesigning my gardens." He grinned at Miss Woodbridge. "You will not forget that I wish to see yours."

"No, my lord."

The housekeeper slipped into the room and whispered into their hostess's ear.

Miss Woodbridge nodded and rose. "Do forgive me. My parents, it seems, need me desperately."

"I do hope they have not suffered a turn for the worse," Fanny sympathized.

"I'm sure they have not." She shrugged. "They crave attention."

Miss Colfield rolled her eyes. "That is certain. *Your* attention."

Darian stood. "Our conversation has been most pleasant. I fear we have overstayed our visit anyway."

"Do finish your tea, my lord," she insisted. "Sally is so at home here that she can act as hostess in my stead."

"I shall be happy to show you the gardens," her friend offered.

"Thank you, miss." He chuckled. "But I believe I would gain more knowledge if I were guided by someone who fully knew the difference between a rose and another flower."

It was a gentle trimming, but she took it good-naturedly. "Of course, my lord. If you are planning to redo your gardens, you must seek the counsel of those of greater experience. Venetia's mother is so skilled. You will benefit greatly by her advice."

"The prospect will cheer her. I am so glad you stopped. Good day." Miss Woodbridge curtsied and breezed from the room, seeming to take all the welcome freshness with her.

Darian and Fanny left shortly after.

"Well, what did you think?" his sister-in-law asked as their carriage rolled down the drive.

"It is quite a pleasure to be entertained by a young lady who is not throwing herself at me," he admitted.

"And Miss Colfield?"

He grinned. "She is like all the others, isn't she?"

They looked at each other and laughed.

Hastening up the stairs, Venetia was unhappy that the visit had been prematurely ended, but she realized that it wouldn't have lasted much longer. Proper etiquette frowned upon overly lengthy stays. Because of Sally's arrival, they had pushed the boundaries of time. Her parents were probably aggravated at her. After all, they hadn't wanted her to go down in the first place. But it was worth their irritation. Oh, how handsome was the Marquess of Enville! And he might come again? Her heart leapt at the very thought of it.

Entering her mother's room, she faced two stiff, pinched faces of disapproval, but even their pique did not take the sunshine from the day. She smiled brightly. "Mother, I wish you had been there. They were interested in your gardens. That's why they came, other than to be neighborly, of course."

Mrs. Woodbridge's expression relaxed somewhat. "Lady Terrell wanted a start from my viburnum."

"Yes, but more than that!" She seated herself opposite them and tried to infect them with her own excitement. "They wish to benefit by your renowned knowledge, Mother."

"Fah! Anyone can grow a flower," her father muttered.

"Now, Father," she sweetly chided. "You know that

Mother is famous for her gardening. You have always been very proud."

"Hunh! That may be the cause of the Terrell woman's visit, but what about Lord Enville? Why is he sniffing about my premises?"

Venetia's heart skipped a beat at the mention of the marquess. "He too is interested in Mother's talent. He is considering redoing the gardens at Enville Hall, his country seat. He hopes to gain some pointers from Mother."

At that, Mrs. Woodbridge looked highly pleased. "I must caution him to think very seriously before destroying old plantings. It takes some shrubs a generation to reach their full glory! They should not be dug up on a whim."

"Lord Enville does not strike me as a man to jump to extremes," she opined.

"I certainly hope not," her mother stressed.

"What do we care?" Mr. Woodbridge demanded. "It has no effect on us."

"Nevertheless," said his wife, "if he wishes my advice, I intend to enlighten him to the best of my ability."

"A man should be interested in the agriculture and animal husbandry of his estate, not the posies," he snorted. "He is sisterly!"

"No, he is not!" Venetia defended. "He is . . ."

They stared at her.

"Masculine," she whispered, lowering her gaze.

Her father audibly ground his teeth. "Enville has nothing to do with you. Read the newspaper to us."

"Yes, Father." Obediently, she picked it up, but the print seemed to blur. How could she concentrate on reading when thoughts of the handsome marquess still crowded her mind? She blinked.

"Do begin, Venetia," her mother prompted. "What is wrong with you?"

"I . . . I don't know where to start."

"On the front page!" her father directed, impatience filling his voice.

"Of course. How foolish of me!" She laughed.

"Your head is in the clouds, girl, because of that man. Remember, he has nothing to do with you." If he had written the last statement, he would have underlined it.

"Yes, sir." She nodded.

Lord Enville had nothing to do with her. Even if she were available, she would never have a chance with such a lofty peer. He was the stuff of dreams.

This was reality. This was her life, present and future. She cleared her throat and began to read.

TWO

On the first day that Venetia's parents decided that they were strong enough to go downstairs, Lord Enville and Lady Terrell came again to call. Venetia was halfway down the stairway, her father leaning heavily on her shoulders, when the marquess and his sister-in-law entered the hall below. She nearly missed a step, rattling the old man, who fiercely grasped the railing and tripped her even further. Recovering, she locked gazes with Lord Enville and smiled weakly. Merciful heavens, he must think her such a nodcock!

He frowned slightly, briefly glancing at the menservants. Starting forward, he bowed. "Allow me to assist you, sir."

"Never you mind," growled Mr. Woodbridge. "My daughter knows how to manage this. At least, she is supposed to know."

Lord Enville hesitated on the bottom step. He looked rather disapproving, but he didn't make further comment. It was obvious, however, that he would have liked to debate the issue.

"I'll go to the morning room," her father announced when they had completed the descent. "I'll be glad to see Mrs. Woodbridge's flowers through the open French doors."

"I thought you weren't interested in posies," Venetia quipped.

"I want to see what all the fuss is about."

She smiled and turned from him to begin proper greetings and introductions for their guests.

Mr. Woodbridge tugged imperiously at her arm. "Under the circumstances, formalities aren't important. Come along, Venetia. You too," he told Lord Enville and Lady Terrell.

Venetia winced as he settled his weight on her shoulders again.

"That's enough," the marquess muttered, then raised his voice. "Sir, I cannot live with myself if you do not allow me to help."

Without another word, he slipped his arm around the old gentleman's waist and shifted the burden to himself.

The relief to Venetia was miraculous. She continued to help support her parent, but the strain was minuscule. "Thank you, my lord."

He grinned crookedly over her father's head.

They settled Mr. Woodbridge in a well-padded chair facing the open French doors. A soft, warm breeze, fragrant with bursting spring blossoms, drifted inside. The room was veritably perfumed by it.

"It's cold," complained Venetia's father.

"I'll fetch you your lap robe when I bring Mother down," Venetia promised and eyed their guests. "You will excuse me momentarily?"

"Of course." Lady Terrell began plumping the pillows at Mr. Woodbridge's back. "There, sir, I shall make you very comfortable. My papa has a bad back and . . ."

With a grateful smile, Venetia escaped into the hall. She was surprised to find Lord Enville following her. "I'll only be a moment, my lord."

He fell in step beside her. "I insist upon aiding you, Miss Woodbridge."

"Truly it isn't necessary," she protested, cheeks warming. "I am accustomed to this."

"Nonsense," he said briskly. "If you keep this up, you'll have the back of an old crone by the time you're thirty."

Sensing that he was quite masterful and used to commanding others, she did not argue the matter. It was nice to lean on someone else, even if it was only mentally and only temporary. But to be an old crone by the age of thirty? That made her feel like crying.

"Miss Woodbridge, forgive me for prying, but you seem to have an adequate number of servants," the marquess observed. "Why are you engaging in heavy drudgery . . . that is, the physical aspect of your parents' care?"

"I am stronger than I might seem," she evaded.

"That isn't what I asked."

She sighed. "My parents prefer it this way. Caring for them is my only mission in life."

"That is ridiculous," he pronounced. "What young lady of your beauty wishes to spend her life as a nurse?"

Beauty? Her heart skipped a beat. He thought she was beautiful!

"Absolutely absurd," he went on. "Aren't you like other women? Don't you want a husband and family, a home of your own?"

Again she tried to evade. "It isn't so bad. I have no other responsibilities. We have a very able steward to manage the estate when Father is ill. And our housekeeper is an absolute treasure."

"Is it enough?" he demanded.

Venetia glanced sideways at him. His lips were pressed rather firmly, and a muscle rippled along his jaw. He was altogether disapproving.

"It must be," she said quietly, "for it is all I have."

"It doesn't have to be."

She halted abruptly. Lord Enville had far overstepped his bounds. Strangely enough, she didn't feel resentful, but she had to stop this trend of discourse. She was running out of answers. And the whole matter made her sad.

"My lord, things are the way they are," she stated with finality, "and there's an end to it."

He opened his mouth as if to say more, but she started up the stairs. He followed. "Forgive me, Miss Woodbridge? I sometimes become overzealous in expressing my point of view."

She smiled, readily absolving him. "You are forgiven, Lord Enville. I know my situation seems odd. People must wonder about it."

Venetia led him down the hall and tapped lightly on her mother's chamber door. The abigail answered. Venetia could have laughed at the servant's wide-eyed gape at the marquess.

"Lord Enville has come to assist," she explained, smiling at her mother, who was seated by the window. "Isn't that kind of him?"

Before Mrs. Woodbridge could reply, she made the introductions.

The marquess bowed over the lady's hand and remained bent. "If you will place your arm around my neck, ma'am, I shall carry you down."

"Oh, my goodness, no! You needn't do that! I am not that feeble," she demurred. "Venetia will help me. She is accustomed to it."

"My back is stronger than hers," he said bluntly and picked her up.

"Oh-h!" cried Mrs. Woodbridge. "This isn't necessary! I can walk!"

He ignored her and proceeded onward.

Bringing two lap robes, Venetia buoyantly walked beside them, spirits soaring. Not only was her aching back being saved, but someone else was in charge. It was wonderful.

Lord Enville carefully seated Mrs. Woodbridge beside

her husband and bowed again. "I am only too happy to be of service, ma'am, especially since I hope to beg your advice on garden design."

"So do I!" Lady Terrell assisted Venetia in spreading the lap robes. "Will you please advise me, Mrs. Woodbridge?"

"You young people flatter me," the older woman chirped, smiling. "Very well. I like nothing better than talk of gardening. I'll be happy to answer your questions. Tell me, my lady, did your bush arrive?"

"Yes, ma'am. Thank you! I had it placed in a special spot by my terrace. I hope you will approve of its positioning." She eyed her appealingly. "I would be so honored if you would view my garden when you are better."

"Perhaps I can do so."

Venetia surreptitiously summoned the butler and ordered refreshments. It was pleasant to have her parents occupied by others. Even though her father looked a bit bored, her mother was cheerfully waxing on and on about her favorite hobby. She wished they'd have visitors more frequently. But the residents of the neighborhood were so accustomed to the Woodbridges being ill, or as was more the case, being sent away by Mr. Woodbridge, that they seldom called.

She moved to the French doors and gazed out at the pleasant vista. Maybe with the influence of the marquess and his sister-in-law, her mother would become fully absorbed by her gardening again. It would take her mind from her troubles, and probably make her feel better. Her father was another problem. But if he saw his wife renewing her interest in life, perhaps he would involve himself more actively in the estate. She'd often wondered if her parents really felt as bad as they acted. Could they have merely decided that they were old and infirm, and fallen into the habit of acting that way?

"Will you take a turn in the garden with me?" Lord Enville said into her ear.

She startled.

"I'm sorry." He grinned.

Venetia blushed. "I was woolgathering."

"Were your thoughts tremendously interesting?"

"Not hardly." She laughed. "I was simply hoping for my parents' further improvement in health. Normal thoughts, I suppose, but scarcely intriguing."

"Indeed, but I hope your wish will come true. Your life would be made much easier." He moved toward the door. "Now won't you show me the famed Woodbridge gardens?"

Instinctively, she glanced past him and caught her father's eye. He was ignoring Lady Terrell's animated conversation and positively glowering at his daughter. He didn't like her chatting with Lord Enville. He would despise her strolling outside with him. Venetia wanted very badly to go, but she was afraid he would pitch a volatile protest. Still, she had the excuse of the gardens. Their guest was interested in the plantings. With such an enticing view from the door, his request was entirely reasonable.

"Let us go." Taking a deep breath, she breezed through the doors and onto the terrace before she noticed Lord Enville's proffered arm.

Her father's voice stopped her, even as her feet touched the flagstones. "Where do you think you are going, daughter?"

It would be impolite to raise her voice in reply, so Venetia was forced to retrace her steps inside. "Lord Enville begged for a tour of the gardens, Father."

"There is time enough for that on another occasion, perhaps when your mother is well enough to guide him," he retorted.

Venetia sensed the marquess standing very solidly behind her. His masculine strength gave her the nerve to debate the matter. How could there be harm in an innocent walk in the gardens?

"The gardens are so pretty today, Father. There are many spring bulbs just bursting with color."

"If I recall your mother's plantings, that is a state which will continue all through the growing season and into the fall," he snapped.

"But the spring flowering bulbs are so very beautiful and fragrant," she countered.

She felt Lord Enville's fingers reassuringly touch her waist and nearly jumped. She prayed her father did not perceive the privy gesture. It was vastly comforting, but it was rather warm.

"Some of the bushes bloom for such a short period of time," she ventured hesitatingly.

"Venetia, you know nothing of flowers." Her father jutted his jaw. "For you to show anyone a garden is patently absurd."

No, she wanted to shout. Arguing over such a minute excursion was what was ridiculous, and terribly mortifying too. Why, Sally's parents would have fairly thrust them out the door! But then, she was not Sally. There was no hoped-for match in her future.

"Mr. Woodbridge," the marquess said pleasantly, "with your wife's famous gardens just across the terrace, I am sorely tempted to see them."

"Oh, you are?" He narrowed his eyes. "Well, young man, let me tell you that I mistrust your motives."

Venetia felt as if the bottom had dropped out of her stomach. There was such an awful silence that she could hear Lord Enville breathe. She wished that a great, gaping hole would open in the floor and that she would fall through it.

"I know exactly what you are about," he pounded on. "You don't fool me, and you won't get away with this."

Lady Terrell halfrose. "I believe that we had best leave."

"Oh, dear," Mrs. Woodbridge murmured.

"Sir, I assure you that my actions are above suspicion," Lord Enville said coolly. "I am an honorable man, and no one has ever said otherwise."

A chill surged through Venetia's veins. Gentlemen had fought duels for less provocation than this. Her father had insulted the marquess beyond all belief. It was uncalled for. And it was more than mortifying.

Mr. Woodbridge worked his jaw in a harsh, grinding motion. "You are interested in my daughter, not in any posies. She may be a naive country girl to a man of your bronze, but she is not an easy piece. Nor is she available, to you or any other man."

"Come, Darian." Lady Terrell crossed the room to the hall door. "Mrs. Woodbridge, I did enjoy our conversation, but it is obvious that we are no longer welcome. Darian, *let us go, now.*"

"Oh, dear," Venetia's mother helplessly repeated.

Venetia blinked at gathering tears. How could her father be so rude? Dear heavens, what if he did cause a duel? What could she do to make amends? She squared her shoulders.

"Father, I resent these accusations!"

"Go to your room, girl."

"I will not!" She gritted her teeth to keep up her nerve. "Your attitude is outside of enough! And you are wrong! You owe Lord Enville an apology."

"Do not!" he fired back. "He knows exactly what I am talking about!"

"Darian," begged Lady Terrell in a slightly hysterical voice. *"Please!"*

The marquess finally heeded her. "Very well, Fanny."

Venetia followed him toward the door.

"Where are you going, daughter?" her father demanded.

"To show our guests out."

"That isn't necessary." He stuck out his lip. "I need you. Come plump my pillows."

Nerves stretched to the breaking point, Venetia burst into tears. She wanted to stand her ground and do as she intended, but her courage suddenly washed away. Whirling, she dashed toward the gardens.

"Daughter!" her father bellowed.

"Leave me alone!"

Running across the flags, she tripped on a jutting stone and fell hard on her hands and knees. The sharp pain momentarily halted her. Embarrassed too, she slowly picked herself up, staring at the bloody scrapes on her palms. The whole scene was perfectly awful.

"Get back in here!" Mr. Woodbridge blared.

"No!" She took to her heels again.

She did not see Lord Enville start to go after her, or his sister-in-law, in an astounding feat of strength, yank him through the door.

"That old bastard," Darian swore as he and Fanny descended the front steps.

"I could scarcely believe my eyes and ears!" she cried. "I have never been so ill-treated and humiliated. And that poor girl . . . what her life must be like!"

He helped her into the landau, then stepped back.

"Darian, where are you going?"

He eyed her grimly. "There's more than one way into that garden."

"No, you cannot!" She leaned out and grabbed for his arm. "That nasty old man might try to shoot you!"

The marquess laughed without humor. "That would require him to leave his damned chair."

"Nevertheless, it is a family matter. It is not our affair."

"That son-of-a-bitch—pardon me, Fanny—that ancient grump insulted me, and I do not take it lightly."

"There is nothing you can do about it, short of calling him out," she shrilled, "and you are too wise to do that. You are, aren't you, Darian?"

He snorted. "The man probably couldn't walk the requisite ten paces."

"Then let us go," she pleaded.

"I'm going to see that garden," he said firmly.

She bit her lip. "And Miss Woodbridge."

"Yes, and Miss Woodbridge." He nodded with determination and turned to the driver. "Take Lady Terrell home. I'll walk."

"Yes, m'lord." He picked up the reins.

"Darian!" Fanny wailed, one last time. "What if Mr. Woodbridge finds out? He will make things even more difficult for his daughter."

"But he won't find out, will he?" Darian stared hard at the attending Woodbridge footman.

"Uh, my lord, uh . . ." The servant winced. "It'd mean my job, sir."

"Then I'll hire you . . . at a better wage." The marquess clapped his shoulder. "Come, my man, I'm sure you can show me a way to the garden in which I will not be seen."

He wavered only seconds longer, then grinned. "Yes, m'lord. This way."

Darian followed him around the house and into a veritable tunnel of vegetation. It was a dense passageway, paved with brick and dotted with benches, apparently extending along the entire side of the building. When they emerged, the footman stopped.

"If you'll go round that fringe of box, m'lord, you should find our young miss."

"Very well. Thank you." Darian tossed him a coin and proceeded.

He heard Miss Woodbridge weeping before he saw her.

He cautiously kept close to the hedge, realizing, even so, that he could probably be seen from the upper floors of the house. If he was, hopefully the witnessing servants would feel enough pity for Miss Woodbridge to keep their tongues to themselves. Rounding a corner, he spotted his quarry.

The young lady was seated in a slatted swing under an arbor of budding roses, her head cradled in her hands. Shoulders shaking, she was sobbing as if her heart would break. She was oblivious to his approach.

"Miss Woodbridge." He sat down beside her and did what anyone would do if wishing to comfort a distraught individual. He put his arm around her.

"Lord Enville!" She briefly gazed wide-eyed at him, then crumpled against his chest. "Oh, I am so mortified!"

"Shh, it is not your fault." He drew her close, watching carefully for the first stiffening of resistance.

"I have never been so humiliated!"

She was a soft, cuddly armful. Darian had embraced many women, but he had never felt quite like this. The caress was not seductively sexual. It was soothing. Strangely, it touched his virility more than an overtly sensual encounter.

"I cannot believe that my father could be so horrid," she moaned. "I did nothing to deserve it, and neither did you!"

Darian did not attempt to explain male rivalry, but that was the likely cause of the contretemps. Her father, albeit for a different reason than most masculine conflicts, saw him as a competitor. More's the pity, he suddenly realized that the old bastard was right in his concern. Darian was attracted to the lady. He truly was a threat to the Woodbridge way of life.

"Your father is being defensive," he simply stated.

"Of me?" she snuffled and suddenly drew back, as if

she were alarmed by the closeness. She searched his gaze with those soul-touching emerald eyes.

He nodded reassuringly. "He doesn't want to overset his routine."

"But I was only going to show you the gardens!"

Darian grinned lopsidedly. "He didn't see it like that."

"I don't understand." She snuffed mightily and tried to wipe her eyes on a wispy, wet lace handkerchief.

He produced his monogrammed linen square.

"Thank you." She took it without hesitation and put it to use. "Do my parents know you're here?"

"Lord, no! A footman showed me the way round the side of the house."

Miss Woodbridge managed a smile. "You were kind to think of me."

"You are easy to be kind to." He took her hand. "I feel responsible for being a part of your distress."

"No." She firmly shook her head. Pretty pink circles appeared on the uppermost points of her cheekbones. She lowered her gaze to her hands, fingering the corner of his handkerchief.

"Lord Enville, my father was perfectly odious. He is often cantankerous, but I have never seen him quite like this. Perhaps you have a point in saying that he was being defensive, but I sincerely believe that his rudeness was due to the state of his health. People who are ill are often bad-tempered."

"Well, you know him better than I," he said doubtfully.

She looked at their clasped hands and gently drew hers away. "Viewing the garden is an innocent pursuit. We all know how interested you are in it. Father will realize how ridiculous he was. I'm sure he will apologize."

Darian could have laughed, but he didn't want to hurt her. He couldn't visualize Mr. Woodbridge apologizing to anyone, especially to him. The grumpy old boar might have sired a lovely young lady, but any other of his life's accomplishments must have been tinged with high-handed, nasty ill humor.

"You are so very kind, my lord," she repeated, "to be concerned about me. Few of my friends would have chanced the risk of being caught by Father."

"I only hope he does not take out his anger on you."

"Oh, he will." She laughed shortly. "But I am accustomed to it. He will blow like a tempest, and I will ignore it."

He couldn't keep from voicing his opinion. "It doesn't sound like a very happy way of life."

"I make do with what I have." She rose. "I fear we must end our chat. We are tempting fate."

Darian stood. "You are right, of course. I don't wish you to incur further wrath today."

"Hopefully, no one will tattle. The servants are sweet about covering my few escapes. Is Lady Terrell waiting for you?"

"No, I told her I'd walk."

"Then come." She spontaneously took his hand. "I'll show you a shortcut."

Miss Woodbridge led him through a maze of tulips to a gate. "This path will lead you to the stream . . . where we met."

"Very well." He paused and took a deep breath. "Miss Woodbridge, I would like to see you again."

Her eyes widened.

"Perhaps we could meet by the stream," he suggested.

"Goodness, Lord Enville, I don't know. It's . . . it's difficult." She frowned slightly. "I do not think I can. No, it is not a good idea."

"Will you think about it?"

"Yes, but—"

"Send me a message if you decide you can." He swiftly kissed her fingers. "Good-bye, for now."

Darian strode through the gate, leaving her standing

somewhat flustered. He knew he was causing her turmoil, but, dammit, he did want to see her. There was something about Miss Woodbridge that fascinated him more than he could say. Whether it was her sweetness, her beauty, her plight, he could not say. But he wanted to find out.

When he arrived at his brother's residence, Daniel was pacing back and forth on the front stoop.

"Good God, Darian, what are you about?"

He grinned. "By that I assume that Fanny told all."

"In minute detail! That old bastard!" He smacked his fist into the palm of his other hand. "I can't believe it!"

Darian lifted a shoulder. "Woodbridge sees me as a rival."

Daniel knew exactly what he was talking about. "Apparently so. If he knew your history, he sure as hell wouldn't. His girl will remain safe within his clutches. Maybe someone will enlighten him."

"Maybe so," he said noncommittally.

His brother narrowed his eyes. "That is true, isn't it, Darian?"

The marquess merely looked at him.

"Darian?"

"The whole situation is absurd," he mused, "and so outlandish. And such a waste."

"That may be true, but it is, of course, no concern of ours," Daniel stated. "My estate may march with his, but I've scarcely seen the man. My few dealings have been with his steward."

"Do you know, I have need of a glass of brandy." Darian sauntered past him in the direction of the library. "I hope Fanny has planned a hearty dinner. The afternoon has put an edge to my appetite."

His brother darted after him. "Talk to me, Darian! Enlighten me on what is going on.

"Certainly, Daniel. What do you want to know?"

He sighed. "Sit down. I'll pour the drinks. You're probably weary from your walk."

"To the contrary, I feel fine." He laughed. "Never better."

His brother shook his head and crossed the room to his liquor cabinet. "Something's strange. I've never seen you like this."

"How am I supposed to be?" He seated himself in a leather wing chair.

"Angry as a stuck bear, for one guess. Frankly, I can't believe you didn't call out the old fool."

"That old man? Are you daft?"

Daniel poured the drinks and joined him. "Big brother, I doubt you've ever been insulted like that. No one would have the nerve."

"The elderly, I find, have a certain immunity." Darian chuckled. "Advanced age seems to grant one the privilege of saying and doing what one pleases. Illness provides even greater latitude. So there seem to be some perquisites to look forward to as we grow older."

"Hell and damnation!" Daniel snorted. "Where did you get that cork-brained idea? Goddammit, in my opinion, even Fanny was insulted! I should call out the bastard myself!"

"But you won't." Darian took a sip of the brandy and rolled it appreciatively in his mouth before swallowing.

"No! More's the pity! But we should get even," he vowed. "Let's write Woodbridge a nasty letter."

"That would make you feel better, I'm sure, but I wouldn't give the man the satisfaction of thinking he perturbed us." He smiled but shook his head. "And it would doubtlessly distress Miss Woodbridge. To say nothing, Daniel, about it being juvenile and unsophisticated."

"I don't give a damn!" He jutted his chin. "I don't like my family being so belittled. Woodbridge shouldn't be allowed to get away with it."

"Forget the entire matter." He squinted through the rich amber of his drink. "You'd only hurt innocent parties. Moreover, if you make a fuss, Fanny will definitely kill you."

Daniel had to laugh. "You're right in that!"

"Consider the fact that I secretly met with his daughter as a grand revenge."

His brother cocked his head. "Yes; what of that?"

"As you might expect, the poor young lady was vastly overset," he revealed.

"And?"

He wasn't about to discuss his encounter with Miss Woodbridge. For one thing, it would lead to speculation and more questioning. For another, Darian wasn't entirely sure how he felt about it all. He had entered a strange, new territory of emotions. He didn't intend to discuss something he himself did not understand.

"It would not have been honorable of me to have left her with such feelings of guilt and humiliation," he explained. "I had to let her know that Fanny and I did not blame her in any way."

Daniel nodded, accepting the reasoning. "Well done, Darian. I feel sorry for the girl and the life she has to lead. She should rebel."

That aggravated him. "How?" he demanded. "What can a young chit of a girl do about her situation?"

His brother shrugged. "I don't know. Run away?"

"To where?"

"To her brothers and sisters?"

"What if they side with the parents?" Darian fired back.

"How the hell do I know what she could do?" Daniel tossed down the last of his drink. "It's none of my business."

"Then maybe you'd best keep your mouth shut about it!" he snapped.

"Damn! I feel like I've poked a bee nest!" Daniel

frowned. "I don't know why you're so riled. I only made a mundane observation."

"Just keep it to yourself."

"I certainly shall. I didn't realize how touchy you are about Miss Woodbridge." He arched an eyebrow. "It's very interesting, Darian."

The marquess abruptly changed the subject. "Let's have another drink, Daniel . . . and another topic for conversation."

He held out his glass and grinned innocently at his younger brother.

In the days following the awful incident, Venetia's parents improved in health, but her father did not ease his vile opinion of Lord Enville. Venetia had hoped that he might realize how unreasonable he had been and wish to make amends, but on the few occasions he had mentioned the marquess, he had done so with rancor. Obviously, he would never extend the olive branch.

Venetia was miserable over the whole affair. She tried to tell herself that her distress was mainly caused by the difficulty of strained feelings between neighbors, but she knew that wasn't entirely the case. She had been flattered by Lord Enville's interest, and she wanted to see him again. The only way she could satisfy her yen was to engage in an outright defiance of her father's wishes. She was, frankly, rather afraid to do that.

At first, she attempted to thrust the idea from her mind, but her yearning persisted. Then she decided to eliminate the notion by work, but her busyness with her hands only allowed her thoughts to run rampant. One afternoon in the garden, while thinning herbs at her mother's direction, she broached the subject with the lady, hoping to find an ally.

"Mother, Father's contretemps with Lady Terrell and

Lord Enville disturbs me more than I can say," she murmured, leaning forward on her knees to pick out springs of rosemary.

"Indeed." Mrs. Woodbridge tugged her light shawl more closely about her shoulders, even though the gentle spring breeze was warm. "I dislike ill feelings between neighbors too."

Venetia sat back on her heels. "I wish there was something we could do about it."

She sighed. "I don't know what it would be."

"Perhaps you could talk with Father."

"Oh, my goodness, I could not do that! Why, he'd snap my head off." She shrugged lightly. "No, that wouldn't do. Nothing can be done."

"But Father was wrong!" she insisted. "He should apologize."

Her mother laughed. "He will hardly do that. He believes he was correct in his assessment, and I'm not so sure that he wasn't."

"That is ridiculous!" Venetia scoffed.

Mrs. Woodbridge frowned. "Do not be pert, my girl!"

"I'm sorry." She lowered her gaze. "I did not mean to be disrespectful. I simply feel so strongly that Lord Enville was merely being kind . . . and madly interested in the gardens."

The lady's expression softened. "My dear, naive child, you just do not understand. You are becoming a very beautiful young lady. Like a delicate rosebud, you are on the verge of bursting into a full-blown flower. You are vulnerable to being picked and placed into a bouquet."

Venetia looked up questioningly.

"You do not glean my meaning?"

"No, ma'am."

Pausing briefly, Mrs. Woodbridge tilted her head and stared heavenward. "A gentleman like Lord Enville possesses a large bouquet, to which he is constantly adding flowers. When he views a pretty blossom, he wants to place it in his collection. He is not content to admire it from a distance in its own garden. Now do you understand?"

"I'm not sure. Can we speak of *people* instead of flowers?" She took a deep breath. "Mother, I have not heard that Lord Enville is a rake, or a . . . a womanizer."

"Where have you heard such a word?" her mother cried.

Venetia bit her lip.

The lady answered her own question. "From Sally, I suppose. That girl is too brazen for her own good, and definitely for yours! Perhaps that friendship should be examined. It does not seem wholesome."

Venetia felt a sense of near panic. Sally was her lifeline to real world honesty. If she was forbidden to see her best friend, she would be so very alone.

"I overheard two maids gossiping about a stableman," she swiftly lied.

Since her daughter never fibbed, Mrs. Woodbridge believed her. "Who were the maids? I must interview them and ascertain the name of the culprit. I shall not have such a manservant on the staff."

"I do not know who they were," Venetia assured her. "Since I was eavesdropping, I did not make my presence known."

"Then I must speak with them all." Her mother pressed her lips firmly together. "I won't have it!"

She nodded. "Certainly not. But to return to the subject of Lord Enville . . ."

"You are correct, Venetia," she said briefly. "I have not heard that he is a gentleman of disrepute."

"Then I don't grasp Father's objection to my showing him the gardens."

Again Mrs. Woodbridge rolled her eyes upward. "The marquess is *experienced.* I'm sure he enjoys flirtations with lovely young ladies. You are just a child, unaccustomed to such pastimes."

"I am twenty-one years old!" she exclaimed.

Her mother laughed gently. "Age has nothing to do with it. I refer to childlike innocence."

"Or that of an old maid," Venetia said bitterly.

There was a terrible silence, broken only by the appearance of the head gardener.

Mrs. Woodbridge was obviously relieved. "Hello, Lefton. Have you completed the transplanting?"

"Yes, madam. I thought you might like to see."

"I do." She rose from the bench. "Do carry on, Venetia. You do not need my approval. I believe you know what you are doing."

On thinning herbs, yes. Venetia watched her mother's suddenly spry departure, then bent again over the bed of rosemary. It was plain that her parents were determined to further her naiveté. They had already limited her access to the outside world, and they wanted to prevent the outside world from intruding on her. It was a wonder that they had allowed her friendship with Sally to continue. Apparently, they were alert to any excuse to halt it. She must forever be on her guard. Thank heavens she'd quickly come up with that lie.

She sighed and shook her head. If she must engage in deceit to maintain some small control of her life, she would just have to practice it. She had to have some freedom.

She thought of Lord Enville's suggestion of a clandestine meeting by the stream. That had nothing to do with garden design. He wanted to see *her*. The idea made her tremble. Was her mother right? Did he merely wish to gather her into his bouquet? Maybe . . . maybe kiss her?

Her heart beat frantically. She should not meet him. A gentleman had no place in the life of a destined old maid. But she'd never been friends with a man before. Her brothers were older. She'd had little to do with them. It had been pleasant to talk with Lord Enville. And when he had comforted her . . . She shivered. When he had put his arm around her, she had never known such excitement and joy.

"I'm going to do it," she whispered. "I'm going to meet him . . . if he still wishes it."

He must not reply to her message. It was risky enough as it was. Weather permitting, she would be at the stream tomorrow afternoon when her parents took their naps. If he still wished to see her, he'd be there. Hopefully, he would not have made other plans.

Venetia stood and resolutely walked toward the house. She was going to defy her parents in a perfectly shocking way. She was going to write a note.

It rained. The morning dawned gray and remained overcast until afternoon, when the leaden skies burst forth with a deluge of heavy showers. Venetia stood at the morning-room window and gazed out at the ruination of her adventure. Perhaps it was for the best. Maybe the Lord himself was punishing her for her deceit. But disappointment washed over her as thoroughly as the cloudburst would have done if she had ventured out. She could not bring herself to write to Lord Enville again. She did, however, decide to go to the stream on the morrow.

The following day progressed in her favor. The sun beamed down brightly, and the air was balmy and warm. Strolling down the woodland path toward the creek, she felt her pulse pounding like a hammer through her veins. On the one hand, she wanted Lord Enville to be there; on the other, she didn't. She was being awfully forward. What did he think of her actions? What would she say? She almost turned to flee in the opposite direction, but she forced herself to go on. If she gave in to flight, she would never forgive herself. Breaking through the fringe of forest, she caught sight of the marquess standing on the far bank, loosely holding his horse's reins.

He saw her at once. "Miss Woodbridge! I was hoping you'd come today."

She smiled bravely. "It was rather damp yesterday."

They glanced simultaneously at the water between them.

It was symbolic, Venetia thought. There would always be a barrier between her and any gentleman. Lord Enville had forded it once. Now that he knew her story, would he do so again? The idea of meeting really was useless.

"I have a plan." The marquess swung up on his horse. "We'll use Fanny and Daniel's facilities, and neither one of us will get wet."

Touching his horse's sides with his heels, he rode through the stream to her side. Reaching down, he lifted her up in front of him. Holding her securely with one arm around her middle, he guided the chestnut back across to his brother's property.

"Perhaps we suffered just a few splashes." He eased her to the ground and vaulted down.

"Very inspired planning, my lord." She noticed a picnic hamper sitting on the wrought-iron table. "In more ways than one!"

"I thought we might like refreshment." He tethered his horse to a sapling. "I hope you can stay a long time."

"My parents nap for about two hours."

"No longer?"

She shook her head, feeling that shadow mar their afternoon. What seemed like a long time now became very short. But it was better than nothing.

"Then I must be content with that." Lord Enville took her hand and led her to a chair by the table. Opening the wicker basket, he withdrew a bottle of sherry and two crystal glasses.

"I don't know if I should," she demurred, unaccustomed to drinking wine except with regular meals. Then she smiled. This meeting had been risky. It wouldn't hurt to be a bit more reckless.

She nodded permission. "Oh, very well."

"Good!" He filled the goblets and set out cheese and thinly sliced bread. "I want this to be a festive occasion."

"Why?" she asked.

He looked at her for a prolonged moment. "I don't know. I just thought it might be a good idea."

"It is." Venetia smiled brightly. "I don't know why either!"

They gazed at each other until she became slightly self-conscious and glanced away. She sipped the sweet sherry. How would it taste on his lips? Even as she scolded herself for such a warm thought, the very notion of it sent a frisson of excitement coursing through the pit of her stomach. She chanced a glimpse at him across the table.

He was watching her. "You are so very beautiful."

"Lord Enville, please," she whispered, heartbeats choking her throat.

"It is true, but I don't wish to frighten you away by my appreciation. Venetia . . ."

She stared wide-eyed at his use of her first name.

The marquess bent his head and studied his hands. "A thousand pardons."

"No!" she said quickly, feeling even more daring. "It's . . . it's all right. Under the circumstances, it seems perfectly normal. After all, everything about this meeting is highly irregular."

"It is that." He nodded. "Will you call me Darian?"

She smiled shyly. "That is a fine name."

"I'd like to hear you say it."

"Darian," she murmured.

Silence fell, and with it an awkwardness. Venetia sipped

her drink, absorbing the glorious sunlight and yet feeling chilly. Was it the coldness of guilt?

"Oh, Darian!" she burst out. "I have practiced such deceit! Why must it be this way?"

He startled.

"I'm sorry." She tried to laugh. "I don't know what caused that outburst. I suppose I must be feeling sorry for myself. Why, I don't know. I am the transgressor."

"I'm not so sure about that."

"No, I am," she said firmly. "I am untrustworthy, and I am a liar. I am a most undutiful daughter."

"I don't know where duty and reality collide. Your parents are demanding that you go against nature and Society. It's a make-believe world they're creating, Venetia. At least, it's not a life which you choose to pursue."

She sighed. He was right, but what could she do? Running away would cast her in worse straits.

"It doesn't matter," she said flatly. "There is nothing I can do about it."

"I wish I could help."

"There is nothing you can do either, my lord, though it is sweet of you to offer that. Please let us speak of other things." She smiled ruefully. "I'm sorry I brought up the topic. I was just overset for a moment. Do tell me of London and all its marvelous sights. How I would love to travel there!"

He complied, verbalizing visions of the historic buildings, the promenades in the park, Vauxhall Gardens, and Bond Street.

Venetia enjoyed the travelogue so much that she scarcely realized the passing time until she noticed the lengthening shadows. "Oh, my lord, you have truly diverted my thoughts far away from this neighborhood. I feel as if I have really seen these marvelous sights. But, unfortunately, now I must go."

"So soon?"

"If only the clock would stand still! For a while, it did," she said wistfully, rising.

"We can do this again," he proposed.

Her heart leapt with hope. Maybe this great nobleman genuinely didn't mind spending time sharing his world with a naive country girl. Or was he just being nice?

"I would like very much to see you again, Venetia."

She took a deep breath, weighing deceit against pleasure. "I would like to see you too," she whispered.

He gazed into her eyes. "Tomorrow?"

"Yes."

Catching her hands behind her back, Venetia waited while he mounted his horse. When he took her up in front of him, it was all she could do to resist allowing her head to drift to his shoulder. *Shameless hussy*, she scolded herself.

"It has been a wonderful afternoon," she told him after sliding down to the ground.

"For me too." He grinned. "I shall look forward to tomorrow."

"So will I." With a last gaze into his eyes, she whirled and ran into the woods, heart singing with the thrill of it all.

THREE

The afternoon meetings continued. As they learned more of each other, Venetia and Darian became very close. When rainy days prevented their rendezvous, they were rather devastated. They grew to need their time together.

Summer commenced, bringing greater improvement and more activity on the part of Venetia's parents. It became more difficult to escape the house and immediate grounds. Venetia was forced to invent more elaborate subterfuges. She decided to take up fishing.

Shoving a rather fishy-tasting fillet of cod to the edge of her plate, she set down her fork. "I am going to endeavor to improve our diet," she announced at luncheon. "Father, I know how you love fish, and this is frankly unacceptable. I am going to go to the stream and catch you a string of fresh fish. Combined with the new vegetables from the garden, we shall have a feast."

Her mother, too, pushed aside her cod. "That would be delightful."

"You don't know how to fish," Mr. Woodbridge complained.

"Of course I do! You taught me when I was a little girl, and I remember my lessons."

"Those were wonderful days," Mrs. Woodbridge reminisced. "No one was ill."

"You don't have time to fish," her father balked.

"You're supposed to be helping your mother in the gardens."

"We only work in the morning. By afternoon it is too hot. If I recall, there are many shade trees by the stream," she replied carefully. "Allow me to provide this treat."

"Oh, do!" her mother seconded enthusiastically.

Mr. Woodbridge lifted a shoulder. "Very well, if there is angling equipment to be found."

"I'm sure there will be." Venetia glanced speakingly at Branson, who nodded in answer to her unspoken request that he send a footman to search. There was a certain wary sparkle in his eye. She wondered if he knew of her clandestine activities. If he did, she hoped she could depend upon him to hold his tongue. These weren't minor escapades, as had sometimes happened in the past when she'd sneaked to the village or to Sally's house. Her meetings with Lord Enville were serious transgressions, and were growing more important every day. She was beginning to question how she would react when he finally left the district.

Someday it would happen, probably sooner than she wished to contemplate. The marquess had already stayed with his brother for a very long time. It couldn't continue.

Venetia finished her lunch with only desultory conversation with her parents. When she left the dining room, a footman was entering the back hall with an assortment of angling devices. Her spirits soared.

"I cannot believe you found all that so quickly," she praised.

"It was right there in the attic." He grinned almost mischievously. "Should land a prize catch with these things, Miss Venetia."

She eyed him closely. "Indeed."

Before she could examine her tackle, the front door knocker clanged. Sally burst into the house, waving gaily. Venetia's cheer faded.

Her friend tripped down the hall. *"Fishing* equipment? What are you about, Venetia?"

"Never mind." She took her elbow and piloted her into the salon. "I am trying to ignite Father's enthusiasm for fresh fish."

"Are *you* going to fish?"

"Oh, Sally, let us not speak of my predicament. You cannot be interested in angling." She motioned her to a chair. "Do tell me of the doings of the outside world."

"Well, if *you* were going fishing, I would accompany you. It would be rather pleasant to sit by the stream and talk," she observed.

"With Father?" she asked.

She shook her head. "No, not if he is going."

Venetia breathed easier. She hadn't told Sally of her tête-à-têtes with Lord Enville. It would cause undue speculation, and Sally just might blurt it out in a moment of excitement. Then, despite the Woodbridges' seclusion, word might reach her parents' ears. She'd never hidden such a momentous thing from her best friend, but this was just too risky.

As Sally began to prattle on about the neighborhood social events, Venetia stole a glance at the clock. Darian would be there by now, awaiting her. She had seldom failed him. When she had, he'd told her that he'd waited a very long time in hopes that she'd finally arrive. She hoped he would do so today.

"Lord Enville certainly has stayed a long time in the area," Sally mused.

Venetia nearly startled at the mention of his name.

Sally's merry eyes danced. "There is gossip that he may be interested in a local lady."

"Oh?" She could scarcely breathe. She had often dreamed that he stayed because he enjoyed her company, but perhaps he was forming a tendre for someone here.

"It isn't me, more's the pity!" her friend lamented. "But

I cannot think who it could be. He shows everyone equal attention."

"Maybe he merely likes his brother's company," she offered.

Sally twirled a curl around her finger. "That may well be, but I shan't give up hope."

Venetia glanced at the clock again.

"That's twice," her friend counted. "Honestly, have I come at an inopportune time?"

She sighed, preparing to lie again. "Yes, frankly, it is. There were some difficulties at luncheon . . ."

"Say no more." She stood. "I shall be on my way. You should tell me immediately, Venetia, when my visit is inappropriate."

"I enjoy your company," she said lamely.

Sally waved the comment aside. "I can come anytime."

Feeling like a traitor, Venetia escorted her to the door. "I wish I was not occupied today."

"Pshaw! Think nothing of it." Kissing her friend's cheek, she skipped down the steps to her horse. "Keep up your spirits!"

"I will."

She waited until Sally had mounted and turned away, then rushed back into the hall. By the rear door, a rod with line and hook stood waiting. With a silent thank-you to the now absent, helpful footman, she grabbed it and darted outside. Strolling nonchalantly until she was out of sight of the house, she broke into a mad dash through the woods, running straight into the marquess's arms at the side of the stream.

"Whoa!" He hugged her briefly before setting her back and picking the hook from his blue, superfine coat. "Are we going fishing?"

"Oh, Darian, these meetings are becoming more challenging. My parents are feeling quite well and are keeping close watch over me."

He tucked a stray wisp of hair behind her ear. "So you came up with an angling ruse."

"Yes." She grimaced. "Do you know how to fish? Oh, please do! I've forgotten everything I learned as a child."

He studied the pole. "The tackle I used was somewhat different, but this seems simple. However, we do need bait."

"My goodness, I didn't think of that!"

"We'll find insects. Come, let's cross." He mounted his horse and reached for her, lifting her up in front of him and fording the stream in their usual fashion. "Sit down and catch your breath while I hunt. Shall I pour the sherry first?"

"I'll do it," she volunteered, relieved that he was going to assume the role of handling bugs.

Sipping her sherry and watching him explore the clearing, Venetia marveled at how happy she was. She thought back on her conversation with her mother and those warnings about Darian's *experience* and could have laughed. How wrong her parent had been! Darian was perfect. He treated her as if she were made of crystal, and other than calling her by her first name, he had certainly never attempted liberties. He was an honorable gentleman, and she . . . she loved him.

He returned with a grasshopper on the hook, tossed the line into the water, and propped the rod between several large rocks. "There. Now I am certain we'll catch a mammoth trout."

"Without working at it?" she queried. "I remember how Father cast and cast, making his bait hop across the surface of the water. Do you know how to do that?"

"Yes, but I'd rather spend the short time with you."

She smiled happily. "Our time isn't particularly short today. Mother and Father know I've gone fishing. Father grudgingly approved."

"Spectacular!" In his excitement, he impulsively bent and kissed her forehead.

Venetia's smile disappeared as her lips formed an O. She looked longly into his eyes. He too had swiftly sobered.

"Venetia, I love you, my sweet girl." He took her shoulders and drew her to her feet. "I think I have loved you from the moment I first saw you across the stream."

Tears blurred her vision of his handsome face. His words echoed her own thoughts. *But it could not be.*

"My darling." He drew her close, his lips gently descending to hers.

Venetia's first kiss was not like Sally's as her friend had once painstakingly described it. She did not feel naughty. She felt as if nothing could be more natural. Nor did she feel like gasping or swooning, even as he deepened the kiss and she responded. She wanted to experience every subtlety of this intimacy, and she ached for more. Her body wildly begged for Darian's touch in the most forbidden places, and that was what drew her up. She gently pressed his cheek.

He lingeringly lifted his head and said in a husky voice, "I won't apologize, for I am not sorry."

"Neither am I," she whispered.

"It was rather inevitable, wasn't it?"

"Yes."

He grinned lopsidedly. "So now what do we do?"

She didn't know. This terrible love had happened, and there was no future for it. They couldn't meet by the stream forever. Love between an honorable lady and gentleman progressed to marriage. But that couldn't happen for them, so what did it leave? Only hurt remained.

She squared her shoulders and tried to smile brightly, pushing the heartbreaking thought from her mind. "Let us try to catch a trout, Darian."

"What?" he cried.

"Please," she begged, her emotions in turmoil. She walked to the brookside, picking up the rod and flipping the bait across the water as she remembered her father doing.

He came up behind her. "I *love* you, Venetia. My God, I've never said that to any lady."

A tear trickled down her cheek. She batted her eyelashes in an attempt to stay the flow. Another tear followed.

"Very well, darling; we won't speak of it now, if that is what you wish." He put his arms around her waist and drew her back against him.

She laid her head in the hollow of his shoulder and closed her eyes. Darian loved her. He wasn't trying to add her to any bouquet. He loved her, and her alone. He had never loved anyone else.

"Just hold me please," she murmured.

"With great pleasure." He lightly leaned his chin on her head, his breath blowing fluffs of her hair. They stayed that way for a long time, then returned to the table and chairs to partake in a glass of sherry. They sat, speaking of everyday matters, as the shadows grew long.

"I really must catch a trout," Darian finally stated. "You can't go home empty-handed. I want your father's appetite whetted, so he'll be anxious for you to come again."

"Yes! Once, he dearly loved fish from this stream."

He shucked off his coat and went further along the bank to the shadows of an overhanging tree. Expertly, he flicked the line back and forth across the water. Almost immediately a trout rose to the bait.

Venetia applauded, watching the rippling of his muscles under his thin lawn shirt as he played the fish to the shore. "You are wonderful!"

He turned, grinning. "Lucky, more like."

"I am quite content to think you are wonderful," she said pertly.

"I'm glad you do. Is one enough?"

"I think it must be. It's becoming very late." She rose. "I should go."

When they crossed the stream on his horse, Darian continued to pilot him through the woods. "I won't have you dragging that big fish all the way home."

"We're taking a great risk!" Venetia wailed. "If they saw us . . ."

He set his jaw. "They are going to have to know, sooner or later."

"No! Father would lock me in my room! He would have me watched night and day!"

"This is archaic," Darian muttered.

"Yes, but that is the way it is!" she cried. "You must let me down!"

He took her to the very fringe of the woods before drawing rein. "Now, darling, isn't this better?"

"It is, but it is so dangerous!" She scrambled to the ground, taking the fishing tackle and the trout. "If Mother was in the garden . . . We are so close . . . Oh, Darian, I couldn't bear never seeing you again!"

"You just don't understand," he muttered to himself, then smiled. "Tomorrow?"

She nodded eagerly. "I shall contrive some way, *any way*, to come."

"Until then." He caressed her cheek, then turned his horse and quietly retraced his steps through the woods.

Venetia hurried to the house, happy to find the garden and terrace vacant. Inside, she learned that her parents were ensconced in the library. They couldn't have seen her with Darian. Her secret was still safe.

Darian rode home so lost in his thoughts that he didn't even notice Daniel's butler on the porch until he almost ran into him.

"Reynolds! Do forgive me. I was woolgathering," he admitted, grinning sheepishly.

The manservant bowed. "Yes, my lord. May I be of assistance?"

"As a matter of fact, you can. I need two or three fresh trout in the morning . . . live, not dressed."

The man was too well versed in his profession to register surprise or curiosity. "As you wish, my lord. I'll see what I can do."

"Excellent." The marquess nodded. "I'll pay outrageously, if need be."

"I shall obtain the best bargain." Reynolds produced an inch-long smile. "May I bring you a drink, too, sir?"

Only then did Darian notice Daniel and Fanny sitting on the porch, both of them eyeing him with something akin to astonishment. They surely had overheard and must think him a total numskull. Explanations would be in order.

"I was woolgathering," he repeated inanely. "I didn't see you."

"Do join us," Fanny invited, her face alive with interest.

"Thank you." Darian glanced at the butler. "Brandy would be fine, Reynolds."

Daniel made no pretense toward subtlety. "Why do you want live trout, big brother?"

He strode across the porch, trying and failing to think of an innocent rationalization.

"Well?" his brother prodded as he sat down. "It's a strange request, for certain!"

"When I go fishing, I want to be sure I catch something," he answered, nearly wincing at his ridiculous excuse.

They gaped at him.

Darian gave up and decided to tell the truth. "You must not tell a single soul."

"We promise," Fanny swiftly avowed, eyes alight with curiosity.

He took a deep breath. "I've been seeing Venetia Woodbridge almost every afternoon since our disastrous visit to her house. We meet secretly at the stream."

Their mouths actually fell open.

"As her latest ruse for escaping her parents, she is pretending to go fishing. Today I was lucky and caught a trout, but I wish to leave nothing to chance. Now that her parents' health has improved, it is becoming more difficult for her to sneak away." He shrugged. "There you have it."

"My goodness," Fanny breathed. "I realized that you were attracted to her, but I had no idea . . ."

"Dammit!" Daniel burst out. "Fanny and I wanted you to have the happiness our marriage has brought us. Assuming your intentions are honorable, there is no future in this!"

"Oh, yes, there is." Unable to remain seated, Darian wrenched up and began to pace. "I am going to marry her."

"It's impossible, brother!"

They went silent as Reynolds brought the drinks, cheese, and small crustless sandwiches.

When Reynolds left, Fanny lifted her glass. "I would like to propose a toast to Darian's marriage, for I do *not* believe that it is impossible."

"Are you a magician, wife?" Daniel asked, but he joined them in clinking glasses and sipping the spirits.

"Gretna Green," she said flatly.

"That's not honorable," her husband pronounced.

"If it's the only way?" she countered. "Think, Daniel! If that had been the only option for us, wouldn't we have flung convention to the winds and gone there?"

He grinned fondly at her. "Certainly, my darling, but

Darian's a marquess. Marquesses just don't get married at Gretna Green!"

"This one will . . . if he must," Darian insisted. "But I will first pursue the honorable way, of course."

His brother gaped in awe. "You'll try to speak with Woodbridge?"

"What choice do I have?"

"Gad." Daniel grimaced. "He'll murder you. You'd best go armed to defend yourself. I am truly serious, Darian. Maybe I should go with you."

"Absurd," he negated. "Neither does anyone need to hold my hand."

"What does Miss Woodbridge think of all this?" Fanny queried.

He sighed. "We haven't discussed the particulars."

Throughout the entire discussion, no one had thought of Venetia's outlook. She had been greatly distressed when he'd left her. She'd worried about her parents' finding out about their clandestine meetings and preventing her from seeing him. Her mind hadn't taken the liaison further. Still, he'd vowed his love. Surely she'd realized that their marriage would be the next step. She hadn't told him she loved him, but he was certain she did. He knew it from the way she'd returned his kiss. She didn't want the kind of life for which she was destined by that horrible Wood-bridge tradition. She had told him that she truly wanted a husband, home, and family. She couldn't turn him down!

He tried to see the situation through her eyes. Even if her father capitulated and gave his permission for them to wed, he would be angry and resentful. If they were forced to flee to Gretna Green, her parents would probably never speak to her again. Either way, the family relation-ship would likely be bleak. If it became necessary, did she love him and trust him enough to sever all ties with the past?

He would make it up to her. He would love her with

all his heart, shower her with everything his great wealth could buy, give her children. His family would adore her.

"I hope I can depend upon your support," he told Daniel and Fanny. "At best, it will be difficult for Venetia."

"We'll do anything," Daniel said readily.

"If you must go to Gretna Green, we would be happy to accompany you," Fanny volunteered. "Our presence might lend a bit of propriety to the event."

"She might like that," he mused. "But you must live next door to the Woodbridges. I wouldn't want to make things more difficult than they already would be."

"When you wed, she will be a Terrell. She'll be ours. To hell with the Woodbridges," his brother sided.

Darian grinned crookedly. "You two are wonderful. Do you know that?"

"I know Daniel is," Fanny laughed.

"As is Fanny," her husband said devotedly. "And I think you and your Venetia will have what we do, big brother. It might be somewhat more formidable to commence, but I promise you, it will be worth the effort."

Venetia scarcely slept that night. Her thoughts were too tormenting. Over and over, she reviewed her situation, which now, of course, had become Darian's circumstance as well. That made her feel even worse. She should never have encouraged him. If she had only been compliant to her parents' wishes and had not initiated that fateful, secret rendezvous by the stream, he would not have fallen in love with her. It was all her fault that he would be hurt.

Staring at the ceiling as the morning light filled her chamber, she despondently reflected upon her motives for meeting with him. Oh, it was true that she had treasured him even then. She'd been flattered by his attention, too. Why, of all the girls in the district, the noble Lord Enville preferred being with her! Also, she'd had a curiosity about being friends with a gentleman. With her brothers so much older, her father had been the only man whom she really knew. The marquess was totally fascinating, just because of his gender. Finally, she must admit that it was satisfying to defy her parents, at least in the initial encounter.

But all those reasons soon became obsolete as she grew to know Darian. She reveled in his company and in their conversations. They had countless ideas in common, and they shared so many likes and dislikes. Her feelings had deepened into love, the kind that lasted and that craved fulfillment. In any other circumstance, their mutual devotion would have been a cause for joy, but in this, it only meant heartbreak.

For the millionth time, she wondered why the Woodbridge family had to have such a dreadful tradition, or why it must be kept extant. And why must she bear the formidable responsibility of it? It was unnatural, and it wasn't fair, especially when there were so many other options. It wasn't as if her parents were poor. They could afford a staff to care for them. If they were very ill, she could come to them. Moreover, the duty should fall on the eldest son, who would inherit the estate. After all, what would she do with her life when her parents no longer needed her?

With a sigh, Venetia rose, dressed, and descended the stairs for breakfast. Entering the dining room, she was surprised to find her parents already present. She greeted them and sat down, smiling her thanks to the footman who brought her tea.

"Will you be fishing again today, Venetia?" her father asked bluntly. "That trout was excellent. I'd like to have more."

"I shall endeavor to supply them," she agreed, actually dreading her meeting with Darian. He would want to discuss their feelings for each other. What would she say?

"You might do better to fish in the morning," he suggested.

Her pulse raced. She might be daunted by the imminent encounter, but she *must* see him. Good heavens, would she be forced to risk another note?

"Oh," her mother said, crestfallen. "I had hoped that Venetia might assist me in cutting flowers for arrangements after breakfast."

"Very well, my dear." He shrugged magnanimously. "I suppose she can fish afterwards, although the trout might not be biting as readily."

"I really think I'll do better," Venetia ventured, "now that I have refreshed my memory on how it's done."

"There is still an element of luck," Mr. Woodbridge pronounced, "but I shall look forward to delicious results."

Following breakfast, she accompanied her mother to the cutting garden, but Mrs. Woodbridge did not commence immediately. Sitting down on a stone bench, she drew her daughter down beside her. Something about her expression put Venetia on her guard.

"My dear, you look so pale this morning. Is everything all right?"

"I didn't sleep well, that's all."

Mrs. Woodbridge frowned. "You look as though something were bothering you."

She decided to chance a comment or two. "I was thinking about my future."

"My goodness, you need have no fears about that! Your brother will always provide a home for you."

"What if . . ." Venetia said hesitantly. "What if I wanted a home of my own?"

Her mother eyed her warily. "It isn't necessary."

"But if I *wanted* it?"

A fleeting glance of sadness crossed her parent's face.

She shifted uncomfortably. "I doubt if you honestly would."

Venetia took a deep breath. "What if I wanted a husband?"

"It . . . it is ridiculous to discuss this." Mrs. Woodbridge rose. "Let us be about our task, and cease engaging in passing fancies."

"But—"

"*Venetia!*" she shrilled. "We have much to do."

"Yes, ma'am," she sighed, wondering why she had even broached the subject.

Stalling for time, Venetia managed to drag out the flower cutting and arranging until luncheon. Mr. Woodbridge was not pleased, but he did not scold her. He did, however, prod her to action, rushing her through her meal with comments about fishes' feeding cycles. As a result, she arrived at the stream some minutes before Darian. Sitting on the bank, she almost wished that he would not come. This tête-à-tête would be horrid. It must be their last. After what had happened, each time they met would make parting even more difficult.

"Hello, darling!" He entered the Terrell clearing, dropped a cloth bag and their picnic hamper, splashed across the stream on his horse, and reached down for her. "This must be a first."

Her mind on endings, she nearly choked. "What do you mean?"

"You are here before me. Your father must be anxious for another trout."

"He is." She tried to smile cheerfully.

"Good, for I have two large trout for him in that parcel. I left nothing to chance." He tilted her chin and softly kissed her. "I have missed you. More than ever, it seems."

"Oh, Darian." She bent her head.

"We must talk."

"I know," she whispered.

Darian slipped from the horse and lifted her down, holding her close. "I love you, my darling."

"I love you, too, but—"

"I want to marry you. I want you to be my wife," he said quietly. "Do say you will."

Her heart wrenched. "How?" she wailed. "How can I do that?"

"We will find a way." He continued to embrace her, gently caressing her back.

"It is impossible!" She pulled away and dashed blindly across the clearing, suddenly finding herself at the edge of the woods. She stared bewilderedly at a large oak, not even recalling her sudden flight.

"Venetia." Darian came up behind her and took her hand. "Let us have a glass of sherry."

She nodded, but removed her hand from his. His very touch made her feel as if her chest would burst. She walked woodenly to the table and chairs and sank down, wearily brushing her wrist across her forehead.

"Darian, you know there is no way," she painfully began. "You know the tradition. I wish we had never met. No, I could not wish that! Every moment I have spent with you will be my most precious memory. I will live on those thoughts all my life!"

He knelt before her and clasped her hands. "Wouldn't you rather live with me?"

"I would give the world for it, but it is a mad dream." Tears flowed down her cheeks. "My love, you will always possess my heart, but my hand in marriage has never been mine to give."

"I will ask your father. I'll beg him to listen to reason!"

"You know what his reaction will be! It will be a terrible thing. And when he learns that we've been seeing each other . . ." She moaned. "He'll lock me in my room and have me watched."

"No, he won't," he vowed. "If he refuses me, we will fly immediately to Gretna Green."

Venetia gaped at him, shock causing her tears to ease their flood.

Proffering a handkerchief, Darian rose and moved to pour them a glass of sherry. "Maybe he will listen to me. I am not so bad a catch."

She had to smile. Wiping her eyes, she sipped her drink. "I am told that you are a *prize* catch."

He grinned. "Hopefully he will agree, but if he refuses, will you fly with me to Gretna Green?"

She lowered her gaze. Elopement carried with it such a sordid stigma. She had no experience with the *ton*, but if the opinion of that august clique was as severe as the neighborhood's would be, it would be just awful. For herself, she didn't care, but for Darian and for their future children, it would be social suicide. He was a high-ranking peer. He shouldn't be faced with such a scandal.

"Fanny and Daniel offered to go with us, for propriety's sake," he urged.

"It wouldn't be right." Venetia bit her lip. "Your reputation would be in a shambles. So would theirs."

"Let me worry about that."

She shook her head. "It wouldn't be honorable."

"My love, honor has gone begging throughout this whole affair." He finished his glass and poured another. "Some things are worth more than honor, especially when it casts people in such absurd circumstances."

He was right, but the price was so very high. Oh, how she wished she could toss convention to the winds and agree! But she couldn't. She had a commitment, and even if she strongly disagreed with her parents about it, she couldn't cause them pain. She made up her mind.

"Speak with my father. Perhaps when he sees how serious we are, he will capitulate."

They gazed at each other, both knowing that the chance was so slim that it was almost nonexistent.

The rest of the afternoon seemed to drag by. There was really nothing more to say. And the dark cloud hanging over them prevented them from merely enjoying each other's company.

Darian insisted upon delivering her to the edge of the woods. Before he set her down, he held her close. "My darling, I shall always love you."

"I shall always love *you*," she choked out, "and I want you to be happy."

"Not without you."

"You will find someone else," she tried to say lightly.

He laughed shortly. "Do you really believe that?"

"You must have children!"

"I might just leave that responsibility to Daniel."

"No," she begged. "You would be such a good father. You could take your sons fishing—"

"Don't, Venetia." He clasped her even more tightly.

She turned toward him and initiated a kiss, tears streaming down her cheeks and her chest feeling as if it would burst. "We can't go on like this."

Regretfully, he let her go. "In the morning, I will see your father."

"Yes." She took one more long, possibly final look at his beloved face and fled.

Seated with her parents in the morning room, the ladies sewing and Mr. Woodbridge reading a London paper, Venetia stabbed her thumb with her needle when she heard voices and footsteps in the hall. Darian had arrived, and soon her fate would be known. But truly, didn't she already know what her future would be?

Branson duly appeared. "Sir, the Marquess of Enville wishes to speak with you."

Venetia's father frowned severely. "I have nothing to say to the man. Send him away."

Venetia avoided meeting his eyes, studying the drop of blood on the fabric. "Father, it would be proper to greet him."

"I am weary of your attempt to be a social arbiter where those people are concerned," he snapped. "Cease the prattle! That man has nothing to do with us."

"It may concern his garden," Mrs. Woodbridge ventured. "After all, I did consent to advise."

"Then you chat with him!" he told her.

She smiled kindly. "He doubtlessly wishes to ask your permission to talk to me."

Venetia held her breath.

"Oh, very well!" He folded the paper and tossed it aside. "You may advise him on his garden, madam, but you, young lady, will stay out of his sight."

She realized then that the small hope was lost. She would probably never see Darian again. Unless . . . unless she agreed to Gretna Green.

Her mother turned to her as her father stomped from the room, and eyed her wounded thumb. "Venetia, what is it?"

She lifted her head, tears blurring her vision.

"You are so ashen you look as if you will faint, and you are never so awkward with a needle."

Venetia wiped her eyes with her index finger. "You will know, sooner or later. Darian isn't going to ask Father about a garden. He's going to request my hand in marriage."

"What?" she shrilled.

She swallowed hard. "We've been meeting in secret, Mother."

Mrs. Woodbridge gasped. "I thought something strange was going on! Down by the stream?"

She nodded miserably.

"And you fell in love," her mother finished. "Is there anything else I should know? Did he . . . ?"

"Everything was perfectly honorable," she assured her.

"Clandestine assignations are never respectable."

"I couldn't help it!" she burst out. "Mother, this . . . this Woodbridge tradition is archaic, and it is against my nature! I don't want to spend my life like a nun. Nor is it necessary! I want a husband to love, and I have found him. And if only Father will consent, I can have a home of my own and children. My heart's desire!"

"Oh, Venetia," Mrs. Woodbridge said sadly.

"He is a marquess!" she cried. "He is wealthy! None of my siblings have gained such stature. Even if my happiness has no bearing, wouldn't the prestige sway Father?"

"I seriously doubt it." She slowly shook her head. "He is a proud, stubborn man. He is a traditionalist."

"He's positively medieval! And he's wrong!" She was almost in tears again. "Mother, didn't you ever wish for the things I do?"

"Of course," she said softly.

"Then help me! If you would intercede . . ."

"It would do no good."

"But will you try?" she pleaded.

"My dear, I think it would only make matters worse. He would think that we were siding against him. It would make him much more furious." She sighed. "Instead, we should decide how we can mitigate his anger against you. If you would beg his forgiveness, he might not—"

"Lock me in my room and feed me on bread and water?" she questioned bitterly. "I don't care about that. Mother, you don't understand. I love Darian very deeply, and it won't end as easily as shedding a cloak. I won't ever forget him. He will always possess my heart."

Both women fell wretchedly silent, staring down at their embroidery.

"I do understand," Mrs. Woodbridge said finally. "You

may find it hard to believe, but I love your father like that. When I was your age, I fell head over heels for him."

"Your parents supported you," Venetia said flatly.

Her mother visibly winced.

"You must think me of little account, to assign me to a life of fetch and carry!"

"Venetia!"

"Well, it's true," she ground out. "I am nothing but a glorified servant. Maybe you don't realize it, but when you are ill, you run me off my feet for totally ridiculous tasks, things that could be done by any ordinary servant! I am happy to help soothe and entertain you both, but I resent the complaining about what I do and the way I do it. And I hate those silly, nonsensical errands! My life is miserable, and it's all because of that damned tradition!"

"Venetia! Such language!"

"I am a bitter old maid, and I don't care about using a curse word now and then! Why should I behave like a lady?" she spat. "It's as ludicrous as a chambermaid trying to act like a countess!"

Her mother grimaced.

"It is pathetic, is it not?" Venetia wrenched to her feet.

"Where are you going?" her mother implored, reaching out. Venetia's heart pounded violently against her ribs. Chewing on her lip, she tried to hold back the sobs. "I . . . I'm going to wait in the hall. To . . ." She took a deep breath. "I will tell Darian good-bye. Forever, I suppose," she choked.

"Oh, my dearest!"

She fled from the room, tears nearly blinding her dash to the entrance hall. She could hear her father's shouting voice through the library door. Darian didn't deserve such a berating. Even a dog shouldn't have to stand for such abuse! Why couldn't her father have merely refused him and sent him on his way?

Mrs. Woodbridge came up behind her and slipped her arm around her waist. "I am so sorry."

Venetia tightly shook her head, groping for her handkerchief.

"I am so sorry for you and Lord Enville, and I am sorry for our frivolous demands. Until you caused me to look back, I didn't realize how oppressive we could be."

"Mother, I can't think of that now." She gritted her teeth and tried to square her shoulders.

Darian left the library and shut the door behind him, walking toward them with the hard strides of a man who has endured too much and still held his temper. He halted before her. Tenderness replaced the harshness in his expression.

"It is as we expected, my darling."

"I . . ." she began, but the need for words was gone.

He caressed her cheek with the back of his fingers, nodded shortly to Mrs. Woodbridge, turned on his heel, and went through the door.

"Go!" her mother suddenly urged, giving her a push.

"What?" Venetia stammered.

"Go with him. Fly to Gretna Green! Will he agree to such a solution?"

"We . . . we discussed it."

"Then go!" She pushed her again. "I will prevent your father from stopping you."

"Mother!" she cried.

"Do not tarry if you wish to go with that gentleman! He is mounting his horse."

"Mother, I love you!" Hugging her quickly, Venetia dashed from the house. "Darian!"

He had just settled himself in the saddle and picked up the reins.

"Let us flee!" she gasped, running down the steps.

A smile wreathed his face. "To Gretna Green?"

"To wherever you wish!"

Before he could reach down, a grinning Woodbridge footman tossed her onto the horse in front of him. "Be happy, miss!"

With Darian's arm secure around her, she looked back. Her mother blew her a kiss and waved. Venetia lifted her hand.

"Thank you, Mother," she murmured. "Oh, Darian, let us go swiftly!"

"Nothing will stop us now, love." He sent his horse into a gallop down the carriage way.

On the porch, Mrs. Woodbridge smiled. "Be happy, my dearest," she whispered, and turned back to the house to think of some way to placate her cantankerous husband.

EPILOGUE

As the carriage drew near the Woodbridge estate, the tension within grew thicker. It had been four years since Venetia had fled from home. Now that they were close by, she wasn't so sure she wished to return this soon. But there were unbound threads dangling from her otherwise joyful life. To be completely happy, she must make the attempt to tie them.

At the first of the month, she had received a communication from her mother, the only letter she'd ever had from the lady, though she had written many to her parents. Mr. Woodbridge had been through a small crisis in health, but he was recovering nicely and expected to return to near normal. Venetia, in accordance with Darian, had decided to make the journey. It was time to bring about amends, especially because of the children.

Venetia smiled fondly at Little Darian, lolling on the seat facing his parents. He'd just turned three and was full of questions about his Woodbridge grandparents. Tiny Elizabeth, riding in the next coach with Nurse, was too young to remember this trip later, but hopefully she would grow up knowing both sides of her family.

With his mother's attention on him, Little Darian bounced on the squabs. "I have to get out."

She sighed. Traveling with a small boy wasn't easy, but

she didn't mind the extra stop. It would give her a bit longer to gather her thoughts.

Darian rapped on the carriage roof to signal the halt and prepared to escort his son into the woods.

"No." Venetia caught his hand. "Let Collins take him."

"I want Papa!" the child complained.

She shook her head. "I must speak with Papa. You like Collins. He will probably even allow you to run about for a few minutes."

He stuck out his lip.

"Do not do that," Venetia warned, "or we won't stop at all. Look! There is a squirrel."

Attention captured, Little Darian gaily went off with the groom, leaving his parents their privacy.

"I'm terrified," Venetia swiftly admitted.

Darian slipped his arm around her waist and squeezed. "Would you prefer to go to Daniel's first?"

"No. I think it is best to go to Woodbridge first, thus proving to my parents that they are the main reason we have come here." She lay her head on his shoulder. "Oh, Darian, I do so want this to work."

"If anything will bring them round, it will be their grandchildren."

"I am hoping for that." She turned up her face to be kissed and was gratified by Darian's willing response. He was the most affectionate of husbands. Even given their perfect nights, she was elated by his everyday gestures of tenderness.

"I hope your father doesn't see us coming and shoot me," Darian mused. "I don't believe our son is quite ready to become the Marquess of Enville."

She quickly glanced up to see if he was serious and saw a grin playing at the corners of his mouth. "If he didn't shoot you when you asked for my hand, I doubt that he'll do so now."

"Well, my love, I didn't want to die then, or now, but you are well worth a serious wound."

She wrapped her arm across him and hugged him. "I do love you so."

"I love you too." His lips claimed hers.

"Mama and Papa are kissing *again!*" cried their son.

The marquess and his marchioness leapt apart to see their first offspring dancing back and forth beside a red-faced Collins.

"Do forgive me, my lord, my lady," the servant managed.

"Of course," Venetia giggled.

Darian stared at the roof of the carriage. "Let us be on our way."

"Indeed, sir." He lifted the little earl into the coach and hurried to the box.

"I don't like girls, except Mama and Cook," Little Darian pronounced as the horses moved into a trot.

"You will when you're older," his father predicted. "Moreover, you shouldn't compare your mother and Cook in the same breath."

"I like Mama!" The little boy inhaled deeply. "I like Cook!"

"You don't understand. Cook is a servant."

"She gives me biscuits!"

Venetia caressed her husband's arm. "Let it be. You won't win."

"But . . ."

Her touch became a clench as they passed through the Woodbridge iron gates.

Darian covered her hand with his. "It will be all right."

"Why are you scared, Mama?" their son asked.

She smiled. "I am not afraid. I am merely anxious because I haven't seen my parents in such a long time."

"Why?"

"That will be enough," his father stated. "Why don't you look at all those squirrels?"

The youngster looked out the window. "There's millions!"

"Father always fed the squirrels," Venetia recalled. "Mother would become quite distressed on the occasions they invaded the gardens. But they usually kept to the woods. See? There are some of the feeders."

Little Darian nodded. "Maybe he'll let me help put feed in them."

"Maybe he will."

The house hove into view. Venetia's stomach tightened. She mentally spoke a brief prayer.

As they drew up in front, the door opened and the butler stepped out. Behind him was her mother. Mrs. Woodbridge squinted at the Enville crest on the door. She hesitated.

Collins vaulted and came round to let down the steps.

"Let me . . . first," Venetia told her family and allowed the footman to help her down.

"Venetia?" Her mother's lips formed the word. "Venetia, my dearest!"

The two women rushed forward to meet each other in an avid embrace.

"Oh, Mother, I've wanted to come home so badly, but I didn't know . . ."

"Well, you are here now, and I am absolutely overjoyed! Let me look at you." Mrs. Woodbridge stepped back. "You are quite grand . . . every inch a marchioness!"

"But, more importantly, Darian's wife and the mother of two marvelous children," she said proudly.

"You surely have brought them?" her mother asked eagerly.

"I would not go anywhere without them." Venetia turned and motioned.

Darian and their son emerged. The little boy dashed toward them. The father followed more slowly.

"Are you Grandma?" the child cried.

"Yes, I am." Mrs. Woodbridge bent to give him a hug. "My, but you are a handsome young man."

"This is Little Darian," Venetia introduced.

"Sometimes they call me Darry," he proclaimed.

"Those are both fine names," said his grandmother.

"They're Papa's!"

"Yes, I know." She straightened to greet her son-in-law. "My lord."

She began a curtsy, but Darian caught her hands and brought her up. "That isn't necessary, especially not when I owe you such a great debt."

Eyes twinkling, Mrs. Woodbridge glanced from her daughter to him. "Then it was not an error?"

"Venetia is the most cherished thing in my life."

"We are the perfect match," Venetia vowed. "We even *think* alike."

"Then all is well, my dear?" she queried.

Venetia studied her toes. "Almost . . ."

"Is that Grandpa?" Darry shrieked suddenly.

She jerked up her head to see her father standing on the steps. Beside her, Darian stiffened. Their son darted forward.

"Grandpa! Can we feed the squirrels?"

For a long moment, the elderly man stared at the scene before him. Then he shifted his eyes to his grandson and patted his head. "I can't walk that far anymore, but if you'll ride with me in my carriage, we'll do it."

Little Darian clasped Mr. Woodbridge's hand and tugged. "We can take our carriage! It's all ready!"

"In a while." He limped down the steps.

Darian moved forward. "Sir, I owe you a deep apology; however . . ." He glanced back at Venetia. "I cannot be honestly sorry. She is my treasure. I hope you will forgive us." He extended his hand.

Mr. Woodbridge gnawed the inside of his lower lip. "She was mine too."

Venetia tensed, nearly praying aloud.

"What's done is done." Her father accepted her husband's handshake. "But it's hard to dispense with traditions."

She walked toward him. "Maybe we can make new ones, Father."

"Maybe so." He embraced her. "You look well, girl. This man must be good for you."

"He is!" she acknowledged happily.

"You have a fine son."

"And a daughter, too!" She turned and beckoned to Nurse, who was descending from the second coach with the child in her arms. "You must meet our Elizabeth."

"My goodness." Mrs. Woodbridge beamed. "Our first grand*daughter*. All the rest are boys."

"Boys are better," Little Darian stated.

"Both are a delight to me," she told him, "but you are still very special. One of each! How clever you are, Venetia."

"Darian deserves some credit." Venetia shrugged eloquently. "Of course, by the first of next year, I shall break the gender tie."

"What?" exclaimed her husband.

She smiled sheepishly. "I didn't want to tell you about the baby, for fear you would forbid me to make this trip."

"Venetia!"

"Oh, no," moaned their son. "Now they're going to kiss. Let's go feed the squirrels, Grandpa!"

"Perhaps I will save the kiss until later," Darian said, "but you, love, are going to rest *now.*"

"I am perfectly all right."

"Obey your husband," Mr. Woodbridge muttered gruffly. "After all, that's what you wanted."

Darian grinned.

"You've got to be more firm with that gel," her father went on. "She's developed a mind of her own. Now come along with me. We three men will feed the squirrels. While Venetia lies down, the ladies can chat."

Venetia couldn't help touching Darian's arm as the group separated. Their exchanged glances spoke volumes. The trip home had succeeded. Nothing could shade their happiness now. All would be well. Amends would be made. Their life together would be complete.

THE
BRAMBLEBERRY
BRIDE

by

Hayley Ann Solomon

ONE

"Miss Anastasia Richmond is receiving morning callers in the cherry salon, Captain. May I take your hat?"

Captain Bertram Ralston was looking particularly dapper in a cheerful riding coat of bright periwinkle blue. His hat—a quixotic creation that just passed for a curly beaver—was of an equally jaunty style. This he handed over with an air of gloom that was sadly at odds with his character.

"Is she?"

"Indeed. Lady Richmond is attendant upon her. They have been expecting you all morning, if I may say so, sir."

Captain Bertram avoided, with difficulty, pulling a rude and thoroughly disgruntled face. Instead, his hands slid into his pockets and his shoulders drooped ever so slightly as he nodded his thanks.

"Shall I escort you up, sir?"

"Gracious heavens . . . Porter, is it? I think I can remember my way about! It has not been so *very* long, after all!"

"Five years, sir. And may I be the first to welcome you back?" The butler's face creased, momentarily, into an infinitesimal smile.

"Thank you." Bertram longed to ask whether Mistress Anastasia had changed much. She'd been such a timid little thing when they had played together all that time ago. A small snip of a girl with mousy hair and a slight lisp. Now he had been informed, on returning from the Peninsula, that his brother considered her an entirely eligible match.

That was the Viscount Waverley all over! Thoroughly autocratic and entirely too overbearing by far. Still, he had the annoying knack of being almost always perfectly right as well as holding the much-coveted distinction of being absolutely top-of-the-trees. A member of the Four Horse Club, he drove to an inch, was an arbiter of all matters of fashion, and, unfortunately, was dearly beloved of his younger brother.

That was why Bertram was standing here now, rather foolishly toying with his cravat and fighting the craven desire to take heel and return immediately to London. As far as he was concerned, matrimony was one of those unpleasant states one contemplated only far into the distant future. It was not the sort of thing that should hover menacingly over one's head like the sword of Damocles. He had not known a moment's peace since his brother had announced this latest whim. And for what? For an heir to Waverley! That was absurd, since his brother was in prime twig and perfectly capable of getting shackled himself.

A shadow crossed the Honourable Bertram's face. Andrew, Viscount Waverley, had been crossed once in love. It was too much to hope he would allow the same to occur twice. No, if the line was to continue, it would, unfortunately, have to be through him. *That* much had been made transparently clear. Bertram sighed. Sometimes he wished he had been born plain Tom Thumb rather than second in line to a venerable peerage. Still, duty called, and the route to the cherry salon was through the gallery, if he remembered aright. With a quickening of his step and a straightening of those expressive shoulders, he waved airily to the butler and started up the great marble stairs.

He did not hesitate on the landing but passed through a gallery of rather garish portraits, hastily introduced by Lady Richmond in an effort to be "civilised." All the fittings were of bright gold and glared out at Bertram as he took step after step on piled carpet in the Egyptian mode. As usual, no expense had been spared in these renovations. Lady Richmond—previously the daughter of a rich city merchant—could well afford them. Unfortunately, her taste, though expensive, could not always be described as pleasing. Bertram thought this an understatement as he finally rounded the corner and found the cherry-salon door. It was open, so he gulped a little, breathed deeply, fiddled with gleaming brass buttons, and reminded himself firmly that he had made Andrew no promises beyond agreeing to "look the chit over."

He stepped forward, then gasped for another breath of air. Not, this time, for fortification of the spirits, but in outright surprise. True, there *was* a lady occupying the room, but she was not seated demurely by a tea tray as he had expected. Neither was she blessed with mousy hair, and as for a small snip of a thing, well! Miss Anastasia Richmond had truly grown, and in the nicest of places. Bertram could tell, for she was dancing with abandon across the length of the room. There was no orchestra, of course, so she was improvising with a merry whistle and the odd interpolation of a hum. Bertram could not tell by the hum whether she still lisped, but he did not care. In that moment he knew that Andrew, as usual, had been strangely, extraordinarily, and unequivocally correct. He *must* marry Miss Anastasia and marry her at once. Just as soon she set down the ridiculous broomstick she was waltzing with. Where had she *acquired* such an object? Surely she hadn't thieved from the scullery maid? But there! If she could dance with a mop, she could do anything.

He was just clearing his throat to make his presence

known when she compounded her undoubtedly error-filled ways by executing a cartwheel. The captain regarded her with no small interest, for the exertion tipped her clean upside down and afforded him a hitherto undreamed-of view of mountains of petticoats and the shapeliest pair of legs he had ever had the bountiful good fortune of observing. These, it might be added, were encased in pantalets. Common in France, but still shockingly fast in England, of course.

"Oh!" The young lady had tipped herself the right way up and noticed, for the first time, that she was not alone.

Bertram watched with amusement for the crimson that must inevitably suffuse her face as she realised her horrible predicament. He waited in vain, for, far from blushing, the lady emitted a gurgle of laughter and patted down her petticoats with all the aplomb of the perfectly at ease.

"I *knew* the pantalets would come in handy! It would have been a shocking thing, would it not, had I heeded Lady Richmond's advice and cast them into the fire?"

Bertram nodded solemn agreement, though his errant mind could not help conjuring up the image she provoked.

"Shocking," he said. "More shocking, in fact, than mentioning your unmentionables to an unknown gentleman."

"For which I will no doubt be sent to bed without dessert for a week if you were so disobliging as to mention it."

Bertram feigned indignation. "I am not, I hope, such a mawworm."

"Good! I suspected as much the moment I saw you. But you are *not,* you know, unknown. I have the advantage of you, sir. You must be the Honourable Captain Bertram Ralston, late of the Sixth Hussars."

"And I fancied I had changed much in five years."

"Your smile gives you away, though you *do* look very grand!"

Bertram was diverted. "I do, don't I? Had the coat fashioned by Weston, and the boots, of course, are by Lobb."

"You are the very pink, my dear sir!" The lady bestowed such a dazzling smile upon him that Bertram, if he'd been entertaining the slightest smidgen of doubt, found that it melted away upon the instant. He was charged with marrying this girl, and marry her he would! For an instant, he wondered whether he ought to formally speak to her parents. In his annoyance, he had forgotten to inquire of such details.

He looked into her bright, merry eyes and decided that such niceties could wait. She was, after all, primed for a proposal. Consequently, he dropped to one knee, quite oblivious of the dust on the appalling strawberry red pile.

"If you agree to wed me, you shall have lashings of plum pudding and I swear I shall insist on the wearing of pantalets at all times."

The lady's mouth twitched. "At *all* times, sir?"

Bertram grinned. "There might be exceptions!"

"Sir, that is the most *splendid* proposal. Not at all stuffy, like one expects. If ever I merited one, I should hope it is framed in just such a way."

Bertram blinked. "What the devil do you mean? This is not a dress rehearsal, my dear. I am perfectly sincere."

The lady cast him a wistful glance, strangely out of keeping with the conversation so far.

"I expect I should have told you sooner. I believe you mistake the matter, Captain. It is not I, but *Anastasia* you have come to offer for."

Bertram looked as though he had been struck.

"And *you* are not Anastasia?"

"No, I am merely her paid companion. Miss Richmond awaits you in the cherry salon. In high fidgets, I can assure you! Her mama, I am sorry to say, is in fine fettle."

Bertram cast his eyes heavenward.

"Exactly so! It is all perfectly ghastly. If I did not utterly *adore* Anastasia, I would commend you to run a mile."

Captain Ralston made a disgraceful face. Lady Richmond's vulgarity was one of the prime reasons he had damned Andrew to perdition for thinking of such a match. He stubbornly persisted. "But *this* is the cherry salon."

The lady's eyes sparkled mischievously. "No, sir! This room *is pink,* a very different thing, I assure you. Lady Richmond has been at great pains to impress the difference upon us. She will be mortified that you don't immediately make the distinction."

"A pox on Lady Richmond! And my offer stands."

"Don't be ridiculous, sir! You have not the slightest notion of my *name,* never mind my eligibility!"

"You are not married, are you?"

"No, but I am confoundedly poor."

"Well, I am confoundedly rich. Tell me your name."

"It is Vivienne. Miss Vivienne Townsend."

"Well, Miss Vivienne Townsend, I ask you again—*will* you marry me?"

"I cannot, not on so short an acquaintance!"

"Yet I collect Miss Richmond told you of my smile?"

" 'Roguish,' if I recall her words correctly."

Bertram grinned. "May I at least pay you court?"

"I think not, Captain. Lady Richmond would undoubtedly turn me off without a character. Here, let me help you to your feet. I would hate those excellent-fitting doeskins to become creased at the knees." She extended her hand, and Bertram took it as naturally as if he had been doing so for years. When he sought to retain it, however, she frowned at him severely. "Let go, Captain! I may be an intolerable hoyden, but I will do nothing to hurt Anastasia. Despite the disparity of our natures, I think the world of her."

"Would *she* countenance my suit?"

'She is certainly *prepared* for it. But you will have to ask her that question yourself."

"I dare not, lest she say yes!"

"Dare, lest she say no!"

"You give me hope."

"I give you nothing, Captain. If you are to wed, I shall wish you joy from the bottom of my heart and endeavour to be pretty behaved at the nuptials."

"A first for you, I will warrant!"

Miss Townsend peeked at him cheekily. "Very likely, though I *do* try. It is just that I somehow always contrive to land up in a fix."

"Like?"

"Like the time I wished to save Lord Richmond the expense of a hack. I drove his Tilbury into town and somehow landed up on the wrong side of the park. The next thing, I was dashing up St. James's Square, clear in front of Boodles."

Even the suave Bertram had to gasp at this example of social folly. "I am surprised you are still received!"

"Fortunately, I was wearing an enormous chip straw hat with three ostrich feathers and a *very* fetching veil. Lady Richmond lives in daily dread the world shall discover it was me! Though why they should care, I cannot conceive. The odds are about that it was Princess Caroline, so I believe I am safe for the moment. I got a thundering scold, I can assure you! Which is why I am kicking my heels in the pink room whilst you, my dear sir, ought to be proposing to Anastasia."

"I don't *want* to propose to Anastasia!"

"You will, when you meet her. She is truly the dearest, cleverest, most capable young lady of my acquaintance."

"Does she tumble into scrapes?"

"Almost never."

"Does she dance with broomsticks?"

"Definitely never."

"Does she hum like a spinning top and whistle through her teeth?"

"No, but she sings like a nightingale, and her brush strokes are exquisite."

"Then we shall never get along. I deplore birdsong and despise samplers."

Miss Townsend's lips quirked delightfully, but her tones were severe. "You are simply being contrary. Go, before we are discovered together. I should undoubtedly be dismissed for keeping you so long from your purpose."

"*And* you are unchaperoned!"

"That's to no purpose! I am only, after all, a paid companion."

"Ah, but a very beautiful one."

Vivienne giggled. "If that doesn't beat all the odds! You must be blind, Captain, not to note my lamentable freckles."

"I have committed each one to memory. And they are not so much lamentable as . . . as . . . kissable!"

It was on this triumphant note that the door was flung wide upon its hinges and Lady Richmond made her entrance.

"Well!" She glared at Miss Townsend.

The captain bestowed his most raffishly charming smile upon her plump person.

"Lady Richmond, how very kind of you to rescue me from my folly. I am afraid five years has addled my wits and rendered me quite incapable of finding the cherry salon. I am not altogether sorry, though, for my error has led me to discover this simply exquisite *pink* salon. Your taste in such matters is quite famous about town." This last was true, although "infamous" would probably have been a more accurate choice of words. Still, he offered her his hand and one of the blandest smiles Vivienne had ever had the pleasure of witnessing. "Miss Townsend has been urging me this age to cross the hall to the cherry salon, but I find it difficult to tear myself away. The beauty in here is exquisite." The said Miss Townsend very nearly disgraced herself by snorting into her handkerchief at this double entendre, but fortunately averted such a crime by looking piercingly out the window.

Lady Richmond was like clay in his hand. She lost a good deal of her bluster and simpered quite coyly, a sickly noise that made Bertram blanch, all the more determined not to have her for a mother-in-law.

"You have such refined tastes, Captain. No doubt your time abroad has furnished you with a little town polish. So civilised." Then, as an afterthought, "I take it you have made the acquaintance of Miss Townsend? She is the paid companion, you must know."

"Is she *really?*" Bertram extracted the monocle he had sworn he would never find a use for from his waistcoat pocket. He eyed Vivienne quizzingly for a moment, then languidly extended his hand in the grand style.

"How do you do, Miss Townsend? Awfully glad to make your acquaintance."

"Captain." She curtsied, but the laughter lines that crinkled her eyes were evident. Lady Richmond eyed her suspiciously before commending her dryly to the resumption of her duties, for Anastasia had been "waiting this age for her company." Bertram was surprised by how tightly his fists clenched at this cavalier treatment. Miss Townsend, however, offered him a deplorable wink which quite restored his spirits. Fortunately, Lady Richmond was too occupied in dragging him through the sumptuous gallery to notice any untoward goings-on, the likes of which she must surely have disapproved.

"My daughter is in a fever of anticipation to renew her acquaintance with you, Captain. She prattles on forever about how you carried her home when she grazed her knee falling off her pony. But I doubt you would remember such little attentions, so gallant as you are!"

"Oh, but I do! Unfortunately, that particular kindness cannot be attributed to me. It was my brother, if I recall, who carried her home. I, if I remember, was sent home in disgrace for letting go of the training reins."

"Tush! It was you, for the viscount was already buying his colours." Lady Richmond wagged her finger playfully in his face. "You cannot gammon *me,* Captain!"

Bertram left it be. He had no wish to become embroiled in a pointless tousle about who did what so many years ago. And since when did Anastasia prattle? She must have changed vastly if she did now, for she had always been such a shy, retiring thing. He wondered, fleetingly, whether she had changed much. And then the moment was upon him.

A footman guarding the door of the cherry salon bowed and swung the door upon its hinges.

Miss Anastasia Richmond took a step forward hesitantly. Her smile was like a moonbeam, shy but bright nonetheless.

"Bertram! Captain Ralston I should say."

"I hope you need never be so formal with me, Anastasia, or shall I say Miss Richmond?"

"Oh, no call for such niceties! After all, you are here to declare yourself, are you not?" Lady Richmond bustled into the room and practically pushed poor Bertram into a chair. Anastasia coloured in embarrassment, and Vivienne shot him a triumphant I-told-you-so look.

"Well, madam, not exactly! Miss Richmond has first to discover whether I have any admirable qualities, and that, I can assure you, will not be an easy task."

He smiled as he stood up, took her hand, and placed it to his lips. She deserved that consideration, at least.

"Mama—"

"Oh, don't be so missish, Anastasia! We all know that Bertram has not come upon us merely to sample my tea, though it is an excellent flavour if I say so myself. No"—

Lady Richmond settled her ample body comfortably into a crimson wing chair—"The Viscount Waverley and I have settled things nicely between us. Is that not so, Bertram, dear?"

TWO

A pin could have dropped on the elegant marble floor and been heard. The silence was prodigious and seemed longer than an aeon, though of course it was no more than a few hammering heartbeats.

"Yes . . . er . . . *no!*" All eyes focused on him in surprise, though Vivienne's held more than a faint sparkle of something else, something quite indefinable. "That is—no aspersions on *you,* Miss Richmond, but I am held to prefer to do my own choosing in all matters of consequence."

Here, the glance at Miss Townsend was just long enough to be poignant. Despite her hoydenish ways, she felt the colour rising to her pretty cheeks, and a frown of anxiety creased her smooth brow as she shot a glance at Anastasia.

Lady Richmond, who was engaged in pouring, spilled some tea over some of her best morning gloves.

"Gracious, Captain! You must forgive me. I am not quite up to such humour this time of the morning." She removed her gloves, tut-tutting in annoyance, though in truth her entire body heaved with a fury that had little to do with the spoiled white satin. She rang the bell, and Porter himself appeared upon the instant.

"More tea, Porter! And do bring in the harp. I am certain the captain will wish to hear Anastasia play. You may take these away." She dropped the gloves onto the tray.

"Mama, I am perfectly certain Captain Ralston will wish no such thing. He has always found sitting still detestable! Besides, it is a sunny day—perhaps Vivienne and I should rather take a walk about the gardens." Was there a faint smile playing around her lips as she glanced sympathetically at Bertram? The captain could have sworn so. At all events, he leapt at this unexpected reprieve with all the vigour of his four and twenty years.

"Indeed, yes What a perfectly *splendid* idea! I should like, above all things, to have the company of two such bewitching ladies. Is there still that waterfall by the south gate?"

"What an excellent memory, sir! We shall fetch our bonnets at once."

The ladies rose from their seats upon the instant.

"Shall you accompany us, Lady Richmond? I do hope so, though I fear your delicate, creamy complexion is too fine a calibre to be exposed to the callous sun. I am right, am I not?"

Lady Richmond forgot her vexation in an instant. The captain was *so* observant. It was perfectly true that the sun could be quite fatal to someone with sensibilities as acute as hers. And the captain spoke the truth. Her creamy complexion *was* very fine. She regarded him speculatively. A turn with Anastasia would be the very thing to remind him of her daughter's charms. She did look becoming in the lawn green dress, though she could wish her daughter had chosen something a little lower cut in the bosom. Sometimes Anastasia was most provoking! She always appeared so meek and obliging, but when it came to matters of importance . . . She sighed, then looked suspiciously at Miss Townsend, who was coughing in a manner not entirely to her liking.

"You are so astute, Captain. I never walk about the gardens without the benefit of at least a parasol and a bonnet. Even then, I am careful never to stay out above five minutes at a time. Beauty is a sore trial, I am afraid."

The coughing became more irritating than ever. She was about to admonish the companion sternly, when the captain retrieved a handkerchief from his stylish morning coat and offered it to Miss Townsend with a flourish. After that, the unladylike noises subsided somewhat, though Lady Richmond was treated to the undignified spectacle of a nose almost entirely encased in periwinkle blue.

"Well, then, my dears. I shall bid you a very good morning. Captain, we shall speak again." With a meaningful nod that made Bertram squirm, she left the room.

Lord Andrew Ralston, the noble Viscount Waverley, looked up from his ledgers, where he was adjusting some entries of an overzealous agent. It was not necessary, he thought, to extract quite so much rent from the Havershams. They had been tenants on his land for as long as he could remember, and good ones at that. He would see to it that their roof was fixed, for he'd detected several flaws in the thatching only yesterday.

The Crowleys were petitioning him for bales of hay, and the crofters on the north side seemed on the verge of dissension. He would have to deal with that sternly, for with the corn price less than eighty shillings a quarter, there was unlikely to be any further importation of foreign corn. *That* should set their minds at rest. If it did not . . . well, if it did not, he would have to, he supposed, deal with it.

"Lockstone?"

"My lord?"

"What time is it?"

"It is nearly noon, sir."

The viscount nodded and closed the ledger firmly, taking care to first mark his place with a handsome bookmark emblazoned with the royal crest. It had been a gift from the prince regent, and though he despised such unnecessary displays of opulence, the object served its purpose.

"I shall take a break. I have a nasty fit of the dismals and cannot bring myself to think straight."

"Very good, my lord." Lockstone was always very formal with his employer, despite all the viscount's efforts to set him at ease. Despite this strange circumstance, he was excessively fond of Lord Ralston and would not have exchanged employers for the world. He regarded him now, swiftly changing from a silk lawn shirt to more serviceable linen in consideration of the mud on the estate.

The viscount grinned, and the smile changed the darkly classical to the breathtakingly handsome.

"Don't look so alarmed, Lockstone. I assure you I shall not change my breeches, though the roads probably warrant something a little more serviceable than cream."

So saying, he tossed the silk on the table, and Lockstone was treated to the brief sight of bronzed ribs before the linen obscured the sight entirely.

"Montrose shall disapprove."

"Oh, undoubtedly! But if I placed myself in his hands, the noon shall swiftly turn to nightfall before he is finished with me. Valets are for balls, not for rides about the estate."

"I am certain Montrose shall be affronted at such a summary description of his talents."

"Ah, but you shall not offend his feelings by repeating this conversation! You are a loyal soul, Lockstone." At times, the viscount knew how to cut a wheedle just as well as his baby brother Bertie. "I am off over the paddocks, and if that does not shake the windmills from my head, nothing will!"

So saying, he nodded a pleasant good day to the secretary and strode from the room. He wished he did not still get so sunk in bleak misery. True, the spells were now much more infrequent, but they nevertheless persisted in haunting him like the plague. Damn Miss Araminda Fallows and her fancy airs! He had been a mere jackstraw to be taken in by her, but taken in he *had* been. And where had that led him?

To being jilted on his wedding day by a polite little note, stained only with one obligatory tear, informing him that Lord Tarradale had finally come up to scratch. The viscount would, she was certain, understand that a marquis—even one double her age—must always take precedence. And so she had become Lady Araminda Tarradale, Marchioness of Crewe, on the very day she was to have been his bride.

The viscount had endured several curious glances, whispered commiserations, and a great deal of pity. All of these had sat on his shoulders like raw humiliation. It was a couple of years at least before he could come to think of the event as a lucky escape. By then, of course, the damage was done. He developed a slightly cynical view of the nature of the female sex and forswore all respectable ones diligently. The less respectable he engaged in casual dalliances of fleeting satisfaction, and for the most part, put the whole of them from his mind completely.

He *did* attend the odd ball, but no lady was ever particularly favoured. He had a tendency to sympathetically—but unselectively—scribble his name in the cards of the season's wallflowers. The belles of the ball never had so much as a sight of him. He was truly the despair of society's hostesses, for it was not often that a peer of the realm combined the attributes of youth, inordinate good looks—if slightly stern—and a handsome fortune into the bargain. These blessings seemed all but wasted, for it was common knowledge that he was relying upon Bertram, Captain Ralston, to stand his heir and continue the line. Not that there was anything *wrong* with Bertram, but he was young yet and did not have the calm self-assurance that sat like a mantle upon his brother's very able shoulders.

Now those able shoulders were wrestling with a barn door. They did not have much of a struggle, for as soon as the head groom caught sight of him, the door was unbolted with alacrity and a good deal of work came to a halt as each man had to stop his shining of leather, his mixing of hay, his sweeping of floors, and his brushing of stallions to murmur "good day," doff his cap and bow as was His Lordship's due. Andrew smiled and waved them all back to work. It was not *their* fault he was maundering in the doldrums. Perhaps he would take Flick, the most lively of his stable. He thought a rollicking good ride might rid himself of Araminda's ghost. Poor Bertram! Andrew hoped he had not been too severe in choosing him a bride. Still, an arranged marriage with no sentimental expectation on either side might just spare his brother the pain *he* had had to endure. He hoped so, and wondered, for a minute, how his suit was progressing.

He would have been surprised to learn that it was progressing very well indeed, but entirely with the wrong lady. Almost as soon as they were out of Lady Richmond's jaundiced view, Vivienne ran on ahead, laughingly pointing to the south boundary, lifting her skirts quite incorrigibly, and fleeing.

"She really is a very dear soul, you know." Anastasia smiled softly as Bertram looked at her, undecided which young lady to abandon, since both were supposedly under his escort. With sudden understanding, she decided for him.

"Perhaps you had better catch her up. With Vivienne's luck, she will slip into the fountain and then we *shall* be in the suds, for explaining that away will tax all of our wits!"

"Can't have that, Miss Richmond! You will follow?"

"But of course, sir! Only do hurry! The ground is still frightfully wet and she is wearing her favourite gown."

"I shall be as swift as the gods!" With this rather grandiose promise, Bertram was off. He left Anastasia with a friendly but entirely unloverlike, grin and she looked thoughtfully after him as his retreating back faded into the distance, until it disappeared entirely behind a series of poplar trees at the edge of the formal gardens.

Anastasia sighed, for in that moment her mind was quite made up. Bertie was the dearest boy, but that was precisely what he was. A boy. Though she was several years younger than he, she felt the weight of her years. Besides—she grimaced slightly to herself—he had not seemed in the slightest bit ready to offer a proposal.

Anastasia sniffed the air with a sense of delicious relief. Life seemed so much less trying when one was not hovering always on the brink of indecision. She could not think how she had let the matter progress this far in the first place. It was her mama, of course. *And* the pointless expense of another season, for what other way *was* there for a lady to contract an eligible alliance? There was no answer to this age-old question. As a lady, it became her to countenance marriages contracted for convenience and pedigree. Anastasia had been brought up her whole life to believe this to be the proper order of things. Still, when it came to the sticking point. . . .

Her thoughts were interrupted by an ominous-sounding splash. This was followed up by a low-pitched shriek, then several squeals of laughter, then some splendid—though ungentlemanly—oaths, and then laughter again.

Miss Richmond forgot about keeping her hems out of the damp and dashed to the scene. It took several moments to cut past the poplars and discover the source of the incident, so she was distinctly out of breath when she finally arrived. Vivienne in trouble again, no doubt! And just when her mama was so *particularly* keen to keep her out of mischief!

Little scamp, there she was, laughing her head off, dangling her sun-browned legs from their favourite rock. Whenever would she learn that that was no way to appear in company? Especially *gentleman* company!

And where was Bertram, anyway? The next moment, all was revealed. Bertram, in his haste, had skidded through the mud and not stopped at the brink of the fountain, which was situated close to the south boundary waterfall. He was consequently now being showered by a spray of water from a marble angel. This was just as well, for his excellent outfit was no longer periwinkle blue but rather a uniform and decidedly gloomy brown.

"Gracious! Captain Ralston, are you all right? Climb out at once. You shall catch your death of cold!"

"Oh, Stasia, isn't it the funniest thing? I think I shall die laughing!"

"I am certain Captain Ralston does not share your sentiments, Vivienne."

"Oh, but he does! Just see how he is grinning!"

Miss Richmond looked back at Bertram. Her companion was right. He was making no shift to restore his dignity by removing himself from the offending fountain. Rather, he had settled himself quite comfortably in the middle of it and was staring at Miss Townsend with sparkling eyes. These, she noted, were crinkled at the corners and held telltale twinkles that were accompanied by dimples in both cheeks.

"Come on in," he invited.

Miss Townsend giggled, and Anastasia glared at her with as much sternness as she could muster without actually giggling herself "Don't you dare! Mama shall have fits and turn you off without a character! Then *I* shall be

saddled with some mealymouthed companion and think
very poorly of you as a consequence!"

"Oh, very well, Stasia, I shall be good! Besides, it is
rather novel to watch some *other* person in a scrape for
a change. How shall Captain Ralston explain himself, I
wonder?"

"I warrant Captain Ralston shall think of something. If
I recall, he wriggled out of many a tight spot when we
were young."

"Yes, but I did not have Lady Richmond to contend
with!"

Anastasia was silent a moment. Bertram realised what
he had just said.

"Oh, Miss Richmond, I am dreadfully sorry! I did not
think—"

Anastasia stopped him. "No offense taken, Captain. I
am more than aware of my parent's shortcomings."

Miss Townsend looked at Bertram in wonder.

"Do you *also* speak before you think, sir? I am *forever*
in trouble over it."

"Then we are undoubtedly kindred spirits, Miss Townsend, because I am a sad trial, I am sorry to say, to my
poor brother Andrew."

"The viscount? Is he awfully stuffy?"

Bertram looked at her in amusement. "Not stuffy exactly, but certainly more circumspect."

"Oh, like Stasia, I expect you mean." Vivienne looked
at her employer fondly. Anastasia blushed a little, for this
was certainly no drawing-room conversation.

"Vivienne, you are a chatterbox! Help Captain Ralston
from the fountain. I am sure he can do with an extra pair
of hands, and since you are already quite damp, you might
as well be the one to volunteer."

It was on the tip of Bertram's tongue to say that he was
a captain in His Majesty's army. He was perfectly capable
of springing from the fountain unaided. Then he sealed

his lips. At last, he was becoming circumspect! He was rewarded for his reticence by the sight of Vivienne gamely coming toward him with her skirts aloft and her hands outstretched. When they touched his soaked gloves, he startled.

The warmth flowing from her hands was indescribable. He wondered whether she felt as shocked as he did. Evidently, for despite her merry, hoydenish ways, she was blushing prettily and had dropped her eyes to cover her confusion. Bertram was confirmed in the knowledge that it was this lady, above all others, who would share his life. It was wonderful, for a change, to feel protective of something, to want to care and cherish. . . .

Crash! Miss Vivienne Townsend gave a yelp of pain as she landed clean on her rather delightful—had Bertram but known it—derriere. She shifted slightly to avoid the angel, but the damage was done. She was soaked to the skin, and her elegant coiffure—insisted upon by Lady Richmond—was now nothing but a hopeless tangle.

"Ha! Now *you* are in the basket!" Bertram laughed and helped the lady from the fountain.

Anastasia groaned. This would take some explaining. She only hoped her mama would be so occupied in quizzing her on the captain's intentions that she would not have the time to scold poor Vivienne. Actually, it was more likely it was *her* she would bewail, for failing to elicit the required marriage proposal. She made a slight face. So be it. It was clear that the whole notion was absurd.

She glanced at Bertram. He was so occupied in fussing over Vivienne's skirts that he did not notice her scrutiny. Just as well, for Anastasia was perceptive as well as beautiful. She perceived, in that instant, the most pressing reason in the world why she could never accept Bertie's addresses. He was clearly intended—destined, even—for another. Miss Townsend, oblivious to these musings, looked up at Bertram with adoring eyes. It did not seem

to matter a particle that her gown's ribbon was trailing on
the ground and that her bonnet was floating merrily across
the fountain toward the current of the waterfall. Her sparkle spoke volumes. It was mirrored, quite unmistakably,
in the captain's demeanor. He cast his beaver into the
water, and Anastasia watched as it bobbed to meet the
bonnet. An excellent, well-matched pair.

THREE

"Well? How did you go on?"

"Andrew, I shall give Waverley the heir it requires! What is more, I shan't wait a six-month, like you suggest, to tie the knot. I shall procure a special license immediately and do the thing as fast as ever is possible."

"Gracious! I had no idea Miss Richmond would be so vastly to your taste. True, I have always thought her greatly underrated, for she has very vivid, intelligent eyes, and when she loses some of her shyness, I believe I have detected moments of great animation. Slate gray, are they not?"

Bertram was recalled from the reverie into which he had sunk. "Sparkling blue."

"Blue? How strange. I felt certain I would notice a detail like that. Still, if you are happy—"

"Oh, I am!"

"Excellent, then! I hope she may not disappoint you—"

"Not all women are as callous as that damnable Araminda Fallows!"

Bertram could have bitten off his tongue. The icy glaze he had come to abhor swept over his brother's features. The Marchioness of Crewe had a lot to answer for.

"Yes. Well, at all events, I wish you happy." The viscount took up a quill, stubbed it hard onto a perfectly good piece of paper, blotted the ensuing blot with vague vigour, then pushed the whole across his desk in distaste.

"She is amenable to your suit?"

"I believe so, though cannot be certain."

"You did not ask her?" The viscount's lips twitched, though his voice held a hint of the peculiar exasperation mingled with amusement that he reserved only for Bertram.

"Oh, but I did! The thing is, you see, she is damnably poor, and though I have told her that such trifles don't weigh with me—"

"Stop! I have lost you, Bertie! Miss Richmond is *not* 'damnably poor.' She is making May games of you if she represents herself as such."

"I am not a clodpole, Andrew! I am perfectly aware that Miss Anastasia Richmond is an heiress!"

"Well, then?"

"Well, what?"

"Well, then, how comes she to be telling such tarradiddles?"

"Miss Townsend? She is not! Her mother was Lady Addersley and her father was a colonel, but—"

"Stop!" Andrew's tone held a fearsome mixture of alarm and authority. *"Who* is Miss Townsend?"

"But I thought I had explained it! She is the lady I am to wed. And, oh, Andrew, she falls into more scrapes in a minute than I do in a day!" With this happy recommendation, Bertram helped himself to a strawberry. Happily for him, he was quite unaware how close he was to being strangled.

"May I come in?"

"But of course, Stasia! I am your companion, aren't I?"

"Yes, but not twenty-four hours a day, whatever Mama may think to the contrary."

Miss Townsend looked downcast for a moment. "I wish I could please her more, Stasia, but whatever I do, I seem to land in the basket."

"Which is precisely why I love you! My life would be tedious indeed if I did not have such a lively companion to spice it up. Take today . . . we might still be talking elegantly about the rainfall if you had not shot off at that spanking pace."

"I thought you and the captain might like time alone . . ."

"Funny, that. I thought precisely the same of you!" Miss Richmond looked at her friend with sudden seriousness. There was an element of truth in the lighthearted tone that caused a flush to rise prettily to Vivienne's cheeks.

"I am sorry. Was my behavior reprehensible? Did I monopolise him? I am truly sorry, Stasia. I never meant it to be so. It is just. . . ."

"Just that when two kindred souls meet, they become inseparable."

Vivienne's eyes widened at the statement, for in truth she had not allowed herself to think too deeply about the state of her heart. *That* would be too disloyal to Miss Richmond, for Anastasia was practically betrothed to the captain. How wretched that *that*, of all things, should be so!

"Don't look so downcast, Viv. I might quiz you, but I shall definitely not eat you!"

"How can you joke about such a thing, Stasia? I am mortified!"

"Mortified? What codswallop! If you were not mortified to appear before the prince regent in ripped skirts and mud-spattered spencer—"

"That was different! It was at the horse sales!"

"But unchaperoned! I rest my case, so don't interrupt," Miss Richmond admonished.

Vivienne grinned, her irrepressible good humour not permitting her to remain in the doldrums overlong. "Very well; you shall say your piece so long as I can answer in kind."

"It is agreed. Vivienne, you should know that I have no intention of marrying Bertram now or ever."

"But why? He is the most fascinating, delightful, handsome—"

"May I interrupt?"

"I haven't finished!"

"Nor will you, if you continue in this vein! And *that,* by the way, is your answer. I shall not marry him for all of those reasons."

"You cannot be so feather-brained! Who can turn down such a paragon?"

"I, though strictly speaking that is not the case, for I have not yet had the felicity of a proposal."

It was on the tip of Vivienne's tongue to tell her friend that Bertram had made her an offer that very morning. She could not bring herself to do so, for fear of seeing pain and disgust line Anastasia's face. Instead, she let her continue.

"I cannot marry the captain, for whilst *you* are kindred spirits, *we* are not! He is fascinating, delightful, and altogether handsome to *you.* To me, he is just dear, sweet Bertie. I thought I could live with that, but seeing the pair of you together, I realise I cannot. I want for myself what I see reflected in your eyes, Viv. I shan't ever get that if I were to accept Bertie. Even supposing he *makes* the proposal, which I now very much doubt."

"You are certain, then?"

"Absolutely."

"Your mama will have fits."

"Not an uncommon practice for her. I shall win her round."

"Even if *I* marry your Bertram?"

"Vivienne! You sly creature! I'll wager my last farthing you are keeping something from me!"

"And so I am! Anastasia, you are certain?" Vivienne's tone was heartrendingly wistful.

"Of course I am, you muttonhead! Now tell me at *once* what you are harbouring in that breast of yours, or I shall scream!"

"You tempt me. I would *love* to see you doing something unladylike for a change!"

"Vivienne, if you do not start talking at once, you will have your wish."

So the irrepressible Miss Townsend began to talk . . .

The next day started off with a great deal of sunshine and much promise for improving weather. Unfortunately, Lady Richmond looked like a thundercloud at the breakfast table, and by the time Miss Townsend and Miss Anastasia Richmond had finished nibbling on some kippers, some leftover game pie, and a plateful of eggs, they were both heartily sorry not to have elected a cup of cocoa in bed.

Lady Richmond seemed to think it was Anastasia's fault that Bertram had been negligent about proposing marriage the day before. She scolded her for being so prim as to wear high-collared gowns when a little décolletage was "all the rage." She threatened to visit the dressmaker herself to have all the spring clothes altered. She wanted to know every sentence that the captain had uttered, and every circumstance that had occurred during their infamous walk to the stream. She scolded Vivienne for getting wet, and, contrarily, Anastasia for *not* getting soaked, for "damped-down skirts would have been the very thing to capture the eye of a man about town."

Vivienne choked into her coffee cup and glanced hopelessly at Stasia. It would have been fatal to giggle at that point, so she stuffed a large piece of buttered toast into her mouth and chewed hard.

Anastasia nodded peacefully as she heard her mama's tirade. There was nothing new in the nature of it, for Lady Richmond habitually threatened all kinds of dire consequences when her will was crossed. The best thing was to nod quietly, appear apologetic, and make sure that the more unsuitable of her threats and plans were never carried into fruition.

"Shall we pick brambleberries today?" Vivienne was eager to change the subject as she looked longingly out the window.

"Anastasia may, for she had best stay close to the house today in case the captain comes calling." Lady Richmond looked at her daughter doubtfully. "And promise me you'll change into a decent gown! The sarcenet, with your new trimmed chip straw—"

"Very well, Mama." Miss Richmond always gave in gracefully in matters of trivia. That way, her mama was mollified and she retained a measure of peace. Besides, the sarcenet was fetching, and on such a crisp, heavenly day . . .

"Miss Townsend, you shall ride into the village with me. I have many errands to run and should like you to meet Lady Peabody Frampton, a most *particular* friend of mine. I suspect she could use a little help about the place, for she is expecting her nieces to arrive any day. Please behave with decorum! She is related to the Countess Lieven, and I would be mortified if you were once again to edify us with a sample of your disgraceful behaviour."

"Yes, ma'am." Her tone was meek, but she pulled such a nasty face behind Lady Richmond's outmoded wig that Anastasia was hard-pressed not to laugh. When her mother treated Vivienne like a serving girl, Anastasia habitually cringed. Today, however, she did not mind quite as much. Very soon Vivienne would be out of her realm. The thought saddened Anastasia, for she treasured the lively companion's company. Still, she was not so poor a creature as to grudge Miss Townsend her happiness. If Captain Ralston had offered for her, she would be a fool not to accept. The couple was clearly made for each other, though how the pair of them would manage without some more sobering influences, she could not imagine. Still, they were the sort that added sparkle to an otherwise proper world. Society needed that.

So it was that Vivienne was dispatched rather glumly with Lady Richmond whilst Anastasia was free to change swiftly into the sarcenet. It was not long before she was walking steadily down the tree-lined path, and out toward the fields of tall grass and fresh poppies.

The brambleberries, when she reached them, were sweet, juicy, and confoundedly difficult to reach. Anastasia might have decided not to bother, for she had so many tumultuous thoughts in her lovely, bonneted head that she would have quite happily plumped herself down on a plot of clover to think.

Unfortunately, the basket that had been thrust into her hand by Mrs. Timmons, the housekeeper, was empty and she would have some explaining to do if dessert was spoiled by a bout of uncharacteristic idleness. She would incur enough wrath on her head when Lady Richmond discovered the errant Captain Ralston was never to propose. She didn't need brambleberries to compound her sin. Accordingly, she muttered a little under her breath and began to pick.

It took only a few moments for her initial annoyance at having fingers and arms pricked unmercifully by leaves, twigs, and sundry stray brambles to subside. When she relaxed into a soothing rhythm, it was not too long before her basket looked a little more respectable. However, there was little doubt that she would have to shin up the apple tree, for vines of brambleberries crept up it and she wanted to reap some greater rewards.

Thankful that no one was about to witness her unladylike actions, she removed her half boots, lifted her petticoats, and slowly clambered her way up to the third
branch. There it was an easy matter to fling brambleberries aplenty into the basket.

"Ouch!"

Anastasia nearly fell out of the tree. She peered through
the leaves to see who had made this unpromising remark.

"Bertram—I mean Captain Ralston! Where did *you* pop
up from?"

"I've been watching you this age, from the hollyhock
hedge."

"And why, pray?" Anastasia endeavoured to sound
grim, but in truth she liked Bertram and found it hard to
scold despite his unsuitable behaviour. Besides, since his
nose was splattered with brambleberry juice it seemed
unsporting to punish him further.

"I wanted to talk with you. The butler said you would
be out here."

"Could you not have talked *before* I exposed my un-
dergarments and removed my footwear?"

Bertram grinned. "Yes, but that would hardly have been
as edifying. No, don't throw another brambleberry. They
are confoundedly juicy!"

"Then cease provoking me, sir! And don't tell me ban-
bury stories! I am perfectly certain that you have no interest whatsoever in the sight of my ankles. It is Miss
Townsend's, I believe, that are more likely to hold your
scrutiny!"

The Honourable Captain Ralston regarded her closely.
"Come down from there. I want to talk to you about that.
I fear I owe you the most frightful apology, not to mention
explanation."

Anastasia waved her hand airily. "No need, sir! You
have my blessings. Vivienne is the most delightful creature, and I have to concede you are perfectly well suited."

"But am I not a cad? There is practically a betrothal between us!"

"Nonsense! You have neither proposed nor I accepted. I believe that is the form required, sir, in such matters. You merely rode to Brampton to review my suitability. That was made quite plain from the outset."

"But I cannot simply say you are unsuitable! Think how it will reflect upon your character!"

"My character can stand the odds." Her lips curved upward slightly. "Now do be a good boy and turn around, sir, that I might climb down and talk to you reasonably. It is passing hard to discuss matrimony—or the lack of it—up a tree."

"Wait! I will join you!"

"No, you will not, you horrible boy! It is *Vivienne* who is as game as a pebble, not I. *I* am the very pink of respectability. Now close your eyes. I warrant you have seen enough petticoats in a lifetime not to have to gaze upon mine."

"Oh, very well." Bertram obediently shut his eyes as Anastasia carefully made her way down the thorny brambleberry vines.

"Oh!"

"What?"

"I am stuck, and the wretched twigs are scratching me. Just wait a moment." Anastasia struggled, but the more she did, the more entangled her apple-blossom sarcenet became with the branches.

Captain Ralston opened his eyes and grinned. "In a nasty tangle, Anastasia?"

"Since when did I give you leave to call me by my first name? We are not children any longer!"

"My, my, my! You sound as cross as crabs. Don't quibble, Stasia. It was only a moment ago that you called me a 'horrible boy' like old times. Come, stop being so missish and let me help you."

"No."

"Very well, then, I shall just seat myself comfortably and watch the spectacle. By the by, your petticoat, though thoroughly delightful, is ripped."

"Oh!" Anastasia dimpled. The boy was very hard to scold. Bertram had never had a proper sense of decorum

"Oh, very well, then. Climb up and loosen me. I think I am caught on that twig."

"You are covered in thorns! I shall have to pick them off carefully. Don't move, I am coming up." This Bertram did, with amazing deftness considering the tight, cream-coloured buckskins he had chosen to wear. As he merrily picked thorns from Anastasia, he found that conversation was easier up than down.

"You are truly not at odds with me?"

"Captain, believe me! I considered a marriage of convenience with you because it was just that—convenient It would have saved me the tedium of another season and Mama the expense. Also, I like you. Or used to."

"I hope you always shall."

"I believe that is possible, if you only refrain from jabbing me with those thorns. You are supposed to be helping, not hindering."

"Ingrate! I have a mind to just leave you."

"Don't you dare. Have you unhitched me yet?"

"No, but if you hold still I will try. Ready?"

Anastasia nodded. The work was absorbing, for Bertram had to crane his neck to see exactly the spot where Miss Richmond was caught. He found he had to climb a little higher, for the twig was in a difficult position. Anastasia held obediently still until the ominous crack of a branch alerted her to a problem. She did not have time to wonder about the precise nature of the matter, for she was very soon tumbling to the earth, Bertram following with a loud gasp and an astonishingly ungentlemanly oath. For an instant, Anastasia wondered whether she had cracked a rib; then she realized, with relief, that she had merely been winded. Bertram, however, was an impossibly difficult weight, for he had landed just short of her head, but quite definitely on top of *something*. Her thigh, very likely, if she could just get herself untangled enough to be certain. She was just endeavouring to sit up when she noticed a dreadful sight. Her heart quickened considerably.

"Bertram!"

"Beg pardon, Stasia; the silly branch was just not strong enough. Just a moment and I'll have all as right as a trivet."

"Bertram! Get off me at once! There is a party of people approaching!"

The captain grabbed at his boot that had somehow been dislodged in the fall.

"God, Stasia! You will be compromised! Get up at once!"

"Pass me my half boots."

"Where are they?"

"Next to the basket—and hurry!"

FOUR

It was too late. The people were upon them, with a great deal of hallooing and waving. Anastasia flushed crimson. There with her mama was no less a person than Elinor Peabody Frampton. Vivienne trailed just behind, with two unknown young ladies Miss Richmond immediately took for the nieces.

"Anastasia!" Lady Richmond's voice was high-pitched as she took in Miss Richmond's indecorous state of disarray. Bertram was fiddling with his necktie, but to no avail. There was brambleberry juice all over him, and telltale leaves about his person.

"Mama, it is not what you think!"

"No, indeed, Lady Richmond!"

Lady Peabody Frampton tittered delicately and looked at the fascinating pair with razor-sharp eyes. Here, she was certain, was delicious scandal.

Lady Richmond's eyes bulged as she looked at Bertram. "What do you have to say for yourself, sir? You have ruined my daughter's snow white reputation with your unwarranted attentions. Do you intend to make amends? Well, do you?" She poked at him with a stick.

Anastasia opened her mouth to explain about getting caught on the branch, but was shushed sternly by her mama, who said she wanted to know no roundaboutation.

Poor Bertram! He cast an anguished glance at Miss

Townsend, who was looking rather more pale than usual. There was no help from that quarter, for she appeared to have lost her habitual merry sparkle and stood stock still between the two young ladies, eyes downcast.

"Bertram, you shall not—"

"Quiet, Anastasia!" Lady Richmond's voice was almost a roar. Her daughter prepared to do battle with her, but was interrupted from an unexpected quarter.

Captain Ralston, his eyes on the brambleberry basket, declared in a low tone that Lady Richmond was right. Anastasia was unforgivably compromised but for one point.

Lady Richmond stepped forward eagerly.

"And that is?"

"And that is, I intend to make her my wife. I shall make formal application to Lord Richmond just as soon as he returns from Brighton." His hollow tone was almost inaudible beside Lady Richmond's sudden smiles and hearty congratulations.

Anastasia was indignant. She was just about to quarrel fiercely with this nonsensical edict when Bertram gave a prim, rather formal bow and set off down the path.

Lady Richmond eyed her recalcitrant offspring balefully and demanded that she return to the house at once to change, for she could not *possibly* jaunter about in ripped petticoats." Lady Peabody Frampton tittered again, so Anastasia held her peace. She had no taste to create a scene in front of strangers—particularly those with a known predilection for gossip. She sighed and obediently set off for the house. Her indignation would have to wait till another time.

"Bertram! Wait!" Anastasia quickened her pace to catch up with him. He cursed, for he knew that no words on earth could extricate him from the tangle. Anastasia would only addle his wits all the more.

"Leave me be, Stasia!"

"No! Think of Vivienne!"

"That is precisely what I cannot any longer do. Now out of my way, Stasia, before this gelding gets frisky." Bertram had reached his horse, who was tethered obediently to a stable post just outside the Richmond mansion. He waved away a willing groom, removed the fastening, and swung himself up effortlessly.

"You are such a gudgeon!" Anastasia's shoulders lifted expressively.

"And you are such an innocent!"

"I shan't marry you!"

"Don't talk such fustian. You shall, because you have to. Besides, you cannot refuse, for I haven't yet asked. Now do go away before I run you over completely!"

"Oh!" Anastasia clicked her tongue in exasperated indignation. "Of all the chuckleheaded, idiotish things to do! Could you not have spoken the truth? After all, we only fell from a branch! It is not as if we—"

"—rolled about the grass in passionate embrace?"

Anastasia blushed. "Precisely."

"Go upstairs and change, Anastasia. I warrant when you look at yourself in a glass, you shall swiftly change your opinion. Even knowing the truth, you shall be forced to doubt! Your hair is unpinned, your hems are muddied, you are covered in twig leaves and brambleberries, and your face is becomingly flushed. No one can possibly put any other construction on your appearance."

"Even when it is patently false?"

Captain Ralston sighed and drew up the reins. "Even then, Miss Richmond." Then, with a rigid back and a bearing that proclaimed him of the military, he kicked in his heels and was gone.

The viscount smiled as his brother entered the hot house. In truth, for all his whirlwind social life—for though he did not frequent balls, he *was* a frequent visitor at Jackson's boxing saloon, at Manton's, at Brookes, at Tattersalls, and at the Four Horse Club—he was lonely. Bertram was a welcome respite from his solitary musings. Besides, he had good news for him.

"Help yourself to a peach. They have turned out particularly well this year."

"Bother your peaches, Drew!"

Lord Waverley raised his brows. "Do I detect an unwarranted note of acerbity in your tone, brother, dear?"

"Yes! No! That is . . . *not* unwarranted! Oh, Andrew! I am in the *devil* of a spot!"

Captain Ralston pushed away some lingering grape vines as he made his way up to the peach trees on his right.

"Well, don't look so glum about it. When has brother Andrew not been able to fix it for you?" The viscount smiled at Bertram indulgently. "By the by, your neckerchief is stained red and you look as though you've been dragged through a bush backwards."

"That is precisely *it,* Drew! I *have* been! And now I am being forced to marry Stasia after all!"

"Good God! Has the chit tried to entrap you?" Waverley discarded his peach stone and regarded his brother with sudden keen interest.

"No! It is her detestable parent and that vile Peabody Frampton woman."

"Lady Elinor? What has *that* witch got to say to anything?"

"That *witch,* as you put it, caught me tumbling in the fields with Stasia."

Andrew's interest was now more than merely arrested. Though there was a slight quirk to his mouth and his eyes twinkled, his voice was stern as he calmly stated that if *that* was the case, then Bertram was indeed to marry the wench; though he added that if he *had* to take his pleasures

in public, he would probably have been better off doing
so with the incomparable Miss Townsend.

"Oh, stop talking such fustian to me, Drew! This is not
a laughing matter, and I'll thank you to know me better than
to imply I *deliberately* compromised Miss Richmond."

"Bertram, nothing about you is *ever* deliberate. Come,
tell brother Andrew all about it and I shall sort it out."

The viscount's tone, though soothing, held a hint of
ready laughter. He was used to fixing Bertram's scrapes,
for they had occurred with great frequency from the day
he was born. It was one of the reasons, he had to admit,
why he'd selected Miss Anastasia Richmond as his bride
in the first place. He'd felt certain that she would offer a
steadying influence to Bertram's giddy, impetuous, and
thoroughly good-natured character.

"Can you?" Bertram's face was filled with youthful
eagerness.

"Of course I can. There is no bridge that cannot be
mended. I trust you did not play fast and loose with Anastasia's reputation?"

"No, of course not! I have already told you, it is Vivienne—"

"Ah, yes! The incomparable Miss Townsend, who, by
the by, is a thoroughly respectable candidate for your
hand. I have checked."

Bertram looked gratified for a moment; then his face
clouded over. "What odds if I am betrothed to another?"

"Oh, we shall see about that. Yes, indeed, we shall see.
Here, try my grapes." With that, and a friendly clip to the
ear, the viscount left his brother and strode to the house
in search of Montrose. Sometimes, he mused, one *did* require the ministrations of a valet.

It was dusk before the viscount arrived at his destination. He was looking particularly imposing, for he had

chosen to wear a dark ensemble, close fitting but offset by a ruby red neckerchief and an Indian ruby pin that sparkled in the last light of the afternoon. The red neckerchief, striking in that it differed greatly from the traditional crisp white, lent him an exotic, slightly quixotic air. His demeanor spoke of unquestionable authority. He handed his cattle over to the Richmond groom, who at once realised the quality of the well-matched team. When he ventured to say so, the viscount smiled and pressed a sovereign into the surprised man's hand. "See to it that they are well watered."

"Oh, certainly, my lord! I shall see to it that they are rubbed down, too. One can never tell with this chill air—"

The viscount nodded pleasantly and made his way up the stately path to the front entrance. He did not feel particularly chilled himself, but perhaps that was because his every fibre was being steeled for battle. He was under no illusions that Lady Richmond was a soft touch. She had a will of granite, and if she could use Bertie's innocent predicament to her own advantage, she undoubtedly would.

As he took in the gold lions guarding the front stairs, the viscount frowned a little. He had no doubt he could pay the woman off, but by the looks of things, the matter would be more expensive than he had first anticipated. Still, Bertie was the dearest of brothers and worth a slight hole in his very costly pocket. Not that anything would really touch sides, for his fortune was prodigious, but still, it was the principle of the matter. Andrew, Viscount Waverley, did not appreciate being milked by encroaching, social climbing nobodies. Whilst her daughter by all accounts was perfectly delightful, Lady Richmond herself fell into this category. Andrew sighed. No doubt it would be a long session. He would have to take a cold collation at Brookes.

* * *

Lady Richmond looked at the viscount's card with interest. Yes, there were the two crowns—one gold, one green, twining into each other as the crest of Waverley had done for generations. So! The viscount had something to say. She hoped it was merely congratulations, for after all, it had been *he* who had masterminded the whole betrothal. Lady Richmond was not one to dwell on particulars. In this instance, the fact that the viscount had only tentatively suggested that Bertram might wish to renew his acquaintance with Anastasia did not signify.

In Lady Richmond's eyes, the whole matter had been settled on his first visit. But now! Why did she get the sinking feeling that just as she was preparing to post the banns all might go horribly wrong? Just because Anastasia was the most provoking creature, indulging a stubborn fit of the sullens, and her companion not much better, though she *had* proven very useful in the apothecary garden . . . Really! The young people of today simply had no gratitude! She looked at herself in the glass, powdered several shiny patches on her nose and cheeks, then sat down with a sigh. The viscount would simply have to wait.

"Bettina!"

"Your Ladyship?"

Betty, by now, had become used to the odd quirks of the gentry. She was as English as Stonehenge itself, and *nothing,* certainly not being called Bettina, would ever change her to French. Still, if it made Her Ladyship happy . . .

"Did you require me, ma'am?"

Lady Richmond nodded impatiently.

"Fetch the curling papers. We shall have to begin again."

The maid tried hard not to groan. It was an heroic effort, but failed dismally. Lady Richmond's sharp ears detected the noise at once. She glared quite horribly, and the maid bobbed a meek, rather apologetic curtsy. It was to no avail.

Lady Richmond began a long tirade on the trials of hapless dressers who were incapable of setting simple coiffures and such like. The maid had heard it all before, so she settled down to undo her work and begin again.

The viscount glanced at the hall clock impatiently. He could just see it from the open door of the antechamber in which he had been deposited. It was well on an hour that he had been left kicking his heels, with nothing more interesting to look at than an abominable collection of porcelain cats, a sampler album of no particular merit, and the most appalling set of gilded neo-Gothic chairs. As a consequence, his temper was more than a little frayed. Had he known that Lady Richmond was even now in curling papers, he might well have flung the only item of any particular taste—a small Sevres vase—across the room in frustration. He might also have stalked out without another word, to the great chagrin of Porter, the butler. Fortunately for this personage, the viscount was happily oblivious to Lady Richmond's state of unreadiness and paced the room in momentary anticipation of her arrival.

At last—at long last—the door opened. The viscount smiled in anticipation, closed his eyes briefly, and prepared for a long-overdue battle of wits.

"Bertie!" A well-modulated but obviously distressed voice titillated his eardrums. It was not, he was aware at once, the rather elder, less edifying, and more rasping tone of the lady he had expected. The viscount opened his eyes just in time to be afforded a quite magnificent view of a willowy back encased to the waist in delicate, pink pearl buttons. Darkish hair cascaded down to the shoulders, secured only by a knot of flowers somewhere near the nape of a very elegant neck.

The damsel was securing the door rather carefully for one as strictly brought up as he had been given to believe.

Intriguing—certainly a welcome relief from the tedium of waiting.

She turned around, and the viscount was quite struck by the quality of her slate gray eyes. For an instant, they had sparkled pure silver.

"Oh!"

Yes, there it was—glorious confusion. If he were less hardened a gentleman, he may well have been taken in by the wide eyes, round with embarrassment and lashed, quite adorably, in featherlike ebony.

Instead, he was the cynic, so his lips curled a little, shadowing his dark features. He elevated his eyebrows a trifle and bowed.

"My lord! I had expected Captain Ralston."

"Evidently."

Lord Waverley glanced at the shut door dryly. There was definitely not the requisite three-inches of open passage visible to preserve her modesty. Anastasia, trembling a little from shyness—and something else, though she could not imagine what—took his meaning immediately and blushed in a high agitation quite uncharacteristic of her calm, decorous nature. Rattled, she answered, for once without thinking.

"*No,* you horrid man! It is not what you think at all! I merely wished to engage Captain Ralston in a few words of private conversation without the benefit of prying ears."

Lord Waverley, unused, even in extreme instances, to being referred to as a "horrid man," looked upon Miss Richmond with fresh interest. She seemed prettier than he remembered from the odd formal dance with her, and certainly a great deal more animated. Strange that he had not noticed before how peculiarly red were her lips, nor how the light caught her strands of deep, honey brown hair and caused it to shine with healthy lustre. True, it was cropped rather short in the Grecian style—he preferred hair to be waist length, as a rule—but still, it held a certain appeal.

He regarded the lips for a moment and was amused to note the annoyed flush that rose to her creamy cheeks. He decided to prompt her, for she was making no attempt to explain herself, only pushing strands of silken hair back from her forehead in some agitation. For a peculiar instant, the viscount felt the urge to help her, to twine the strands in his fingers, then smooth them down over the crown of her well-brushed head. Then he regained his composure as well as his habitual sternness.

"Well, then, my dear? In the absence of my brother, I beg you to regard me as a suitable substitute. If you wish to say something, say it now. In a few moments, confidences shall be too late. I imagine it will not be long before your mama and possibly a whole *entourage* bursts into this room. Shall they entrap me, too, I wonder?"

Lord Andrew regretted the words the instant they were out. The pain that crossed her features was unmistakable. He saw the shadows and realised instantly that it would be unfair to blame the daughter for the parent's all too transparent vulgarity. Before he could make amends, however, she was speaking.

FIVE

"I shall be brief. With respect to my betrothal . . ."

The viscount's face hardened. "Yes?"

"If Captain Ralston had not left upon the instant, he should have heard my reply."

"That being?"

"My reply was no. I did try to tell him later, but he was being idiotish and high handed and . . . and . . ." Her voice trailed off.

The viscount eyed her for a moment in silence. Then habitual suspicion raised its twisted head.

"You've never entertained the notion of marrying Bertram?" The viscount's tone was disbelieving and a little patronising. Anastasia's eyes flashed, but she retained her courtesy, despite a slight tremor of her long, slender fingers.

"I have, my lord. Of course I have! It would have saved Mama a great deal of worrisome trouble, and Bert . . . I mean, Captain Ralston, was a good friend to me when I was a child."

The viscount eyed her closely. Her voice held a ring of truth. One he suddenly found unpalatable. She was fond of Bertie! The sudden stab of jealousy caught him quite by surprise. To suppress it, he allowed sarcasm to drip from his tone.

"Ah, an adequate reason for marriage, then."

She caught the dryness, and her eyes flashed. *"Just* as adequate as thrusting us together for the sake of an heir!"

He chose to ignore this sally. "But you rejected him."

"I did."

"Why, pray?"

"We did not suit."

"Oh, come, Miss Anastasia! You can do better than that, surely? Recollect, you had only just *met* the adult Bertram, back from the wars. Too soon, surely, to decide on rejection, when you admit you had countenanced this marriage of arrangement?"

There was a moment's silence as Anastasia chewed her lip speculatively. Then she nodded, almost imperceptibly, though Lord Waverley sensed it upon the instant. Though he was loath to admit it, he was intensely aware of every breath, every gesture, that the Honourable Miss Richmond appeared to effect.

"I admit it, my lord. Had Captain Ralston's affections not been otherwise engaged, I might have embraced the notion.

"Though it might appear calculating, I *am* eager to have an establishment of my own. This confidence—and I beg you to treat it as such—is immaterial, however, since Bertram's feelings *were* engaged and I am not such a shimble-shamble, mutton-headed pea-goose to countenance any connection upon such terms."

In spite of himself, the viscount could not help admiring her spirit. There were many in her position who would not be overscrupulous when it came to catching a husband of Bertram's stature.

"And how do you know his sentiments are otherwise engaged?"

"Why, it is plain as a pikestaff! Besides, I am entirely in my companion's confidence. She, as I am sure you are aware, is the true object of Captain Ralston's affections.

At least I can conclude that Bertram has grown to be a man of high good sense!"

"How so?" The viscount had idly removed a pinch of snuff, but his movement was arrested now as he regarded Miss Richmond intently.

"Oh, Miss Vivienne Townsend is a perfect honey! One simply cannot help loving her upon the instant, despite, I must warn you, some rather high spirits. I had to assure her umpteen times that I am not fiercely downhearted by Captain Ralston's fickle intentions!"

"And you are not?"

"Good God, no! The pair were made for each other, though I cannot help owning I would have liked to take up the wedded state. Sometimes—though I am quite dreadful to say it—I find this place oppressive."

Lord Waverley had no difficulty believing her, especially when confronted by the gilded chairs whose feet each depicted a rather monstrous gargoyle. He noted, however, that she said nothing against her vulgar, overeager, social climbing parents, and he found this reticence strangely to her credit, though the omission was as obvious as if it had been spoken. Yes, it was understandable that the lady found herself inclined to marry, however contrived the match.

Lord Waverley resisted the urge to lean forward and kiss the soft, inviting lips that were being nibbled, at present, by perfect, ice white teeth. Instead, he drew out her confidences a little further and surprised himself at his interest.

"Had you no suitors prior to Bertram? I find that very difficult to credit, since you are hardly an antidote!"

"Oh, there were suitors, but I turned them down, much to Mama's—and even Papa's—great annoyance."

"May I inquire why?" The viscount's interest was piqued.

"Oh, though they had rank, they were no more than

fortune hunters and utterly humourless besides. I can countenance many shortcomings in a husband, but not, I believe, *that!*" Miss Richmond made a face. The viscount just caught sight of a pink tongue before noticing how the impudent action lighted her features with a gay sparkle that he, who had seen her several times at formal occasions, would never have dreamed possible.

"I can tell, then, why Bertram would have served your purpose. A more spirited sense of the ridiculous you could not possibly hope for. But tell me, what did the good Miss Townsend do when he so publicly offered for your hand?"

Miss Richmond smiled. "She nearly fell into a dead swoon, of course, but happily was self-possessed enough not to make a dreadful spectacle. Sometimes she has more sense than she is credited for. Of course, as soon as I was able, I indicated that such a drastic solution to a pocketful of brambleberries was as bumble-headed as it was idiotish. She was grateful but sadly doubtful, and I *still* have to impress upon her that it is nonsense that Bertram and I should wed on such a flimsy basis. Why, I should not know a moment's happiness!"

The viscount's eyes danced. "I should say not! And Bertram? He seems to have been remarkably silent through all of this."

Anastasia shook her head, impatient at the memory. "Unfortunately, the captain marched off before I was entirely disentangled, and Mama bundled me off at the first sign of my shocking want of conduct in not immediately accepting the proposal. I did eventually catch Bertram up, but he was deaf to all my pleas."

For an instant, the tips of the viscount's very handsome lips curved upward. He was beginning to enjoy himself. Miss Anastasia Richmond, delightfully attractive, was slightly less retiring than he had thought. Also, she appeared to have a sense of fair play which, since the debacle of Miss Fallows, he had not expected to find in one of her sex. He looked at her curiously.

"Is your mother furious?"

"Oh, spitting livid! I should not say it perhaps, but she was very pleased with herself for wrangling such an eligible alliance. Though my fortune is prodigious, it was always thought that I should attract the eye either of an improvident peer or one of the merchant class. My mother, as you know, was a merchant's daughter herself."

"Yes, I am aware." Lord Waverley certainly was, for he had looked carefully into Anastasia's credentials before selecting her for Bertram. Lady Richmond had been a sad blot on an otherwise spotless record. He had chosen to overlook it, for in truth there was no young candidate who was perfect, and at least Bertram had the advantage of childhood affection for the chit.

For an instant, a memory that had lain dormant in his mind for some time flashed into his consciousness. He had the sudden vision of a pale, slender little maid in a royal blue dress and matching riband climbing carefully onto a dear, clean-smelling pony—a Shetland, if he recalled—with hair as burnished brown as its young owner's. Bertie had been holding the reins but had dropped them to catch a butterfly in his net. The girl had lost her concentration to see and had taken a dreadful tumble on the grass. Though her little knees were horribly grazed, she had not cried, only clung to him—for he had scooped her up at once—and snuggled softly into his arms. He could not quite recall, but he thought he might have carried her home after that.

She was looking at him now with wide, strangely luxurious eyes, and he wondered if she recalled the incident at all. Probably not, but memories played tricks. Twenty years on at least and he could recall her softness with vivid accuracy. He wondered if she would melt into him now, as she had done so unthinkingly then. Suddenly, he wanted very much to try. He took a step forward, then stopped himself short. Whatever could he be thinking of? And was it his imagination, or was she staring at him with an intentness that caused the atmosphere to charge to a tension he had not expected to feel again?

He picked up her fan and played with it idly.

"Is she still angry?"

"Who—my mother?"

Lord Waverley nodded.

"Oh, undoubtedly. She plans to hold me to this betrothal, if I might call it such, for as she repeatedly tells me, otherwise I will have committed the dual sin of compromising myself to no avail *and* ruining all possibility of an eligible connection."

"Not necessarily." The viscount surprised himself with the vehemence of his words. They seemed to have rolled off his tongue without being invited to do so.

"I have already told you, my lord, that I shall not marry Bertie!" Anastasia tried to be patient, but there was something so compelling about his eyes that she felt a fluttering in her chest. Why did she get the dizzying notion that they were no longer speaking of Bertie? She felt light-headed as she stretched out her arm to reclaim her fan. When the viscount returned it, their gloved hands touched briefly. Though there was doeskin and satin between them, Anastasia was more intensely aware of him in that moment than she had ever been of anyone in a lifetime. She fiddled with the clasp, and gasped aloud at the viscount's next words.

"Who said anything of Bertram?"

She unfurled the fan and dropped her eyes, not quite daring to match the quiet intensity of his gaze. Surely, *surely,* she must be mistaking his meaning! The viscount was an incomparable; it was as natural as breathing for him to be charming. He probably had no notion of the sudden, head-spinning effect he was having upon her. With a sigh, she dismissed her suspicions as groundless.

"There is no one else suitable, my lord, who has paid the slightest interest in my bountiful charms. I have already told you that."

"Ah, yes. The humourless fortune hunters. No one else?"

Anastasia shook her head mournfully, though the viscount noted at once the irrepressible dimple peeking out from rose-hued cheeks. So! The unusual Miss Richmond was not without humour herself

"No one, I am afraid. I am sad to have to report, sir, that I am practically on the shelf!"

"Practically is not the same as *actually*, Miss Richmond!"

"You talk in riddles."

"Do I?" He regarded her with such a strange mixture of avidity and self-mocking cynicism that Anastasia was startled from her self-imposed composure. Again, there was that tightening in her stomach and the heady sensation that she was missing something quite outrageously important. There was no way around it. She would have to tax the viscount on his meaning, for, though veiled, it seemed unmistakable enough. She dared not read to much into it, though, for fear of vast, untillable loneliness. Strange that losing Bertram had not had such an effect on her.

"You cannot meant that . . . that . . ."

The viscount looked at her closely. Then he took her chin in his hands.

"Why not, Miss Richmond? Since Bertram cannot, unfortunately, oblige, I shall offer you the next best thing. I shall marry you myself."

Anastasia was still gaping when Lady Richmond swept into the room. Her hair was piled high upon her head and billowing out little cream puffs of curls, all set rigidly in place with the help of layers of pins and other contrivances designed for just such a purpose. Her face was powdered white, but she had taken care to thoroughly rouge her cheeks for the occasion, so she could by no means be described as pale.

The viscount blanched, for he was a man of natural sensibility and found the spectacle unnerving. Still, he recovered his poise sooner than most gentleman of his acquaintance would have, and stepped forward politely.

"Lady Richmond, a thousand apologies for dropping in on you at such a time. I had not thought still to be here so close to the dinner hour . . ."

In spite of her odd predicament, Anastasia could not help admiring him. At one and the same time he mollified her mother whilst drawing attention to the unconscionable length of time he had been kept waiting. Adroit, very adroit!

Unfortunately, Lady Richmond was not one for subtleties.

"Well, if you are expecting an invitation to dinner, sir, you are far out! There is nothing more than a smidgen of pheasant, and besides, you can take yourself off to an inn. If you have come here to plead for your brother, you are far out. Whatever my wayward daughter may say, she *shall* be married." With a dramatic gesture, she announced in stentorian tones that "No amount of money could *possibly* compensate me for the loss of my dear daughter's reputation."

"I never said it could."

"Then you have *not* come here to buy us off?" Lady Richmond set down with some surprise the china kitten she had just taken up.

"Absolutely not." The viscount surveyed her with some distaste. He ordered his features, however, for he did not wish to distress Anastasia with a scene. For some inexplicable reason, he felt protective of her.

"Good. I shall have the banns posted at once. Now, no more sulks, Anastasia! You hear what the good viscount says!"

"Just a moment, ma'am."

Lady Richmond glared at him. "You cannot go back on your word *now,* my lord!"

"I shall not. I merely wish to clarify matters a trifle. Anastasia shall be married, but not, I am afraid, to Captain Ralston. His affections, I am told, lie elsewhere."

"Well!" Lady Richmond spluttered. "Well! I will have you know, sir, that Anastasia is not a common parcel to be passed hither and thither! And who, pray, is the gentleman you have in mind? I trust, of course, that he *is* a gentleman?"

The viscount ignored the high colour on Anastasia's cheeks. More than ever, he felt confirmed in his decision. Miss Richmond should not have to live a moment longer with this harridan, parent or not.

"Indeed, I hope so, ma'am. I can vouch for him absolutely." He was rewarded by the light he saw reenter Anastasia's eyes. Good girl! She was amused.

"Well, that is all very well, but what *I* say, sir—"

The viscount was never to know what Lady Richmond had to say—or not in this instance, at least, for the dinner gong rang at precisely that moment, drowning out her undoubted invective.

"Well?" Lady Richmond glared at him and pointed with her stick. The viscount understood, all of a sudden, why Lord Richmond was said to practically haunt his clubs. Home must be hell.

"Well, what?"

"Well, stop winking at my daughter—yes, I saw that, sir, and I must tell you that your behaviour is abominable—and tell me who this suitor shall be. If it is not a respectable connection, Anastasia shall have Bertram. That is my final word on it."

"Very well, ma'am. I respectfully present myself for review."

"You? Stop funning this instant, sir, before I have your carriage called round myself!"

"I am not funning, Lady Richmond. Pending Miss Richmond's approval, of course, I shall make application to Lord Richmond upon the instant."

"Well!" Lady Richmond was speechless as she reached for her sal volatal. "Well!" After a little more along these lines, she finally recalled herself to her senses, drew herself up straight, curtsied graciously, babbled endlessly, and grabbed the viscount's arm in a viselike grip he did not even care to try to extricate himself from.

"Oh, *Andrew,*" she gushed, tapping him playfully with her stick. "You shall lead me in to dinner. You shall stay, of course, for Cook has rustled up the most heavenly buttered lobster with oyster cream sauce. You will enjoy it prodigiously, for it is prepared exactly to my directions . . ."

Lord Waverly cast an anguished glance at his unexpected affianced. She winked back with the most remarkable insouciance and announced that she would just "fetch out Miss Townsend." Then, with a sudden skip to her normally very proper step, Miss Richmond left him most cruelly to his fate.

SIX

Dinner was a strange affair, for Lord Waverly was not used to being surrounded by a bevy of females, all of whom—except, perhaps, the more reticent Miss Richmond—were eyeing him with lively interest. Anastasia must have hinted to Miss Townsend of what was about to occur, for that young lady by no means sported the pallor and die-away airs that Lord Waverley had fully expected. Indeed, she tucked into the lobster with gusto, announced herself "very pleased indeed" to make the viscount's acquaintance, and proceeded to surreptitiously dig Anastasia in the ribs on every occasion that he happened to glance at her.

Anastasia, on the other hand, was far quieter, her lovely gray eyes sparkling with just the hint of tears. The viscount had the peculiar desire to damn the company to perdition, take her in his arms, and kiss her tears away. He was certain that she was now beset with uncertainties, doubting his intentions, wondering, perhaps, why he should have taken so bold a step. He had surprised himself—it was only natural that she, too, should be astonished. He hoped that reassurance was all the lady needed. The uncomfortable thought had just struck him that he had never given her a chance to say no, for in his desire to knock the wind out of Lady Richmond's blustering sails, he had announced his intentions as a fait accompli.

"May I say something?"

"No, Anastasia, you may not. Leave all the details to me, if you please!" Lady Richmond picked up a gilded spoon and turned to Lord Waverley on her right. "Oh, you have no notion of how I have longed for such an event! Anastasia is forever reminding me of the time you rescued her from her poor pony . . ."

Anastasia blushed crimson and stared at her plate. The viscount, a little amused, glanced her way but failed entirely to catch her eye. Miss Townsend, however, was indignant.

"I thought you said yesterday that it was Captain *Ralston* who had rescued her."

"Bertram? What nonsense! The whole matter was his fault. I recall it perfectly."

Vivienne giggled, in high spirits. "I declare, Lady Richmond, you jest! Yesterday it was most certainly—"

"Miss Townsend! Do you not have any chores to occupy yourself with?" Lady Richmond frowned at her crossly and set down her spoon. "Do take yourself off, and Anastasia too, if you please! The viscount and I have much to talk about."

Vivienne gestured to Anastasia and they both made their curtsies, despite Lord Waverley's earnest urging of them to stay.

Lady Richmond then held him in her thrall so long that he began seriously to doubt his actions. What could have possessed him to make so rash an offer? He, who had forsworn womankind, to propose marriage when he'd had no more pressing thought in his head than to buy the young woman off. He must have been seized by a sudden passing dementia! Not that Miss Richmond was not very comely in her own way, and he found, to his surprise, that her slight, lilting lisp was rather more attractive than offputting. Still, a wedding on the scale Lady Richmond planned for him had been exactly the sort of agenda he had assiduously avoided since the fatal mistake of his youth.

He wished Miss Richmond would return so that he might remember what it was that had given rise to this bizarre chivalrous impulse. Not, surely, the fact that she made his pulses quicken? Many a woman had done so in the past most satisfactorily. No, it was not purely his baser instincts at work here, despite Miss Richmond's almost unconscious charms. What, then? Bertram would tease him heartily unless he could reason the matter out. He looked at Lady Richmond in veiled distaste. Oh, would she never, *never* stop talking?

"Yes," he nodded at her politely, for he was, after all, a gentleman. Had he but known it, another one hundred and fifty peers of the realm were instantly added to the guest list. Andrew returned to his pensive state. Lady Richmond thought he looked like a veritable god, for his face was immobile and his aquiline features were very much in the classical mode. She rather daringly said as much, fluttering her white, rather stubby lashes coyly. Fortunately for her, perhaps, Andrew did not hear her. He was lost in a reverie of his own.

What was it, he wondered, that had made him throw caution, reason, even sense to the wind? He waved away a tray of macaroons and thought on the matter whilst Lady Richmond went on about trousseaus and bridal gifts.

It was Miss Richmond's smile! True, he had not glimpsed it often, but when he had, it had been dazzling, causing her cheeks to glow and animation to creep into her eyes like little fairy lanterns. Perhaps its rarity itself made it a precious prize to seek. But no!

The viscount slapped his thigh vigorously, much to Lady Richmond's genteel surprise. Happily, he was oblivious to her sentiments, and it was not long before she was prattling on about settlements.

No, it was not just her smile. Lord Waverly had been

confronted, in his life, with many a pair of cherry-ripe lips. It was more than that . . . Andrew mused over the lady he'd only just met, for the past could not be counted; she had been a mere child then. Perhaps it was her obvious candour, her complete lack of guile.

The viscount thought of Lady Araminda Tarradale and went stiff. *She* had not been guileless. He must beware, lest he fall into a similar trap. His eyes shuttered for an instant, but when they opened again, they were clear.

The matter was all so simple. Miss Richmond wanted a marriage of convenience, and he was in the unique position of being able to offer it to her. His feelings, he was sure, stemmed out of pity. What person of breeding could, after all, be expected to contemplate with equanimity a lifetime under the same roof as the insufferable Lady Richmond? Oh, it was his duty to rescue Anastasia! And, since it neatly extricated his brother from a scrape, it served the purpose nicely.

He must just take care to impress upon Miss Richmond the nature of their dealings. It would not pay to have her under any illusions. And the Honourable Lady Richmond on his left? She was still penciling in dates, gushing effusively, and breathlessly exclaiming. Andrew sighed and reached for his coffee. He would have done much for a sample of Lord Richmond's renowned burgundy. He'd never needed it more.

Lord Andrew Ralston, Viscount Waverley, had been right. Bertram *was* pleased to tease him unmercifully, though in a spirit of such profound relief that his brother had not the heart to scold—or not *too* awfully, at any rate.

"Have done, Bertram. Your exuberance is tiresome."

The captain beamed as he picked a few prized cuttings from the viscount's well-stocked herbarium. "Mint and lavender. I have been trying to pick it, but I believe Miss Townsend smells of both."

"You shall soon know, for I have invited both ladies to tea this evening."

Bertram's eyes lit up, but then he regarded his brother wearily. "Does that include the dragon?"

"I fear so."

Bertram threw the cuttings on a heap with the violets he had purloined and looked at his brother miserably. "Perhaps I shall claim a violent headache."

"Don't you dare. I've not gone to this enormous deal of trouble for nothing."

"Come, Andrew. Don't be coy! You *like* Miss Richmond! Vivienne says she is a darling."

"Perhaps she is, though I care not for such particulars. She will make a suitable wife, and it seems to be her earnest desire to marry. Leave it at that."

"How dull! Perhaps you should pick the lilies. I believe that is her particular scent."

"No. It is essence of rose water and a hint of something a little more sultry. Lilac, perhaps."

Bertram's eyes twinkled with unholy glee, though he bit his tongue in uncharacteristic restraint. He was certain that, after all, his brother's cold heart was melting. It had been a long time since he had noticed such a particular.

"Have you spoken to Lord Richmond?"

"I shall tomorrow, before Her Ladyship preempts me by posting the banns. I would not be surprised if she has managed to wrangle an announcement in the *Gazette* for tomorrow. She is the most interfering, managing—"

"Oh, I know! That is why *I* wish to speak for Miss Townsend at once! Her position in the house would be unbearable if Anastasia were gone."

"Has she indicated she will accept?"

"No; she was quite positive that she would not. But *that* was when she thought I was to marry Stasia."

"And now? What are the odds?"

Bertram grinned. "I deem them excellent. Oh, not to stand on my own consequence, but really, the girl was made for me!"

"Heaven save us, *one* of you has always been more than sufficient!"

"Yes, but I am not beautiful, like Vivienne."

The viscount privately thought Bertram was mad, for how could any lady—especially one with a profusion of freckles across her nose—possibly compete with Anastasia's breathtaking looks?

True, Anastasia was not handsome in the usual way, for her hair was brown rather than the obligatory blonde, and her curves were more subtle than voluptuous, but she was pleasingly slender, a willowy beauty with bright intelligence behind gorgeously lashed eyes. She was softly understated, but sultry, with wide lips that must surely lead any man—even Bertram—to passion.

But no. Evidently not. Bertram was still prattling on about Miss Townsend as if there were not a girl in the world who could match her. The viscount sighed. That was as it should be. And as for himself—well, he had better look to his own heart. He would move heaven and earth not to be hurt a second time.

The evening tea was rather stilted, with Lady Richmond monopolising the conversation, insisting on charades, and generally thwarting all Andrew's efforts for private conversation with Anastasia. Lady Richmond was so preoccupied with the forthcoming nuptials and with "chaperoning" Anastasia, as she coyly put it a dozen times, that she did not notice the captain engaging Miss Townsend in the most scintillating—if highly improper—of conversations. Neither did she notice them sneaking out to renew their acquaintance, or the fact that Vivienne's eyes were suspiciously bright when she returned indoors.

Lady Richmond was so preoccupied, in fact, that she

did not notice what Vivienne's dresser noticed almost at once upon her return. The dreaded pantalets were back. The strange thing was, though, that whereas Vivienne's had always sported a wisp of lace, these sported several very merry white ribbons and a band of exquisite seeded pearls that had cost a quite improper fortune.

Vivienne's eyes had danced with such naughty mischief that the dresser had not felt in the least bit inclined to report the circumstance. It was there, then, that the matter had, most fortunately, been allowed to rest.

At least the tea was a success for *someone,* the viscount thought with no small measure of irritation. Certainly it had not been for *him.* With the dragon's eyes upon her, Anastasia had answered most of his questions in monosyllables, assiduously avoiding his gaze and blushing painfully at every vulgarity uttered by her voluble parent. There had been no chance to quiz her on her feelings, or on whether she truly felt herself able to proceed with the momentous step. She had curtsied sweetly to him at the doorstep, and allowed him to tuck her snugly into the carriage, but beyond these minor attentions, there had been nothing to hint at any intimacy between them.

With resignation, he had bowed elegantly and murmured all that was proper to Lady Richmond and the more ebullient Miss Townsend. That young lady had then had the confounded impudence to wink.

It took several turns round the garden to cool Andrew's rather strained temper. Bertram, of course, was no help. He had vanished like the veritable Cheshire cat, not to be glimpsed again until morning at the earliest.

Though Lord Richmond needed to be hunted high and low in all the men's clubs to be found the following afternoon, he looked upon Andrew's suit with favour. His large Roman nose behind a newspaper, he seemed glad enough to welcome the viscount into the family, muttering only that he wished Anastasia happy and hoped that the nuptials could take place quickly.

The viscount, mistaking this comment for an indication that Richmond feared he might change his mind, raised his dark, besettingly handsome brows loftily.

"I do not renege on my obligations, sir! Unseemly haste, I assure you, is not necessary for a positive outcome to this affair."

Richmond looked at him with a slight twist to a once handsome mouth.

"You do not know my wife, sir! I beg pardon if I have offended, but I assure you my life shall be unbearable until this thing is done. I have heard nothing but nuptials all morning till my head rings, and what with the entire house needing rehanging in silk drapes—I am assured this is definitely the case—and a thousand hangdog relations invited to witness the splendour, I fear I am quite overset. If you wish to do me a kindness—and I assure you, Viscount, that I am in need of kindness—you will take Anastasia and marry her over the anvil tomorrow."

The ice melted from Andrew's eyes. He found he rather liked the man who was so unexpectedly to become his father-in-law. "Very tempting, I am sure, but your daughter may have something to say to that!"

"Anastasia? Pooh! She might have a few scruples, for she is always inclined to be a little retiring, but I am convinced she would forgo the fanfare at the snap of a finger. She has always, I am afraid, been a sad disappointment to her mama."

"Oh?" Amusement lit up Andrew's tone.

"Yes, indeed. Lady Richmond seizes the limelight at every opportunity. Anastasia shrinks from it like a wallflower."

"Wallflowers are not without a charm of their own."

"You have noticed, then?" For the first time, Lord Richmond's eyes sparkled with a hint of animation.

"I have noticed, sir, though I will not humbug you into believing I am in love with Anastasia. Rather, let us say we appear mutually compatible and have interests that shall both be served by this union."

The old man eyed him closely. "That is good enough for me. Lady Richmond and I were swept away in a swirl of passion, and I am not convinced that that was altogether such a good thing. Passion dies, but compatibility must mature with the passing of time."

"Like your burgundy?"

"Exactly so." Richmond smiled, his teeth gleaming surprisingly white in the light that streamed in through the arch windows. "The cellars are the one place that Lady R does not meddle. If you stop by, I shall be happy to allow you to sample some of my finest."

"An intriguing prospect. And now, my dear sir, I must bid you good day. You may find this remarkably behindhand of me, but I have yet to elicit an affirmative response from your daughter. The whole matter seemed wrested from our hands entirely."

Lord Richmond nodded sympathetically. "Lady R, I suppose. If you wish to speak with Anastasia privately, try the back entrance and the first flight of stairs. A twist to the right will see you in the nursery passage. Right again will take you to her quarters."

"Good God!" Shock mingled with amusement and a new respect for the unsuspected wiliness of the man before him. "You cannot be suggesting, sir, that I solicit your daughter's hand in such a thoroughly disreputable manner?"

"Desperate times call for desperate measures, sir! If you compromise her, you shall marry her. Since that is, at all events, your intention, take the risk. You shall never

separate her from Lady R any *other* way that I know, short
of poisoning the old . . . ahem!"

Lord Richmond cleared his throat apologetically.

Andrew's eyes twinkled. It was years since he'd had a
more edifying conversation. Life, though possibly running
far ahead of him, at least had ceased being boring. Even
the leaden pain he had carried with him since Lady
Araminda's defection seemed suddenly easier to bear.
Truth to tell, he had almost forgotten it.

"Very well, sir, I shall take your advice. And I promise
you, if Anastasia has any second thoughts, I shall not press
her in the matter."

Lord Richmond grunted slightly, though his lips curved
and his eyes appeared gratified. "It is well." He picked
up his newspaper as Andrew prepared to leave. Just as
the viscount was placing a particularly elegant beaver and
velvet hat upon his head, Richmond spoke again. "I have
often thought Anastasia needs to be thoroughly kissed."

The viscount forgot the hat and twisted round in sudden
shock. "Beg pardon, sir?"

"You heard me. You don't look to me to be a namby-
pamby boy. If the filly needs convincing, convince her!"

Waverley eyed him for a moment in silence. Then he
threw back his head and roared with laughter. His future
father-in-law, it seemed, was full of surprises.

Lord Waverley decided to ride to Brampton that very
day. With a moment's regret, he declined his delightful-
looking new tilbury, with its fresh, high-stepping team for
a more sensible bay. The ride might be a trifle exhausting,
but at least he could tether the horse inconspicuously. If
Lord Richmond's advice was to be heeded, he needed a
little stealth, a great deal of cunning, and an ample measure of impudence. The day was so cheery that he felt up

to all three. Thwarting Lady Richmond added piquancy to the challenge ahead.

Stopping only to press a posy into his saddlebag, he had no time to notice the announcement that had been hastily inserted in the *Gazette,* nor to see the hordes of interested morning callers who were even now lining his marbled corridors and elegantly carpeted morning rooms. His butler and housekeeper, had he but known it, were at wit's end. Fortunately, his groom had not seen fit to apprise him of the matter, he being a taciturn character who liked to keep himself to himself. Consequently, the viscount set out, looking, as usual, as fine as nine pence, and entirely oblivious to the fact that his affairs were now known to all of London and half of Brighton at the very least.

Lord Richmond had not lied. The back entrance of the Richmond home, set apart from the servants' entrance by a tall trellis covered in vines, was easily accessible if one was prepared to muddy one's Hessians in several flower beds and one particularly annoying cabbage patch. Andrew braved both, and was rewarded for his intrepidity by the sight of a winding series of stairs in polished mahogany.

SEVEN

"Can I help you, Your Lordship?"

Drat! Foiled by a housemaid in crisp, clean linen who eyed him coyly and bobbed him the slightest of curtsies.

"No, I believe I am perfectly able to help myself. *You,* on the other hand, need a great deal of help!"

The maid stared at him in suspicious befuddlement.

"I daresay you could use some sweetmeats and several fripperies for your half day." The viscount treated her to his smile-to-swoon-for look—a countenance he had not bothered to assume for several years—and the maid was suitably bemused, such that she began to flutter her eyelashes archly and utter half sentences that were entirely unintelligible to the Honourable Viscount Waverley.

He felt around in his greatcoat and extracted a coin. Her eyes widened as he pressed it into her hand and bade her "be a good girl and run along." As she turned to do so, he pulled her back gently and placed his finger to his lips meaningfully. The maid giggled a little and swore she wouldn't "tell nobody nuffin." Whereupon the viscount grinned, told her she was a woman of fine good sense, and turned once more to the stairs.

Andrew strode through the nursery quarters without hesitation, though his heart beat quite considerably fast and he was reminded of the clandestine work he had undertaken several times on behalf of the king. Not many were aware of these activities, but in certain circles Viscount Waverley was known as more than simply a peer of the realm. He had proven himself many times over in the courts of Paris and on the battlefields of Spain. A man of rough justice, perhaps, but one whose integrity was unquestionable and whose wiliness was legendary among those privy to his actions.

Now some of that wiliness was in force once again. Andrew ignored the drumming in his chest as he veered to the right. This, he presumed, was Miss Richmond's private wing. He must tread carefully so as not to startle her—or, worse, trigger a farcical situation that might utterly compromise her good name. The viscount was not aware of why he went to such trouble, only that her good opinion mattered to him. He was also painfully aware that she had never had a chance to rebut his proposal. It would be unsporting to marry her out of hand without offering her this simple courtesy.

He was just debating whether to continue on down the passage or try the handle of the gilded door before him when the lyrical notes of a harp assailed his senses. He left the gilded door at once and strode a little further down the corridor. There, by a window, sat Anastasia. The light streamed in on her unbound hair as long, ungloved fingers plucked at the strings. The melody trailed off as the young woman sat, her back quite impeccably straight, staring into the middle distance. To the fanciful it might have seemed that she was gazing into the unseen strands that tangled into her future.

The viscount stared at her a long moment before striding into the room and making his presence known. When he did, she startled so profoundly that Andrew was forced to steady her a little, the twang of a harp string echoing in the charged room.

"Oh!" Anastasia put her hand to her hair and realised that it was shockingly unpresentable. Andrew's warm eyes crinkled a little at the corners, though he was not unaware of the tightening of his rib cage as their eyes locked.

"My lord!" Anastasia set down the harp and took two paces backward. It was a useless gesture, for the viscount closed the gap upon the instant. His perceptive eyes noticed a telltale pulse in her neck, and he wondered whether it was the shock of the unexpected or the shock of confronting him alone that caused the heightened anxiety.

"I did not mean to frighten you."

"I am not frightened, only surprised."

"Pleasantly so, I hope?"

"I am not certain." Anastasia regarded him closely and removed a wisp of recalcitrant hair from her eyes. They were not slate gray, anymore, the viscount noticed with interest. They appeared to be a silvery green. He wondered what that meant, for Anastasia was one of those rare individuals whose moods were reflected in her countenance. Even her lips, wide and unconsciously sensuous, seemed to be bearing a message. The devil of it was that the viscount could not, at that point, decipher it. Perhaps that was because the pink tongue, only just visible, was maddening to his unsuspecting senses.

"Can I *make* you certain?"

"I mistake your meaning, sir."

"I think not." The viscount ignored her trim, willowy body—though he was aware of every inch of it—and concentrated fully on her eyes.

She seemed mesmerised by him, and their glance held quite beyond the proper, acceptable limits. Though she said nothing more, the viscount had the gratification of seeing her pulses quicken even further. It was *her* eyes that were the first to flutter downward, affording the viscount a heavenly view of dark, lustrous lashes.

"Come here. I wish to talk to you."

"You can talk where you are."

"Not with a gilded harp between us."

"Very well, I shall set the harp against that chair." Anastasia's fingers clutched the instrument, her eyes everywhere but on those of the viscount. She placed the harp gently out of the way and folded her hands.

"Now, sir, you may talk."

"Not with your silvery eyes fixed on this abominable carpet."

"It is not abominable! Mama had it brought in from China."

There was a silence between them as the viscount regarded her sternly.

"Oh, very well, then, it is hideous," Anastasia allowed. "I tried to have it removed to Mama's suites, but she would not hear of such a thing, for her own rooms are decorated in the Egyptian style."

"Spare me the details!" The viscount shuddered, though his eyes were alight with sudden laughter. Anastasia found herself dimpling in return, though she could not think why.

"There, that is better. You are looking at me directly now, and I must tell you, I find the sensation charming." The viscount surprised himself, for truly he had not meant to engage Anastasia in a flirtation. He had sworn never again to let his head be ruled by his heart, and by God, he meant to live by that! Still, there was something about Anastasia that quite overset such well-laid plans.

"Come here."

For some reason, Anastasia felt compelled to obey. She took three steps forward and rather shyly stopped when confronted with the small obstacle of Lord Waverly's very handsome chest.

Now it was Andrew's turn to feel his pulses run riot. He quelled the urge to crush her into his arms and very properly stepped back, though he took both her hands in his in the process.

"My lord!"

"We are practically engaged, Anastasia. I shall take such liberties because I find it extraordinarily pleasant."

"Do you always do things that please you?"

"No . . . I've been known to take cod liver oil upon occasion, and I also, very infrequently of course, feel obliged to put in an appearance at a ball or two."

"Which you find irksome?"

"Impossibly so."

Anastasia digested this in silence. "I once danced with you, you know."

"I know. It was at the Havershams' soiree. But I have the advantage of you, for it was not once, but *twice,* that we danced."

"Oh! You remember!" Anastasia pulled her hands from Andrew's and placed them on her flushed cheeks.

He smiled. "I take it from that edifying remark that you remember, too. After, we strolled to Lord Carmichael's aviaries and I brought you a glass of lemonade. It was then that I decided you would be suitable for Bertram."

"How kind!" Anastasia's eyes flashed. She remembered the moment well, but Bertram had been far from her mind at the time. She blushed to think of what *had* been on her mind.

"Temper, temper!" The viscount's tone was teasing, but he eyed Anastasia closely. She seemed more than unusually overset at a simple passing memory. Perceptively, he wondered why.

"Anastasia, I took you by surprise the other day. Truth to tell, I took *myself* by surprise. I have always thought Bertram would make an excellent heir and have never considered marriage for myself."

"Except to Lady Araminda Tarradale." Anastasia's heart beat wildly at her impertinence, but her eyes held his steadily. If she were to leap into this thing, there must be no ghosts to stand between them.

She had touched a nerve, for His Lordship's back grew rigid and there was a faint twitch in his cheek.

"Yes. Except for Miss Araminda Fallows, as she was then."

"She betrayed you."

"Not, I would hope, common schoolroom gossip, but yes, she did." The viscount's tone had become uncompromising, and Anastasia felt she had lost the sudden warmth that had sprung up between them.

"*You,* however, shall not."

"No."

"That is all I ask, Anastasia. I cannot hope for love, for that is a gift that is not, I believe, destined to be mine. Love is a mutual matter—mutual madness, one might say. It is not in my power to give it, so I cannot, in all honesty, expect to receive it."

He watched the light die out of Anastasia's eyes and wondered if he had been the cause. He hoped not. Still, he was not prepared to offer her Spanish coin. He liked her too much to dally with her affections as *his* had once, in the past, been dallied with. Yes, he had strange, romantic, soaring feelings for her. These he attributed to passion. And passion, he hoped, had a place of its own.

"Do you know what *I* think?"

"What?" Her voice was almost a whisper.

"I think I should immediately take your good father's advice."

"Papa?" Anastasia looked bewildered.

"Yes. It was he who directed me to your chambers, though I shall have something to say to him for not warning me what was to become of my boots!"

Anastasia looked down, virtuously avoiding an overlong glimpse at handsome thighs encased in buckskins. Too late, she realised that his calves, too, were an affront to her virtue, for their sharp, firm lines were definitely distracting to her intentions. These, of course, were to view the state of Lord Waverly's elegant Hessians and pronounce judgment.

Since the boots were still gleaming, despite a few flecks of dry mud, she took leave to declare she had little sympathy for his plight.

To which he replied that she was clearly a shrew and he had little choice but to tame her.

Which was when the very proper Miss Richmond eyed him warily and asked how he intended to do that.

Lord Waverly grinned rather wickedly and murmured that he would either spank her or kiss her and since he was in an excellent humour, she had the choice. Miss Richmond then suffered a severe relapse of heightened pulses and chose, rather gingerly, the latter option.

"Come a little closer, then."

"I am not sure I should!"

"Afraid?"

"Definitely not!" Anastasia sounded indignant, though in truth she was trembling, despite the fact that it was not at all cold in the hopelessly ornate music room.

"Well then?" The viscount made it a little easier by taking a pace forward himself. He was strangely surprised by the tension he himself felt, for all his numbed heart and experienced ways.

Anastasia stumbled forward, and he caught her rather tenderly for a man determined on a loveless path. Then, positioning her firmly, so that her head was cradled quite comfortably, he bent his lips close to her own and proceeded to tease her with kisses close to her mouth, but not quite touching her delicious, deep pink, lush lips. At first, Miss Richmond seemed happy to comply. Then she shook herself out of his arms and admonished him soundly.

"That is not fair, sir! I shall suspect, in a moment, that you are merely a tease!"

"And *I* shall suspect you are a siren, for I have never

before taken such pleasure from a chin, I will have you know."

Anastasia afforded him one of those breathtaking smiles that quite illuminated her features.

"Cry truce, then! Are you satisfied, or shall we try again?" She startled herself with her brass-faced boldness, but somehow the viscount peeled off her layers of properness and stripped her down to truth. And the truth was, quite definitely, that she found the viscount more attractive than her very decorous dreams, and more magnetic than any human being she had ever before encountered. The discovery made her quake with apprehension, yet a part of her yearned quite brazenly for more—much more—of the same.

What of the odds that he did not love her? Plenty of marriages were built on less, yet the tension between them could not be denied. She could see by his eyes that he hungered for her, she had no need for the confirmation of his touch. Still, now that she had felt the warmth of his hands, had tasted—or almost tasted—the sweetness of his mouth, she knew that the hunger was reciprocated, for why else, even now, would she be pulling him toward her, tipping his head forward, drowning in the very caress that moments before he had denied her?

Neither noticed the door opening, but both heard the crash that followed. It was Vivienne, of course, smashing a prized vase—though it was so gaudy Lady Richmond was well rid of it—in her haste to make a quiet, unobtrusive exit. Poor Miss Townsend! She started to make a thousand apologies as she picked up the pieces, not sure whether to go or to stay. Wondering, too, how on earth the viscount had managed to slip past the butler, the housemaids, and Lady Richmond herself.

The moment had been broken, but the lingering effect of it remained as a curious testament. Anastasia, when she had recovered herself sufficiently to look up, regarded

Lord Waverley with wondering eyes. The smile she received in return was most gratifying, for it held none of the reserve that she had previously sensed.

"No! Don't leave, Miss Townsend. Allow me to help you. If you are not careful, you shall be cut by the glass. I have the advantage of gloves."

So saying, the viscount smoothed out the moment and dropped to his haunches. Neither woman could help noticing how firm he looked, with his straight back and modish buckskins so tight that they creased slightly as he sifted through thorns and glass and long, speckled stemmed roses.

Vivienne was the first to lose her shyness. She leaned over toward Anastasia and winked. Then, with a merry lilt to her voice, she declared that for once she had got things right.

"I, Anastasia, am your companion and chaperone. Just *think* how pleased Lady R will be when she hears what a scandal I have just averted!"

The viscount raised his head at that, but he noticed at once that the very proper—or latterly *not* so proper—Miss Richmond did not seem at all perturbed by this announcement. Instead, she threatened to throw Vivienne out the window, at which the miscreant giggled and declared that that would not be necessary, since the spectacle itself had been its own reward.

The viscount's lips twitched. The little varmint needed a good spanking, but she *was* adorable! She would lead Bertram into so much mischief his head would spin, but somehow Andrew did not think Bertram would consider this an impediment. Though she was by no means the sultry beauty that Anastasia was, she was nevertheless sufficiently shapely to catch the eye. She also possessed a vivacity that was both pleasing and—he hated to even think it—entertaining.

His eyes caught Anastasia's in amused indulgence. Her

own reflected his, and he was pleased at the sudden understanding that had sprung up between them. True, he
could not offer her his heart, but he could give her his
home, and he was determined she would be happy in it.

He picked up a few last petals and splinters of gild and
glass and placed them neatly on the occasional table. Then
he stood up, looked around for his hat which had,
strangely, been dislodged from his smooth, dark head at
some point or another, thanked Anastasia as she handed
it to him, and executed a delightfully formal bow. This
only served to make both ladies notice how trim his waist
was and how deliciously hard his torso.

Fortunately, he was oblivious to these unmaidenly
thoughts as he prepared to nimbly return from whence he
came. Just as Anastasia was feeling a most disproportion-
ate pang of loss at his leaving, he turned round, walked
straight up to her, and laughed. "I have taken a great deal
of trouble, at risk to both *your* impeccable reputation and
mine, to ask you a question. I'll be *damned* if I leave
without the answer!"

Anastasia's heart beat a little more wildly, if that was
possible. He was again breaching the proper distance between them, and it was hard to think under such grossly
taxing circumstance.

"The question . . . ?"

"Yes. I am afraid I have rather taken matters for granted.
There is still time to draw back, if you wish. I have a posy
of flowers in my saddlebag for this exact purpose, and do
you know, I have forgotten it?" The viscount was beset
by a sudden nervousness that Anastasia found touching.
If there were any reservations she might have had, they
vanished completely at this simple indication that though
he did not love her, he was not, at least, indifferent.

"Will you marry me, Miss Richmond?"

"Even without the posies, my lord, I shall marry you."
Neither noticed Vivienne creep from the room. It was

only when they heard a dull thud followed by a muttered and thoroughly unladylike curse somewhere down the hall that her absence was observed. The viscount's eyes twinkled and his shoulders shook a little. Anastasia's mouth twitched and a tiny, telltale dimple appeared in her cheek.

Then all was forgotten as the viscount very ingeniously sealed their bargain with a small sampling of the sweetness that was to be theirs for a lifetime.

EIGHT

The wedding day dawned crisp but fine, a state of affairs Lady Richmond declared "providential," though she continued to peer endlessly outside for any signs of rain. Carriages had been rolling in an almost carnival-like procession from Brampton to the splendid cathedral just off Grosvenor Square. True to form, Lady Richmond had seen fit to invite the world and his wife to witness what she rather inaccurately described as *her* big day. Lord Richmond had earlier preceded the wedding party, ostensibly to attend to minor details of space and choral arrangement. No one who knew him was deceived. Lady Richmond, in her element, was proving as unbearable as anyone had predicted.

At precisely eleven, she knocked on her daughter's door and burst in, in a swathe of crimson robes and a turban that defied belief, concocted of peacock feathers of varying dimensions. Her rather podgy neck was banded by diamonds of the first stare, and these were mirrored in the large bracelets that adorned her arms.

"Good Lord, Anastasia! Whatever are you thinking of? You cannot simply wear a posy of cornflowers on your head! People will think you a debutante at her first ball, not a young lady about to be elevated to the ranks of the nobility!"

In truth, Anastasia looked charming, radiant even, for

the cornflowers were interspersed with little dewdrops and violets that matched exactly the colour of her gown. This was a delicate blue that cascaded gently from the waist, ribboned beneath the bust but permitted to remain uncorseted, so that Anastasia's own soft curves were outlined gently. The sleeves were a flowing, wispy white satin, caught up in a puff that was accented by royal blue ribbons. Lord Waverley had bribed her ladies' maid to reveal the exact shade of the nuptial gown. Accordingly, the flowers he had sent, together with the note, had been perfect. Anastasia had placed the note in tissue paper and scented it with lilacs and some merry blue cornflower petals. Though it did not speak of love, its tone was all that she might have wished for. She had never, in all her tender years, looked more splendid.

"Lord Waverley was thoughtful enough to send me the bouquet and the coronet of flowers. I would like to honour him by wearing them, if I may." Though she was polite, her words spoke of a firmness that brooked no argument. Lady Richmond eyed her for a moment in silence. The diamond tiara would have been *so* much more gratifying, but there! Anastasia had the same stubborn flaw as her father. Perhaps *she* should wear the tiara, though the cost of the turban had been perfectly appalling. Lady Richmond weighed up this unexpected dilemma just as Vivienne tripped lightheartedly into the room.

"Ready?"

Anastasia felt light-headed. She glanced around at the room which in a few hours would no longer be her own. There were the familiar potted plants, the bedstead with its heavy oak carving, the elaborate drapes, the great arch windows with their lead lighting. Soon to be memories. She suffered a moment of panic that was transparent to her companion but fortunately not so to her imperceptive parent. Vivienne stepped forward and gave Anastasia's hand a squeeze. For once, she was tactful enough not to say anything, though she did laugh a little when Miss Richmond threatened to become a "watering pot" and spoil her elegant finery. At this, Lady Richmond dropped the tiara she was fingering and looked at her daughter in horror.

"Don't be absurd, Anastasia! I shall never hold my head up again if your gown does not do me credit!"

"Then I shall stop sniffing at once and prepare to depart." With these resolute words and a smile to her dresser, into whose hands she had placed herself entirely, Miss Richmond allowed herself to be led out to her waiting carriage.

Lord Waverley was heart-stoppingly handsome as he waited for her, hands clasped elegantly behind his back. His valet, a notable personage of considerable talent, had not given him a moment's peace all morning. Still, it appeared that his efforts were not for nothing, for Lord Waverly looked spectacular in a dovetail morning coat of dark black that hinted, ever so slightly, of a sultrier blue. To everyone's surprise, his waistcoat, contrary to prevailing fashion, did not sombrely match. Rather, it was contrived of a glimmering brocade, the colour strongly evocative of cornflowers and violets.

His starched white shirt points were pristine, of course, but their impeccable height was matched only by the most perfect rendition of the mathematique, clasped handsomely with a brilliant sapphire that shimmered in the light of the cathedral's many flickering candles. As even the most bucolic of people knew, this style of neckerchief was hell to achieve and almost impossible to carry off with due aplomb. Lord Waverly did both, though his manner did not in any way indicate he was preoccupied with the fall of his cravat. Neither did it reveal that he was overly concerned with the gleam of his top boots, though these shone in a most gratifying manner.

Lady Jersey, always a wit, whispered behind her fan that there was no need to seek a mirror in the powder rooms, for Lord Waverley's footwear was more than any lady could require. Lord Waverley, catching the smiles, raised his brows a little and saluted. This caused several heart flutterings and wild blushes, for in truth he was the very devil of a man and a sad loss to all who had leanings toward the personable gentleman.

And then there was a hush as the bride and her family made their entrance. Lord Waverley, catching sight of Anastasia, drew in his breath. Though he had bribed her maid handsomely, nothing had prepared him for the spectacular vision of beauty that now confronted him. Many who had regarded Miss Richmond as a wallflower in the past, now swiftly—in bewilderment even—revised their opinions. The choir, on cue, began their chant.

Bertram, supporting his brother on this quite unlooked for occasion, grinned madly and glanced about the hall for Vivienne. She, being only the companion, was relegated to a stone pillar toward the back of the church, despite Anastasia's earnest protests. On this point, however, Lady Richmond had prevailed, citing the numerous calamities that Miss Townsend had been privy to, if not the direct cause of, in the past.

In this edict, she had a surprising champion. It was Vivienne herself, who declared she would be mortified if she disturbed the proceedings by giggling—a failing her lively temperament made her unfortunately prone to—or worse. She could trip over the potted palms that lined the aisle; she could sing out of tune and make a spectacle of herself in the front row; she could step on the hem of Anastasia's gown . . . oh, the list was endless and had ended in Anastasia throwing a book at her and finally agreeing.

Of course—and here Vivienne's delightful eyes spar-

kled mischievously—she could regard Captain Ralston's
extremely pleasing visage quite brazenly from the back
of the cathedral. In front, she would be on pins that her
close interest would be remarked upon.

Thus it was that Bertram did not waste his time gazing
out at the front rows but rather peered quite shamelessly
across the hall, twisting his head to see if the heavenly
vision in soft pink was, indeed, the love of his life. He
also wondered, as Andrew stepped forward to take his
vows, whether he could possibly twist his head a little,
for the confounded pillar was disturbing his view. His reverie was unceremoniously cut short by a sharp dig to his
ribs as his brother, a wry look of amusement upon his
perfect features, reached for the ring a second time.

"What? Oh! Yes, of course!" Bertram forgot Vivienne
at the back and searched his pockets. Good Lord, the thing
was not there! He tried the other pocket as a slight murmuring began about the room. Needless to say, his luck
not being prodigious, the matrimonial band was nowhere
to be found. The archbishop, an imposing figure, looked
a trifle nonplussed. It was unthinkable that he should
marry a peer of the realm without the requisite ring to
bind the couple in their vows.

Anastasia stood immobile at the altar, her lovely eyes
fixed unwaveringly on the viscount. In the solemnity of
the moment, she knew undoubtedly that she wanted this
man, ring or no. This marriage was not simply an escape
from spinsterhood or a respectable alliance, as she had
told herself a dozen times. She knew with a sudden blinding clarity, that she yearned for it with a passion.

"Anastasia." The viscount stepped forward and clasped
her gloved hand in his own. "I made a trip to Waverley
to procure for you the family jewels. Now, it seems, by
peculiar circumstance"—he threw a darkling glance at
Bertram—"I have nothing to offer you save my signet. I

hope you shall accept that in lieu of the other, more valu-able, offering I'd intended."

He glanced at her then, and she thought she saw uncer-tainty cloud his vision. Surely he could not imagine she would refuse his personal signet? Yet in the act of remov-ing his gloves, she saw his fingers tremble a little. Un-doubtedly, too, his dark brows were furrowed in tension. Bertram, at his side, looked suddenly stricken, and she wondered why. So much hue and cry, it seemed, over a little gold! True, the bridal party must now be offering a degree of entertainment to all the witnesses, but surely nothing to occasion the pain she glimpsed in Lord Waverly's devastatingly magnetic eyes. They were shut-tered now, almost as if an impersonal mask had dropped over them.

The viscount was struggling with the ring, which had sat on his finger for more years than he cared to count. The archbishop was attempting to make light of the matter to the gathering, but Anastasia was paying no heed. Sud-denly, she believed she understood.

How stupid of her! He must be thinking of Miss Araminda Fallows, who had left him in precisely these circumstances. The whole morning, with all its fanfare, must have been evoking the memories of that other, less auspicious event. How unhappy a reminiscence it must be, and how sad that he should suspect *her* to be as callous and as grasping as that other young woman had been. "Sir, if you had no signet, no gold, and no coat on your elegantly clad back, I would *still* have you."

There was a hush in the hall, for she had spoken with such sudden, unthinking passion that her voice had pealed throughout the cathedral, causing a scandal. Most in the flower-festooned pews beamed indulgently, but there were several high sticklers who looked significantly at each other in aghast horror. Ladies—especially well-nurtured

young ladies—did not proclaim themselves in such a ram-
shackle fashion, wedding or no.

Even Vivienne, seated at the back, understood the sig-
nificance of what Anastasia had done. Instead of being
shocked, however, she offset her excellent friend's sin by
standing up and committing a social solecism of her own.
She removed her bonnet—a delicious confection of rosy
chip straw and cheery ribbons—and threw it into the air
with an animated whoop of encouragement. In the front,
Bertram's lips twitched. Lady Jersey turned around and
stared rather coldly at the miscreant. The archbishop
looked as if he'd have an apoplexy until Captain Ralston
joined in Miss Townsend's applause.

Then a strange thing happened. Lord Richmond, ignoring his wife's furious glares, stood up and clapped. Then
it was the turn of Beau Brummel, the most notable arbiter
of fashion in all of London. Of course, after that it was
pandemonium as almost every person who was anybody
followed his lead. Even Lady Richmond, noting that the
starchy Countess Lieven was smiling, declared that perhaps, after all, Anastasia might be forgiven her outburst.

None of this mattered to Lord Waverley or the lady who
had just, amid all the bustle, quietly become his wife.
Whilst Bertram winked at Vivienne and Lady Jersey contemplated etiquette, whilst the great Beau clapped and the
hall resounded with cheers, applause, gossip, whispered
predictions, and significant nods, the viscount had slipped
the signet on Anastasia's finger and softly declared her
his bride.

This had been duly attested to by the archbishop, whose
head was still spinning with the strange circumstances of
the affair. Still, the matter of the ring had been happily
resolved. He now felt free to proceed to Brampton, where
he was eager to sample a modest glass of Lord Richmond's legendary red.

As for Anastasia, suddenly shy, her hand trembled as

she felt Lord Waverley's chaste kiss upon her ungloved palm. It burnt like fire, but she did not immediately draw away as was proper. A smile crept into Andrew's eyes at this defiant gesture. Her eyes were sparkling silver and held tremulous tears he wished to kiss away. At that precise moment, his cold heart melted. Lady Araminda Tarradale was consigned, at last, to the devil. His future lay with this woman, his wife. He had dismissed her once, rather offhandedly, as decorous and demure. He did not think he could ever again make that same mistake.

NINE

"Anastasia!" Lord Waverly called.

"My friends call me Stasia," she answered, joining him.

"Ah, but I am not just your friend."

"No."

"You are pleased with this match we have contrived?"

"I am pleased, sir."

"Then come here and let me exchange that paltry little signet for something more suitable."

Anastasia saw the flash of diamonds as Andrew opened the casket. It contained a multitude of pieces, all of them the hereditary jewels of the Viscountess Waverley.

"No!"

"Beg pardon?"

"I will not exchange this ring for all the gems of England!"

"It is a man's ring, my love."

My love. Anastasia glowed at the sound of the word on his tongue. Had it just been a fortuitous turn of phrase? The new viscountess's eyes crept to the viscount's, but he seemed unconscious of any particular slip.

"You gave it to me, and I should like to keep it." Her chin took on a stubborn tilt that the viscount found fascinating.

"Very well. You shall have it. Here, I shall put it on your third finger, for it is so big it will fall off otherwise."

Anastasia meekly extended her hand. The viscount took it, slowly slipping off her long sarcenet glove and removing the heavy rose gold from her ring finger. Anastasia felt strangely bereft without its comforting weight, though the intimate gesture caused her virtuous senses to reel in shock. Then Andrew, Viscount Waverley, slipped it, lingeringly, onto the third.

Her fingers felt cool and shapely. He bent to kiss each one, and Anastasia stood stock still, willing herself to remember that though she adored him dearly, the feeling was not reciprocal. The ice white heat between them was real, but ephemeral. Somehow, though she forced herself to think it, the thought did not ring true. She closed her eyes, and though the viscount was now rather daringly kissing her arms—and yes, her shoulders—she willed herself to be satisfied with what she was receiving. Unashamed passion that begged only for a response. She was not unwilling in that regard, as the viscount was soon to discover.

Later, much later, when she was in truth his viscountess, he drew her closer and announced that he had a horrible secret to confess.

Anastasia paled, for she was certain it had something nasty to do with the countess of Crewe. Perhaps, though she had jilted him, he still wore the willow for her.

"I am not certain you ought to tell me, sir."

"Andrew would sound better on your tongue, my lady." He drew a strong, bronzed arm around her slender form "And whilst we are on the subject of tongues. . . ." He smiled at her wickedly.

Anastasia could not help a tiny, wisp of a smile in response, though her heart was fearful of the confession to come. Once spoken, the words would be difficult to retrieve.

"Andrew." The word was at once strange and intoxicating. She did not dwell on it, however, for her mind was set on taking a more serious turn. "You need not confess a thing to me. I am not, you must remember, your keeper."

"Oh, but I wish you were." The words, though flippant, were accompanied by a darkening of his eyes that made Anastasia tremble.

"You are a rogue, sir! You see fit to tease me!"

"Indeed, I have to confess, there *is* a certain diversion in that!" The glint in his eye was unmistakable, but Anastasia disentangled herself from the heavenly warmth of his arms to sit up. Sad to say, her pins, long since removed, were now nowhere to be found, so she had to resign herself to hair that tumbled hopelessly about her face. Andrew thought the effect charming, but she pushed the locks back crossly.

"I am glad I am such a source of amusement to you!"

The viscount laughed, his head somehow closer to her body than was quite sensible for one determined to scold.

"So am I," he whispered. Somehow, his tone was so intimate that Anastasia shivered and had to forcibly push him away to continue her self-sacrificing train of thought.

"I know that you have a tendre for Lady Tarradale . . ."

Now it was the viscount's turn to sit up.

"What stuff and nonsense! The only inclination I harbour in her direction is the recurring need to throttle her undeniably pretty neck!"

"See! You call her pretty!"

"Shrew! Shall you be a very jealous wife, I wonder?"

"I shall try not to be." Anastasia's voice was so low the viscount almost missed her words.

"I shall be disappointed if you are not, for jealousy indicates caring, and I want, very much, for you to care for me."

This time, there was no more teasing in his tone. Anastasia looked up to see an earnest honesty in his breathtaking features.

"You mean—"

"Yes, widgeon! That horrible secret I have to confess. I have loved you from the day you tumbled off your pony. You complained not a whit, despite the fact that it was so obviously Bertram's fault. You spared him a whipping that day, I am very certain of it."

"But Lady Tarradale—"

"Was a young greenhorn's silly mistake. I was cutting my eye teeth then, and clearly had not a groat of sense."

"But you cannot love me! You have said so yourself—"

"I *told* you I was a mere greenhorn! Silly gudgeon that I am, the truth only revealed itself to me today, when we took our vows. You were magnificent."

"And highly improper!"

"Deliciously so. And now, Lady Waverley, since you are already so wreathed in smiles, may I tempt you again to impropriety?"

And of course he did.

Lady Brandoven's ball was always the most august affair on the social calendar. Bertram took especial care with his neckerchief, for he wished to look particularly dapper for the event. Three months, he considered, was a long enough interval to allow Viscount and Viscountess Waverley their privacy. He had been languishing in the country all this time, loath to act the spare wheel in his brother's home whilst he entertained his lady wife. Now, by all accounts, matters were settled most amicably between them. It was only today, after all, that Bertram had been told, rather shyly, that his standing as heir to Waverley was about to be usurped. He had whooped with joy at this pronouncement, and had begun cosseting Anastasia so solicitously that she finally had to tell him to go away, she could not stand nine months of such treatment.

Bertram untied the neckerchief and began the provoking knot again. He was not sure why he bothered, for

Vivienne was bound not to notice whether the wretched thing looped over or under. Still, pride was pride. He did not wish to be behindhand in any attention. Besides, one could not be expected to recite poetry—the captain had diligently learned one of Byron's verses—if one's shirt points drooped.

Captain Ralston was cured of his loathing for matrimony. This was due largely to the fact that he was convinced Miss Townsend would be a most unwifely wife, a fact that redounded quite inordinately to her credit. As a consequence, he'd decided that tonight would be the sticking point. He would formally request her hand—for up until now he had only *informally* done so—and see to it that they were wed at once. The special license bristled invitingly in his pocket.

He wondered how Vivienne did, for by now she must be heartily sick of running errands for Lady Richmond. Despite Anastasia's good-hearted pleas, she had refused resolutely to relocate to the viscount's London town house after the wedding. Like Bertram, she did not believe that three made company.

"Will you be taking the tilbury, sir?"

"No, Siddons. Send down for the barouche, will you? I have no idea where the evening will take me." With these cryptic words, Bertram wedged his hat on over his merry curls and prepared to leave.

Lady Richmond was agonisingly slow. She dithered unmercifully over her toilette, changing this and that until Vivienne thought she might either die from impatience or pour a pitcher of water over her. Fortunately, she veered toward the former, for she would undoubtedly have been dismissed without a character had she tried the water trick.

She had been ready an age ago, having thrown on a discarded gown of Anastasia's and piled her bright, irrepressible hair on top of her head. Had Lady Richmond only known it, it was being secured by no more than three pins. Still, it appeared to be holding, and the bright peonies she had added to the ensemble looked very merry indeed, if slightly unusual. Roses and violets were customary.

"Shall it be the emeralds or the rubies, Miss Townsend?" Lady Richmond asked, suffering yet another spasm of indecision.

"Oh, undoubtedly both," came Vivienne's impatient reply.

"Both? How clever of you! I declare you are right. Bettina! Fetch both boxes, will you?"

Vivienne sighed with relief. They might not be so terribly late, after all. She had not minded being tardy for the masquerade or Lady Davina's card party, but tonight was different. Tonight, she knew, Bertram was back. Her eyes shone at the thought. She imagined his splendid shoulders encased in a perfectly fitting coat styled by Weston, his top boots gleaming. He would notice her at once across the room and would sail over to her and say . . .

What would he say? Her heart hammered quite painfully at the thought.

"The Viscount and Viscountess Waverley, the Honourable Captain Ralston . . ." The names announced were endless, but Bertram paid them no attention. He made his obligatory bow to the hostess, Lady Amelia Brandoven, then went off in search of Lady Richmond's party. Bother! They had not yet arrived.

Anastasia regarded her new brother with some amusement and more than a little twinkle in her sparkling eyes. Commending her excellent husband to the card room, she

marched up to him and demanded the first dance of the
evening.

"It is a quadrille, Stasia! Dreadfully boring, and I wish
to preserve my boots."

"How churlish of you, Bertie! Come, come, you will
not deny me! A certain young lady has not yet arrived. If
I know Mama, it will be ages before they are finally announced."

In this she was wrong, for Lady Richmond and Miss
Vivienne Townsend were at that precise moment in the
process of being announced. Lord Cowper, a kindly sort
of man, solicited Miss Townsend's hand at once. He had
an astute notion that if he did not give her the cut direct
for her behaviour at the Waverley wedding, no one else
would. In this surmise he was correct, though Vivienne
remained happily oblivious to all these manoeuvrings. She
did offer him a very pretty smile, however, and adjured
him to "watch his toes," for she was a deplorable dancer
and only ever successful with a broomstick.

Though Lord Cowper's lips twitched at this refreshing
confession, he obligingly reassured Miss Townsend that
he would be careful. Thus it was that when the set was
formed, both Bertram *and* Vivienne were participants.
Neither noticed the other, however, until it was too late to
do anything but grimace deplorably and wink.

"Bertram! I have great plans for your wedding. You
shall marry from Waverley with due pomp and splendour.
We can have the most fabulous wedding feast out on the
lawns—"

"Spare me, Anastasia! I would not marry Vivienne that
way for all the tea in China." Unfortunately, Miss Townsend, dancing quite close to the couple and unable to resist
indulging her deplorable habit of eavesdropping, heard
most, but not all, of Bertram's reply. Mortified, she stumbled a little, causing Lord Cowper to wince as his foot
took the brunt of her misstep.

"After her behaviour at *your* wedding . . ." Vivienne's ears burned as she heard his words. She took a step backwards to execute an entrechat, thereby missing the remainder of the sentence, which was that he could *"quite* see that pomp and splendour was not her style at all, and that a runaway marriage would be far more to her taste."

"Bertram! You cannot be serious!"

Vivienne heard those words, but not, unfortunately, the reply.

The roof of her mouth was as dry as sawdust. When Lord Cowper bowed and thanked her politely as the music faded, she stared at him blankly, extended her hand quite unthinkingly, and received a chivalrous kiss for her trouble. This made the dowagers raise their eyebrows significantly, but strangely had little effect on Vivienne, who had no notion of the honour that had just been conferred. She smiled wanly, turned tail, and fled.

"Vivienne! I have been searching for you everywhere!" Captain Ralston breathed a sigh of relief. Thank goodness he had thought of searching the gardens. Though they were dark, several newfangled gas lamps lit a path down to the lake.

"Have you? Then come here and get what you deserve!" Despite her devastation, Vivienne was still a woman of spirit. Bertram grinned and readily obeyed, fully expecting a most intoxicating outcome for his trouble.

"Ouch!" Certainly he had not expected the stinging slap that seared his cheek.

"Ouch again!" The other side this time.

"Vivienne, have you lost your senses?"

"No. Have you lost yours? Trifling with the house servants is not considered comme il faut!"

"House servants?" Bertram was bewildered.

"I believe companions are considered as such in some households." Vivienne had never held herself so breathtakingly erect, though her miserable pins were now giving up the ghost. As a consequence, her hair was falling about her face in the most inviting of fashions, and Bertram was torn between kissing her thoroughly or throwing her bodily in the lake.

"I have no notion of what you are talking of."

"Yes, you *do!*" Vivienne replied hotly. "Oh, I know your sort, Captain Ralston! Were you hoping to give me a slip on the shoulder? I may not *appear* respectable, but I *am,* I will have you know!"

"Which is precisely why a special license is burning a hole in my pocket. Also, though I don't personally care for such trifles, I have just spent the ungodliest of fortunes on a betrothal ring that matches exactly the shade of your eyes. Viv, do be sensible. And, oh, please, please stop crying! You shall ruin my shirt points."

Quite suddenly, Bertram found he did not mind about his shirt points, for the delectable smell of mint and lavender was assailing his nostrils and a pair of very desirable lips were parting invitingly. He seized the opportunity, for he would have been a veritable gudgeon had he ignored it. After a while spent in this thoroughly agreeable fashion, he pushed Vivienne from him and managed to unravel where the misunderstanding had begun.

"You said you would not marry me for all the tea in China." Vivienne's lips quivered at the memory.

"Widgeon! I said I would not marry you that *way* for all the tea in China! You would not want a huge society wedding, would you?"

"Heaven forbid! Anastasia's was quite enough. I detest the things."

"There you go, then! I *thought* you'd feel that way." Vivienne nodded, and sighed with quiet contentment. Her hand stole into Bertram's. The captain, whose self-control was now reaching its limits, thought it high time to mention that he had arrived in a closed chaise rather than in the more usual tilbury.

"And why, pray?" Vivienne was not in the mood to talk of transportation, but being an obliging soul, she decided to humour Bertram, just so long as she could fiddle with his silver buttons and nuzzle a little at his neck.

"Because I am about to abduct you!"

"What?" Vivienne stopped nuzzling and looked at Bertram in shock. He was not put off, however, because her eyes were twinkling delightfully and he could just make out a dimple peeping in her cheek.

"It is as I say. I have just compromised you quite horribly—look, there is that Peabody Frampton woman walking in the shadows and I bet any *number* of people can see us in the lamplight. Besides, they are in an uproar inside because they can't find you. Lady Richmond is currently indulging in a fit of hysterics."

"I will bet she is!"

"Yes, and like as not Lord Richmond, in the absence of any brothers on your part, will challenge me to a duel."

"Well, we can't have *that,* can we?" Vivienne's eyes creased at the thought of the timid Lord Richmond challenging anyone to anything.

"Well, then, we have no choice. We shall be married immediately. There is a bishop at Holebury awaiting us this very hour."

Vivienne's eyes opened wide. Then she chuckled delightfully, obligingly allowed herself to be thrown over Bertram's shoulders like a sack of potatoes, and made one comment only. "Abduct away!"

Very obligingly, Captain Ralston did.

More Zebra Regency Romances

Put a Little Romance in Your Life With
Fern Michaels

__Dear Emily	0-8217-5676-1	$6.99US/$8.50CAN
__Sara's Song	0-8217-5856-X	$6.99US/$8.50CAN
__Wish List	0-8217-5228-6	$6.99US/$7.99CAN
__Vegas Rich	0-8217-5594-3	$6.99US/$8.50CAN
__Vegas Heat	0-8217-5758-X	$6.99US/$8.50CAN
__Vegas Sunrise	1-55817-5983-3	$6.99US/$8.50CAN
__Whitefire	0-8217-5638-9	$6.99US/$8.50CAN